HIDE AND DIE

HIDE AND DIE

Stella Whitelaw

This first world edition published in Great Britain 2003 by
SEVERN HOUSE PUBLISHERS LTD of
9–15 High Street, Sutton, Surrey SM1 1DF.
This first world edition published in the USA 2003 by
SEVERN HOUSE PUBLISHERS INC of
595 Madison Avenue, New York, N.Y. 10022.

British Library Cataloguing in Publication Data

Whitelaw, Stella, 1941-
    Hide and die. - (Jordan Lacey series)
    1.   Lacey, Jordan (Fictitious character) - Fiction
    2.   Women private investigators - Fiction
    3.   Detective and mystery stories
    I.   Title
    823.9'14 [F]

    ISBN 0-7278-5893-9

Typeset by Palimpsest Book Production Ltd.,
Polmont, Stirlingshire, Scotland.
Printed and bound in Great Britain by
MPG Books Ltd., Bodmin, Cornwall.

To Anna Telfer, dedicated editor and friend

One

The weathered capstan had been embedded in the shingle on Latching beach for almost a hundred years and yet this was the first time I'd really noticed it. Call me bat eyes.

A brass plaque told visitors that local fishermen had once used it to haul their boats up the steep bank of pebbles. Now they used motor driven winches. The capstan had been made from the boom of a ship wrecked off the coast in 1896 during a violent storm.

I needed a walk to shake the day into the right shape. The sea would light windows in my mind. The air felt strange, disordered.

The promenade was strewn with debris after last night's storm. Pebbles, driftwood, plastic bottles, upturned supermarket trollys. A couple of poorly secured boats were skewed sideways across the promenade, their youthful owners without the experience to know that a very high spring tide plus gale force winds adds up to disaster.

Even the gulls were walking.

It had been some storm in the night, the sky the colour of dark slate. The sash windows of my two bedsits had rattled for hours until I had the sense to get up and stuff them with folded cardboard. The wind blew the drenching rain horizontally along the road. Gutters became swirling rivers of debris. As I looked out of the rain splattered window, I was glad I wasn't night-working on some case. This was time off for good behaviour. Mine.

Mavis would be biting her nails, worried for the safety of

her current fisherman lover. But he would have the experience to know not to launch his boat from the beach. They all listen to the weather forecasts, are addicted to every isobar nuance. Her bronzed and brawny fisherman might lose a few hundred pounds worth of nets overnight, but he would not lose his life.

So I walked the promenade, a landscape of desolation, stepping over piles of stones, skirting ropes and nets and the tarred planks they used for runways down the shingle. Planks tossed about like matchsticks. It was a mess, pebbles halfway across the road, littering the decking of the pier, strings of lights hanging in broken clusters, cans and drums rolling around the seafront.

Still, spring was coming and my feet were slowly getting better. Slashed feet pounded by an old watermill take a long time to heal, especially when they get stood on most of the time. I am no couch King Edward and cannot accept the role of invalid.

I wanted to keep active. DI James might get seduced by a female WPC in black seamless if I prolonged the hobbling. That was definitely not on. Feet do not inspire sympathy, especially male sympathy. Walk if it hurts like hell, girl.

My cases had run down but I was not alarmed. New ones had a funny way of arriving on my doorstep like homeless cats. I only had to wait and they appeared out of thin air. This was mental recovery time. And for feet healing. Sometimes I did not know where to put them. My feet, that is.

It was not long before a client arrived at First Class Junk, my corner shop. She pretended to be interested in an antique fan in the tiny window display, but actually she was wondering how to broach the subject of First Class Investigations, my undercover private investigations business. She came in.

'Are you the detective? Can I speak with you? It's very personal,' she began, wringing her hands. Her nails were painted a vibrant Royal Red, a bit chipped. The liver spots were a testament to time. Nothing works, not even lemon juice. 'My husband is, er . . .'

'Oh dear,' I said. 'That sounds ominous. Would you like to come into my offfice where it is more private?'

'Thank you,' she said, heaving a sigh of relief. 'I was told you are very discreet.'

By whom? I could not think who might have recommended me and this was mega-think time. 'Please come in. Would you like some coffee? I make good coffee.'

'Thank you. This has been very stressful.'

'Yes, I do understand. Please sit down and make yourself comfortable. There's no rush, no hassle. Take your time.'

She sat on my Victorian button-back, a beautiful pink velvet chair that had cost me a lot but had been worth every penny. I loved every inch. And my Persian rug was all blue and red muted colours. It sat on the floor of my back office like something from another world. I'd never tested whether it would fly me across the sky but the thought was there.

'My name is Gill Frazer,' she said, still hesitating over the words. 'My husband is Brian Frazer.'

Oh shucks, not another errant husband/wife case. Latching is a hive of domestic drama. I prayed for something different. Was there ever anything different? Life kept repeating itself.

I smiled and asked how did she like her coffee? She was small, brunette and compact. Her clothes were ordinary and hung on her without appeal. I did not like her skirt and jacket. Taupe does nothing for me as a colour. More like being dipped in mud.

'It's not the usual sort of thing,' Mrs Frazer began. 'No liaisons with blonde secretary, hotel receipts in pocket, weird phone calls in the middle of the night. Oh no, nothing like that. And yet, I do want him investigated and followed, and I want proof.'

I nodded knowingly, still at sea.

'Things keep disappearing, you see.'

'Really? What kind of things?'

'Unless I'm imagining it all. It might be early dementia setting in. I look for something at home and it's not there.'

'I doubt it,' I smiled. Mrs Frazer looked about forty plus. Too early for brain cell loss. 'What sort of things are disappearing?'

'Clothes mainly, my clothes. Make-up sometimes and jewellery. Mostly earrings, bracelets. Nothing valuable. I've only got paste jewellery but I've got some pretty pieces. And I couldn't find my cashmere sweater this morning and I really wanted it. The colour matches this suit exactly.'

More mud. 'How strange,' I said. 'Do you have a teenage daughter?' I asked. 'Daughters have a way of borrowing things without asking.'

'We only have a son, Max. He's grown up now.'

'Do any of the things ever come back?'

She nodded with a sort of resignation. 'Yes, they do and that's strange, too. Months later. When I've almost forgotten them. And I know what you're thinking. And it's what I'm thinking, too. And I want to find out and stop it before everyone knows. It's so humiliating.'

'So you think your husband is cross-dressing?'

Mrs Frazer was blinking back tears now. Her eyes were a watery blue for a start. 'Maybe. But I don't know why. He's such a good-looking man. There's no need to be anyone else other than himself. We've always been very happy, but obviously our marriage is not enough for him. I don't know what's going on.'

'I'll find out,' I said confidentially. 'And I promise I'll be very discreet. The neighbours won't know a thing.'

'I didn't say anything about neighbours,' she said, quite sharply. Her tone took me back. It had just been a throwaway remark. 'I'm not worried about my damned neighbour even if she is a stuck-up madam.'

Ah, so she was worried about the neighbours. People who deny things with such vehemence are usually hiding something. It wasn't only the husband who had a secret life wearing

4

his wife's dresses and earrings. Perhaps mud-coloured Gill Frazer was also hiding something.

I got out my contract form and trotted through my charges. 'I charge £10 an hour or £50 a day. You can choose. But I feel the hourly charge would be right in this case, since it'll be mainly evenings. What does your husband do for a living?'

I imagined stockbroker, banker, insurance, something nine to five.

'He's the manager of the new Community Shore Theatre. You may know it. It used to be the old Odean cinema.'

Know it? I practically live there when there is any big band jazz playing. Save me a seat please, row J, I'm paying. Save me two. DI James might come with me if he hasn't been called out. Come with me? He hasn't been anywhere with me, except to Skyliner's. That memorable late evening at Christmas when he took me to the rooftop Skyliner Club and ordered the best red wine. My knees went weak at the memory.

'Sure, I know it,' I said. 'One of Latching's most valued assets. They put on some great shows. I love the place.'

Gill Frazer seemed to relax. My enthusiasm was genuine. I love all the theatres in Latching almost as much as I love the beach, the sea, the shore, the shingle. Sorry, there I go again. A sea freak. My hair will be turning greeny-blue any minute. Seaweed coming out of both ears.

'The hourly rate then . . .' She hesitated. 'It would be mostly evenings, I suppose, but then he also works evenings. You know, down at the theatre. It could be any time.'

Tricky hours. 'Let's try a week at the hourly rate and then make adjustments if necessary. I will invoice you each week but I need you to sign this contract first. It's easy to read. No small print.'

She took out glasses to read the contract and signed it straightaway. 'That's fine,' she said, very matter of fact. 'I agree to everything. Just let me know what you find out about Brian. And soon. I'm really worried.'

I filled in the rest of the contract with her name and address and phone number. The actual details of the case I would put in when she had gone. My memory was good for details. I always write everything down.

'How did you find me?' I asked. 'I don't exactly advertise.'

'It was through a firm of solicitors in Chichester. One of the secretaries on the staff mentioned you as being reliable and discreet.'

Cleo Carling. My first case. Bless her. I must give her a ring and thank her. Perhaps we'd have lunch together, but no carrot cake, please. That last slice had been poisoned.

I took a few more details then Mrs Frazer left. She looked longingly at the antique fan but the £6 price tag put her off. I put £6 on everything. It makes life easier.

So I had a new case. Great. Evenings only, by the look of it. But . . . Brian Frazer might have a different persona during the day. That was a possibility and I would soon find out. Research, Jordan. Library: find books on cross-dressing deviations. Avoid looks of librarian.

I shut up my shop. We were still in the post New Year sales paralysis even though it was early spring. No one wanted to buy anything. Most people never wanted to see a shop again. Shop overdosing.

This style of surveillance did not need charity box dressing. I could wear my own laid-back, plain and workmanlike gear. Jeans with everything. Stroll about taking in the evening air. The clocks would change soon and the evenings become lighter. That's always a magical time, my time of the year. Skies shot with the setting sun, rays of orange and rose stabbing the sea, turning it to quicksilver.

The Frazers lived in St Michael's Road at number three. I averted my eyes from the church. My friend, Oliver Guilbert's funeral was still too fresh in my mind. Number three was a small detached house, fairly new, a brash red-brick, built in the garden of a sprawling Edwardian villa. The big house was old and elegant, white stone with a pillared porch and bay windows and carved lintels. They had sold off a parcel of land and some developer had put up the Frazers' house. It was like a red carbuncle growing on a fold of lily-white skin.

I pretended to read the notices on the board outside the church. I made it last half an hour. Slow reader. I tried reading the notices from the end backwards. They still made sense. I wondered if they knew that.

A man came out of number three, closing the gate behind him. He was short, slim, and nicely made. Not my type, of course. I'm pretty choosy. My men have to be topping six foot, with crew-cut dark hair, broad shoulders and called James James. This cuts the numbers down pretty quick.

Brian Frazer wore a belted fawn raincoat over a normal dark suit. Not a wisp of frock or jangle of bangle. St Michael's Road was walking distance to the theatre, a long walk but not more than ten minutes. I followed him leisurely, keeping a few other pedestrians in front of me but never letting them block my view. He walked with an easy swinging rhythm.

The box office was already open and people were queueing to buy tickets. There was some big pop group on stage tonight with pounding amplification. *Pop Idols* with chin growth. Mr Frazer nodded to his staff and went through a door marked Private. He looked as if he was gone for the evening. Goodbye work.

Still, I hung around in case Mr Frazer emerged dressed as a female programme seller. They might be that short of staff. They were. I spotted a notice asking for volunteers for front of house at shows. Volunteer seriously means no money involved. Perhaps they gave you a free ice cream instead. Make mine chocolate chip flavoured.

The last of the punters had their tickets inspected and the perforated bit torn off and were ushered into the auditorium. I was still in the foyer, reading everything in sight. A crescendo of clapping greeted the arrival of the rock musicians. Then the pounding music began. The walls shook.

'Are you really short of help?' I asked the girl in the box

office, having to raise my voice. She booked seats on screen these days, and printed out the tickets with name and customer number.

'Always,' she said. 'We get lots of volunteers but they don't stay long, or they don't want to sit through shows they don't like. Why, are you interested?'

'Could be,' I said cautiously.

'Would you like to have a word with our staff supervisor, Maggie?'

'Why not.'

'She'll be free in about ten minutes. I'll tell her you are here. What name shall I say?'

I hate this bit. Lies again. 'Lucy,' I said, using my alias as the young woman who went round looking at graded fisherman cottages with a clipboard. She had served her apprenticeship.

I sat on a plush bench reading the programme of events. It looked good although I was not much into wrestling or clair-voyance. Could one pick on which nights one volunteered? I did not want some medium pointing at me in the crowd and saying loudly, 'My guide says you are not who you say you are. You have another life.'

I could say I was allergic to plasma.

Maggie, the staff supervisor, was an efficient no-nonsense woman in her early forties, crisp manner, crisp, tinted henna hair, name badge on her white blouse. Her eyes swept over my casual outfit and they said, no way, buster, get going.

'You know it's unpaid, don't you?' she said, thinking state benefits, homeless, vagrant.

'I have a regular job,' I said, digging up dignity. 'And I have my own shop in Latching.'

She thawed two degrees, her hair defrosted. 'Oh, that's a bit different. Do I know it?'

'I don't suppose so. It's a specialist shop.' Let her think what she liked, herbal, optician, disability aids.

'I'm very short tonight,' she remembered, more talking to

8

herself. 'Two haven't turned up. I've no one at all to sell ice cream in the interval at the back.'

'I can do that. I handle money all the time.' Slight exaggeration. I only handle money on a good day.

'You'll need a white blouse and black skirt,' said Maggie dubiously, as if I might never have heard of these garments.

'I can go home and change. It's only a short walk.'

'OK, I'll give you a try out tonight. Come back and we'll see how you shape up. You'll have to stay on afterwards and help clear up. Litter and stuff. Lost property.'

'No problem.' I hadn't bargained on cleaning.

I hurried back to my shop. My charity box had a long narrow black skirt trimmed with braid, very classy, designer label. There must be a white blouse of some sort. I could only find a man's shirt, but since it was minimum iron, it was wearable. My hair went up into a knot. It looked quite stylish. Mascara. My appearance was improving by the minute.

Maggie was clearly surprised when I returned. 'OK,' she said. That phrase was the mainstay of her conversation. 'Load your tray from the icebox five minutes before the interval. Stand at the back of the stalls. This is your float. Everyone offers notes. The ice creams are all priced at one pound each. Makes giving change easier. OK?'

I nodded. 'Thank you.'

'There's a staff room at the back. You can make tea or coffee while you wait. You don't have to watch the whole show.' She had mellowed. It must have been mentioning my shop or wearing the expensive skirt.

'This is a bit noisy for me. I like jazz, smooth soul.'

'You'll get used to it. A lot of people like loud music. We're sold out tonight.'

'Whoever runs the theatre must be pleased.'

'That's Mr Frazer. He's the new manager. He's very nice. But it's owned by a company called CC Entertainment. The faceless ones with the money.'

I smiled. 'There's always a few of those.'

9

'Fill in this form before you go. Name and address, phone number, so we can get in touch.'

Maggie hurried away and I was left holding the float. I could have walked out with it. She was trusting. It was definitely the expensive skirt. Memo to self: clothes talk.

Jazz is my music so I found the rock and rollers hard going. They were an enthusiastic group, leaping about the stage, and occasionally I recognized a tune, with difficulty, hiding somewhere underneath the thump, thump of the percussion. It would be different if it was a play. I'd be enthralled in the plot, forget about selling ice cream and programmes, be showing people to the wrong seats.

I wandered about the corridors of the theatre, wondering if I would catch sight of Mr Frazer in a dress. But I never saw him at all. The door marked Private was very private.

Selling ice creams was demanding and fun. Except for those who could not make up their mind which flavour before they joined the queue. Surely they knew which kind they preferred? Some couples hesitated and pondered, the interval ticking away while they argued over chocolate or vanilla. I'd sold out before the second half began. Obviously charming smile plus elegant skirt worked. I had to count the money and put the coins into plastic bank envelopes. I was now an accountant.

'You've done well,' said Maggie afterwards. I'd found a lost glove, too. 'I'll give you a call when we're short. We could use you.'

'How about tomorrow?' Could I charge for this time? I was still on surveillance.

'OK, tomorrow. 7 p.m.'

I stood outside waiting for Mr Frazer to leave. He walked home with a carrier bag that he had not arrived with. Interesting. But it did not look as if it carried a dress. More like a takeaway supper. Perhaps Mrs Frazer did not feed him late at night.

I followed discreetly, stopping in shop doorways to stay out of sight. It was drizzling, a sort of early April shower. I hurried into another doorway, not wanting to get valuable skirt wet.

A car drew up alongside. It was a police car without the flashing lights. A window slid down.

'Mini . . . You are supposed to wear a mini, Jordan, preferably made of latex or leather. Long skirts don't give out the same message.'

It was DI James, a look of amusement on his stern face. I was not amused. The grey in his crew cut was gleaming like silver under the neon street lights. His ocean-blue eyes were hidden. He did not look as tired as usual. Perhaps he had got some sleep recently. I had not seen him for days.

'I'm not giving out any message. This is not what it looks like,' I said. 'I'm on surveillance.'

'It looks like loitering to me,' he said, still leaning out of the window. 'But you've got the gear all wrong. Granny skirt and hair scraped back in a granny bun? Unless this is a new trend. A granny-hooker?'

'Excuse me, officer, but this is Latching, West Sussex, not Soho or Shepherd's Market. We have a different class of nightlife on the coast.'

He was leaning over and unlocking the passenger door. 'Get in, you idiot, before you get mugged. There's a lot of villains around. I've just locked up a couple.'

'I hope they didn't spit on you,' I said, climbing into the passenger seat with as much elegance as the tight skirt would allow. 'I'm particular who I travel with.'

'Not any more than usual, I hope.'

'If you've been spat at, then I don't want you coming in for a coffee and dripping on my carpet.'

'I wasn't coming anyway,' he said, throwing the car into gear. 'I've better things to do. Have an early night, girl. You look as if you've been dragged up.'

He left me outside the front door of my two upstairs bedsits and drove off. I stood on the pavement and watched the tail lights of the car disappearing into the night drizzle. I had loved every minute of being with him. It was quite pathetic. Even insults went to my head.

Two

The man waiting outside my shop, pacing the pavement, looked like a client who could not make up his mind whether to come in or not, wanting to do a runner. A bit like Gill Frazer yesterday pretending to inspect a fan. Instant replay situation.

He had a honest-looking face if honesty can be deduced from the shape of a face. Receding brown hair revealed a furrowed brow and the sheen of the skin told me he was nervous. A quick flurry of window dressing gave me a chance to throw a reassuring smile in his direction. It seemed to work because he opened the door, letting in a spray of pre-April shower at the same time.

'Can I speak to the lady detective?' he asked.

His voice was pure Sussex. Born and bred, schooled and slippered, coated and coasted. I would have liked to tape his voice and decode the vowels.

'I'm Jordan Lacey. If it's First Class Investigations you are interested in, then my office is through the back.'

'You're a bit young to be a detective, aren't you?' he said, following me. 'I thought detectives were always a bit older.'

'I didn't know there was a minimum age,' I said, going for the jugular. 'You've either got it or you haven't. Have a seat.'

No coffee. Twenty-seven, knocking twenty-eight, is not old enough to make coffee. I might have missed a year somewhere. Women do that. Kettle far too dangerous in such youthful hands.

I opened my notebook and uncapped a pen. Note the joined-up writing. Quick learner. 'May I have your name, please?'

'Phil Cannon. I'm an electrician. I could fix that doorbell for you. It doesn't work.'

'No one ever uses it.'

'They might, you know. You get post, don't you?'

'It has been known. Well, Mr Cannon, how can I help you? Perhaps you'd like to tell me in your own words. Take your time.'

Debt collecting? Difficult neighbour? Dispute over a hedge? It was not easy to classify Mr Cannon. It could be anything.

My deskside manner was not putting Mr Cannon at ease. He looked as stiff as a board, rigidly perched on my button-back. I bet his pulse rate was up.

'I've got this son, see. His name is Dwain. Only I don't think he's mine.'

I waited patiently. There must be more to it than this. Mr Cannon was having difficulty in finding the words. Had he being doing some calculations on a calendar and found he was out of the country at the crucial time of Dwain's conception?

'And how old is little Dwain?'

'Twelve.'

'Twelve!' How long had it taken him to decide that his son was not his? Wasn't he a bit slow? How long did it take to notice colour of hair, eyes, skin? 'He's almost a teenager,' I added lamely.

'And I've been paying for him all these years,' Phil added bitterly. 'It's cost me a fortune. Thousands.'

'Ah . . . perhaps you'd better start at the beginning. I'm not quite sure what situation we are talking about or what you want me to do.'

'I met this woman – I wouldn't call her a lady – nearly thirteen years ago. We had a brief affair, very brief. Just a long weekend in fact and I don't remember much about it.

It was all over before it began. Too much to drink at some party and I woke up the next morning with this skinny blonde flaked out in bed beside me. It was tacky all right. We didn't get up much. We stayed in bed all weekend. Only got up for another beer or a pee.'

My face stayed straight as if I was used to hearing about entire weekends spent in bed. That my clientele are always sexually active. Latching's underworld is seething with rampant sex. A whole weekend? I'd be lucky if I got as much as thirty seconds of DI James in range of a duvet.

'Then what happened?'

'A few weeks later she phones me, all upset and crying, and saying she's pregnant. Well, I believed her. I hadn't used . . . you know . . . one of those. I thought she was on the Pill, when I was sober enough to think of anything, that is.'

'But now you don't think that Dwain is your son. What's made you suspicious?'

'I've found out that about that time she was going out with some other fella. Some chap that kept hopping off abroad on jobs. That weekend, the weekend of the party, he'd gone to Amsterdam.' Phil Cannon was getting really worked up now. He clenched his hands. 'She might have known she was already pregnant and fitted me up for the daddy role.'

I swallowed a sigh. I could see where this was going. An old trail, thirteen years cold. He was going to ask me to find out if Dwain's mother had been sleeping with another boyfriend just before said weekend of illicit joy. Brilliant as I frequently am, this was asking too much.

'That's very difficult to find out, thirteen years on, Mr Cannon,' I said, paving the way for a regretful no thank you. 'There's hardly likely to be any evidence.'

'Dwain's the evidence,' he snapped.

'True. If you say so.' I drew a stick picture of Dwain with twelve fingers.

'And I've been paying support maintenance all these years. Some weeks it's been bloody hard. Bled me dry, she has. And that damned Child Support Agency. They follow me around wherever I go. I couldn't escape if I tried. It's been driving me mad. Sometimes I wanted to kill myself. Finish it all. Drive off Beachy Head.'

This sounded genuine. 'Have you ever seen Dwain?' I asked.

'No, I thought it better not to see the kid. I didn't want to get involved. I'm no father figure. Next thing she'd have me taking him to football matches.'

I finished writing up my notes. I needed the mother's name and address, also boyfriend's, if he knew it. Lucky I had the ladybird. Have spotted car, will travel.

'I shall need names and addresses, also any photographs of you as a child and about aged twelve, the same age as Dwain.'

'I expect my mum's got some.'

'Will you get them, please? Names and addresses now. Mother of Dwain first. You must know her name at least.'

'Her name is Nesta Simons. And I know where she lives. Down East Latching way. A ground floor flat in a terrace. Near a duck pond. I followed her home one day. Nearly pushed her in the sodding pond, pardon my language.'

Near a duck pond . . . I couldn't be that lucky, could I? My friend Mavis, she of the Oscar winning fish cafe and bronzed lovers, lived in a first floor flat in a small terrace of villas near a duck pond in East Latching. But East Latching could be teeming with duck ponds, a positive duck sanctuary. I'd visited Mavis a couple of times, once after her face had been bashed in and secondly to take her a doggy gift (the untrainable Jasper).

'Boyfriend's name?'

'Don't know.'

'Date of party and Dwain's date of birth?'

'Don't know. I was drunk, I told yer.'

'Is there anything at all you can tell me?' He was not being much help. Yet it sounded like a real story. He was obviously fed up with paying support. It must run into thousands of pounds over twelve years and an electrician would not earn that much.

'Are you married, Mr Cannon?'

'No, couldn't afford to, could I? But I've got a girlfriend now. And no, I ain't telling you her name. She's got nothing to do with all this. I want to keep her out of it.'

But I did see a connection. He wanted to stop paying support now that he had a girlfriend to take out. Perhaps they wanted to get married or go on holiday. Perhaps the girlfriend was pushing him to take these steps.

I pulled out a contract form, filled in a few details, explained my rates of pay, and asked Mr Cannon to sign on the dotted line.

'Hourly rate,' he said. 'I can't afford any more.'

'No problem,' I said. 'Of course, you could solve all this quite simply. Have a DNA test. You have to provide two samples . . . one from you and one from Dwain. It can be anything. Blood, saliva, hair. The genetic profile is accurate to a millionth. But it's a complicated procedure and takes a couple of weeks.'

'Can I get it done on the NHS?'

'No, you have to pay. It costs about £200. There are several private diagnostic firms which do it. Would you like me to find out for you?'

He shook his head, pursed his lips and got up. I looked at my button-back quickly to see if his depression had left signs on my chair. Note: keep an eye open for second-class chair for second-class clients. Cancel note: Jordan, you are a snob.

'£200? I'm paying out enough already,' he muttered. My sympathy was evaporating. How come it had taken him so long to do anything about the situation? Any man with guts or doubts would have challenged Nesta a long time ago.

'I'll do my best,' I said insincerely. 'I'll phone you as soon as I have any news.'

'It had better be good. And I want reports. Written reports. I want it in writing.'

I put on a tape of James Last as soon as the morose Mr Cannon had gone out of the door. I needed some brass. Soon 'Perfidia' shook the gloom out of my office and the confident trumpet dusted off the cobwebs. A few Latin steps had my circulation bouncing in time.

'Dancing with yourself again, I see,' said Doris, passing my open door, her arms full of shopping. Her general grocery store was two doors down from me. She often looked in, mainly to check on my state of health. 'You'd better see someone about it. Could be catching.'

'I've got two cases,' I said cheerfully. 'I'll be able to eat this week. Stock up on food. Frugally.'

'Do you ever eat any other way? My shop'd go bankrupt if all my customers lived on tinned soup and soya. Seen Miguel recently? He's your best bet, you know. Hasn't he been feeding you in his classy restaurant?'

I shook my head. 'He's gone away, taking a holiday in South America. Checking up on the old homestead. Didn't you know? I thought you knew everything.'

Doris sniffed, rearanging her heavy bags. 'You forget, the Mexican only opens in the evenings. I'm closed by then. Too late for the likes of me.'

'I'll carry those,' I said, following her.

'No, you won't. I'm not an invalid.'

I let Doris go on ahead and open up her shop. I gave her time to empty the bags of bargains bought at the cut-price supermarket at the back of town and put them out on her shelves with a new price. I'm sure it was illegal.

'Two cartons of soya milk, two tins of lobster soup and three apples and three oranges,' I listed as I sailed in.

'Lobster? What do you think this is? Fortnum and Mason? I got tomato, vegetable, mushroom.'

'One of each.'

'That makes three tins, not two.'

17

'I'm feeling extravagant.'

'There's a fine line between being extravagant and being plain wasteful. You'll never touch the mushroom. It's all listed chemicals.'

'If you say so,' I said meekly. Doris and I got on well. It was a benevolent friendship. She said what she thought and I agreed.

'So what are these two new cases?'

'Sorry, client confidentiality. Like a doctor.'

'Doctor, my foot. You are the one who needs to see a doctor. Get a proper job, girl. That nice man, Francis Guilbert, would give you a job in his store any time.'

'Excuse me, didn't I solve who bashed up Mavis's face? Aren't that unsavoury pair coming up before the Old Bailey any month now? At present residing behind bars, en suite, smoking, playing snooker and watching television. Even the wife is up for GBH.'

'One of your few successes, if I may say so, and more by luck than deduction, Jordan.'

This was not one of my days for deep discussion. I paid for my purchases, sent Doris a cryptic smile and departed. I was hungry. I ate an apple, unwashed, on the way back to my shop. How I loved my shop, the feel of the place, the old things full of memories and people long gone. They were still with me, something of them lingered, intangible. Don't ask me how I know, but I do.

I didn't know where to start. Surveillance, surveillance. I'd got two lots of surveillance, fortunately not overlapping. The theatre manager and the single boozy mother. DI James . . . please help me. Give me a clue. Lend me two minutes of your professional mind. Give me two seconds of your personal attention. Let me use the computer unit. Hold my hand. Touch my face. I don't care which. Anything.

The apple made me feel even hungrier. I put up the CLOSED FOR LUNCH sign and made tracks for Maeve's Cafe. It was beginning to feel mild. She grinned at me as I went in, Jasper thumped his tail. I stroked his head. He looked a happy dog now.

'Look who's over there,' she whispered out of the side of her mouth. 'Your detective friend.' I did not need to look. I already felt his presence. I could see him without looking.

DI James had my favourite window seat. He was staring out of the steamy glass, a chip halfway to his mouth. He did not know I was there and I could watch the way his vulnerable mouth took the chip in a sweet, pleasurable curve. He would kiss like that. A curve that would seek sweetness from your lips, like a honey from a flower.

'Hi there,' I said, keeping my voice steady, sitting on the spare seat at his table. 'How's Latching's most famous cop? Still hitting the headlines?'

He had been mentioned in the arrest of the Sussex gang who'd been targeting the big stores, Guilbert's being one of them. I could not resist reminding him that I had given the police their first lead.

'Hi there, Jordan. No more headlines. How are you? Been taken hostage recently? You haven't phoned me.'

I couldn't answer. I had to look at him first. Drink in that chiselled face, those ocean-blue eyes, the cool look, the granite chin. When would he ever look at me properly? See the real Jordan Lacey, my tawny hair, windblown and unfussed, the woman who loved him to distraction but never let on. Always a lady hiding the tramp within. My knees buckled.

'Not recently, James. It's been pretty quiet. Latching has gone into its pre-spring conception lullaby. You know, little things planted and growing, like babies and bulbs. Watch the birth columns later in the year. And you know I never phone you.'

'I don't know what you are talking about.'

'Those chips look nice.'

'Try one. Be my guest.'

I had not seen him since the lift home. Where had the time

gone? Had he even noticed? There was never a day when I did not think of James. But the time kaleidoscoped into now as I chewed one of his chips and Mavis brought me a plate of today's special: scampi and chips. Real scampi, not bits scrounged from other fish, golden and delicious flesh of the sea.

'Put that inside you,' she said like a nanny.

I flashed her a thank-you smile. Since her face-bashing, we did not always need words. First-class female bonding. Things had progressed.

'James. Can you look up a name for me, on the PNC? I've got to start somewhere with my two new cases. I've no jumping off point. I hope you'll be able to help me.'

'You know I can't do that.'

'You've done it before.'

'Did I? I must have been out of my mind.'

'It isn't much to ask. Just one little name. It would only take a minute. Half a minute.'

James added some more tomato sauce, tipping the plastic bottle upside down. He was a ten gallon sauce man. 'What's one little name in the great scheme of things? But I'm not promising anything,' he said, forking another chip.

'Phil Cannon, Nesta Simons, Gill Frazer and Brian Frazer.'

James choked. It was either a chip or the sauce.

'I thought you said one name,' he spluttered. I poured him some water from the jug Mavis kept on the counter. 'That's four names.'

'Yes, just one name. You can pick which one. You choose. I'd be so grateful.' I put on my grateful face.

He finished his meal then got up, all rangy and suppressed energy, ran a hand over his cropped hair. He was going already. So soon. A cloud gathered and that was just inside Maeve's Cafe. My appetite disappeared even though the scampi was delicious.

He lent over and took a chip from my plate.

'One of mine, I think,' he said.

He put a tenner on the counter and spoke to Mavis. 'I'll treat Miss Moneypenny over there,' he said, nodding in my direction. 'Add a cup of tea and a chocolate ice cream. Her stamina needs building up.'

'I don't want an ice cream,' I said.

'Typical,' he said, with relish. 'That woman is never grateful.'

Grateful. What had I to be grateful for? That he'd allowed me to breath the same cubic foot of air? His carbon monoxide. Pause for cough. Nasty police station breeds germs.

I could hardly finish that meal. Each morsel had to be forced down. Mavis looked at me suspiciously. She probably thought I was pregnant. Father unknown. The chips got smuggled out in a paper napkin. The beady-eyed gulls would appreciate them. They could smell food a sea mile off. They honed in like Exocet air missiles, practically snatching the chips out of my hand. It was unnerving. I swear they had grown bigger beaks over the winter. Any minute they might take a fancy to my fingers.

It was like living on a seesaw. Up one day, down the next. My feelings swung giddily from one emotion to another, from one man to another but not in a promiscuous way. There were four courses of alternative action open to me:

1. Embark on passionate Latin–British affair with dishy Miguel, owner of posh Mexican restaurant. Money and wine.

2. Embark on unkempt, downbeat affair with besotted Jack, owner of Pier Amusements and flashy metallic blue Jag. Money.

3. Embark on marathon cook-in for Joshua, scrounger supreme, sweet charmer and part-time inventor. Pass.

4. Embark on becoming sexual plaything of Derek, violent, possessive, moody, sulk expert supreme. No safe conduct.

All of whom said they adored me to different degrees.

Thank you, but no. I'd stick to a good book.

Note I have not mentioned DI James or divine jazz

trumpeter, both of whom have a key to my heart. That left DS Ben Evans in the talent parade, unknown factor on the fringe, but nice enough. Perhaps I would take in Sunday evening jazz at Shoreham airport. If the Detective Sergeant was there, then what a coincidence.

State of heart solved temporarily. I threw the oily paper napkin in a bin and walked the pier. My eight minutes of solace. The sea below was a deep green, splashing the rusted girders with lazy insolence. The balmy temperature was a signpost to spring. A gaggle of five geese flew over my head in perfect formation, long necks craning. I was entranced, stood with my head tilted back. They flew parallel to the sea, seeking some inland pond for a romantic rendezvous. All the creatures of the earth knew that spring was coming. Why should I be the only one left out?

The Brian Frazer surveillance was more than a dead end. It was a complete fiasco, a black hole of zero results. I followed him regularly, sold ice cream at the theatre, watched a couple of plays, followed him home. I was beginning to think Mrs Frazer had made it all up. Wives can be devious. She could have got me watching him for a completely different reason, not wanting to tell me in actual words. It has been known. The police often get called out to domestic affrays only to find that the real reason is hiding in a wardrobe without any pants on.

Then I got lucky. I was combing the charity shops for stock. My shop was a bit low on classy stuff. It needed a lifesaving injection, a lift, some overlooked Dresden or Art Deco Clarice Cliff pottery. Quality has a way of winning out. I was sifting through cigarette cards and had found some of the Lambert & Butler Aviation series. It was not complete. I was looking at Graham White's five-seater biplane, awed by the elegance of the design, when I became aware of a man beside me.

How did I know it was a man? The hands, of course. Usual giveaway. Knuckled and square, nails blunt, slightly bitten. But the sleeve cuffs were floral and the coat crimplene.

'Do you collect cigarette cards?' I said brightly.

The watershine raspberry-pink lipstick parted in a polite smile, solid black mascara fluttered. The pitted skin was hidden under Estee Lauder's Enlighten, shade Outdoor Beige.

'No. But they are most interesting, aren't they?' agreed Brian Frazer. 'I don't collect them, of course.'

I could definitely charge for this encounter.

'Don't I know you?' I said artlessly.

'No, I don't think so. I'm new to this area.'

I had a kind heart and he was panicking. So I let him go.

'See you around,' I said.

Three

B rian Frazer, or was he calling himself Briony now? Brian Frazer toured the charity shops, buying tasteful little items. Anyone would think he was setting up a love nest. A velvet evening bag? An embroidered traycloth? A mirror decorated with pastel flowers?

How he managed in those shoes, I'll never know. I gave him a six for determination. I rarely wear high heels. I'm a trainers or boots person. But Brian Frazer valiently tottered round in a pair of ankle-strap wedges and I bet his feet hurt. Still, if you gotta do it, you gotta do it.

I logged my sighting and route march and wondered how Mrs Frazer would take the news. It might be hysterics and smelling salts, or she might hit the gin. A double gin and low calorie tonic was my bet. Two ice cubes and a slice of lemon.

Was I about to draw a double line under the job, too? Would she instruct me to continue following her husband or was confirmation all she wanted? Perhaps she had a quick divorce in mind. And I'd hardly earned enough to pay my shop expenses. I might hang on in there a couple of days longer. No harm done. He might do something spectacular, like impersonating Liza with a 'Z', busking on a street corner near Marks and Spencer.

The hospice charity shop had a wedding room upstairs. A heavy red rope hung across the stairs so that grubby fingers could not mark the merchandise. Brian Frazer was actually asking an assistant to show him the wedding dresses. She looked at him with some astonishment.

I turned to another assistant and smiled, all shy and virginal. 'May I also see the wedding dresses, please? I'm planning a June wedding. Three small bridesmaids too. It's going to cost a fortune.'

'Certainly. Perhaps you'd like to follow Julie up the stairs. We're a bit short-handed down here.'

Upstairs was a room full of utter luxury, frothy, elegant and expensive beauty, pearls and lace embroidery, glistening and glowing, cascades of dreams that had walked down an aisle towards the man they loved. I could almost hear Mendelssohn's triumphant wedding march.

A whole wall rail was hung over with a row of wedding dresses, brocade, lace, silk, taffeta, elaborately embroidered, pearled, trains trailing yards, bouffant skirts spilling over the floor. White, cream, ivory, magnolia, champagne, tucked, flounced, ruched. Empty, armless sleeves held out pearled cuffs to me. Wear me, they pleaded. We've only been worn once.

I'd never wear one. I was not the fluffy type. The nearest I'd get to a wedding outfit would be white jeans. Besides, no man would walk with me to church. Left in the porch more likely, making small talk with the vicar, that would be my fate. And left with the bills to pay, no doubt.

I felt quite faint. How could a display of dresses affect the emotions? I was getting soft. The adjacent wall of bridesmaids' dresses steadied my nerves. At least they were in rainbow colours and designs, some flowered, long and short, puffed and innocent, skirts swishing as Brian went along the rail. He pulled out an extravagant lilac taffeta.

'No, no, not exactly what I was looking for,' he said, hastily. 'Sorry. I can't explain. I want something really unusual and spectacular.'

You bet, I thought. How unusual could a man get? Veils and headdresses filled an alcove. Floral garlands, white lace gloves, white brocade shoes lined up on shelves. Huge brimmed hats with overblown roses in boxes. It was all too much. I was walled in by weddings.

'We get new ones in all the time,' said Julie. 'Come in again.'

'Yes, thank you. I will.'

I fled down the stairs. My endurance was nil. I needed sea air. My asthma was coming on, airways constricting. All the old deodorant, talcum powder and perfume was clogging my airways. There must have been a pint of perfume lingering in that room.

The pier walked in eight minutes and Maeve's Cafe was my next call. The cafe was full but with no one that I knew. No dark crew cut silhouetted against a window. I leaned against the counter and drank a cup of tea, my style, weak with honey.

'Mavis, can I ask you about the terrace where you live?'

'Sure, thinking of moving? One of the houses is up for sale. Don't ask the price. It's monopoly money.'

'But you have a flat?'

'Yes, number five is the only house that has been divided. All the others are still lived in as houses.'

'Do you know all your neighbours? Isn't there another that's divided into flats?'

'What's all this about? Are you asking me to snoop on someone?' Mavis looked susicious. She was trying a new hair colour called Burnished Blonde.

'No, of course not. But I'm interested to know if a woman called Nesta Simons lives near you.'

'She does indeed, a couple of doors down. And the son from hell. Nesta and Dwain, a right little tearaway. That's a house, not a flat. My goodness, that kid is spoilt rotten. I know what I'd do to that young man. He needs a firm hand.'

'Would you say . . .' This was difficult. 'Would you say that Nesta has a lot of visitors?'

'You mean, men visitors? She sure does. Like a bus station at times. In and out all day long.'

'The same men?'

'Jordan, get off it. Are you interrogating me? I'm not answering questions like that. How should I know if it's the same men? I don't stand at my window, making a list. And I won't, not even for you.'

'Would you let *me* stand at your window?'

I could see her thinking. She poured me another cup of tea. I'd be awash with caffeine. She did owe me. If it was me doing the snooping, then she was not involved. But what about her own visiting fishermen? She would not want me around then, getting in the way. I could always pretend I was the cleaner or take Jasper for a walk.

'I'll think about it.'

'Please don't take too long or I'll be driven to hiding in the bullrushes.'

'You'd have to tell me when you're coming.' She was giving in slowly. 'I'd have to know.'

'By arrangement, I promise, Mavis. No dawn or midnight swoops. I could walk Jasper. Surrogate walker.'

She gave me a sharp look. 'You didn't say anything about midnight.'

I backed off. 'Sorry. Joke, Mavis. Just a joke. Not one of my best.'

It was an extraordinary moment. I was laying on cold, wet pebbles on a darkened beach, looking up at the stars in the night sky.

'Can you see Venus?' DI James asked me. He was on the shingle slope beside me, bundled up in jersey and anorak, only the shape of his face showing, half in shadow. In repose, he looked Greek classical. His straight nose, the jutting jaw, forest of eyebrows forever etched in my mind. The stern look had gone. His deep-set eyes, if I could see them, had probably lost their usual disapproval. They held no colour. I was mesmerized by the plane of peace resting on his features.

'No, where is it?'

'Low down, on the horizon, over there. That red light. Venus is a red star.'

I sat up on the shingle and looked at the glowering black of the horizon. There was definitely a red light, faintly twinkling, a bit low down for a star. So that was Venus. I was looking at Venus. How many other people in the world were doing the same? A thousand, a hundred, a dozen, or was it just me and James?

'No, not that light, idiot woman. That's a ship in the Channel. Can't you see that it's moving? Slightly higher, to the right.'

There was another light, swathed in cloud, with only the faintest tinge of colour. I suppose it was tinted pink in comparison to the icy blue of the rest of the stars in the galaxy.

Then I felt the cold sharpness of pebbles pressing into the bareness of my back. It was extraordinary. I could not understand how my skin had got bare. I thought I was fully dressed in my usual head to toe cover-up, suitable for a cold spring night, nearing a bleak midnight.

How did I know it was midnight? Mavis had given me the thumbs-down for midnight. Was that why I was here? The chill of the pebbles jabbed my thoughts and the base of my spine. My jeans were round my thighs. Had the zip fractured? Had I wriggled down the slope in order to find a more comfortable hollow?

A clothed body was moving against me with urgency, pressing hard. I could not believe it. Here was I on a black, deserted pebbled shore, half undressed, in a perishing easterly wind and someone was making love to me. Should I fake a tidal orgasm? Half of me was delighted, the other half convulsed with hysterical laughter at the absurdity.

Of course, it wasn't DI James. Or Miguel. Or Jack. It wasn't anyone. Just a fragment of dream that punctured my continued starvation. I rolled over in bed, my T-shirt wrinkled up, a large tortoiseshell butterfly clip jabbing my bottom. So much for passion. It was a lump of cheap plastic.

But I would look tonight for Venus. See if it was really there. Pink.

Jasper was appointed surveillance aid number one. Mavis lent him to me. We walked the duck pond in endless perambulations till even Jasper lost interest in the ducks and begged to be taken somewhere else. Dwain appeared from his house, a noisy boy, kicking a ball and playing a loud ghetto blaster at the same time.

He did not look like Phil Cannon but then it was hard to tell at that distance. He looked like a normal, scruffy boy, hair spiked, clothes too big and baggy.

'Yeah, yeah, yeah,' he intoned to the ball's bouncing.

'Hi,' I said. 'Are you a Beckham fan?'

'I don't rate footers,' he said scornfully. 'I'm into rugby, man's game, doncha know nuffink? Yeah, yeah.' He turned away with indifference.

End of conversation.

Jasper came to my rescue. The dog saw the ball as an end to boredom, suddenly tugged the lead out of my hand, and tore off with the ball, joyfully yelping and leaping into the air.

'Strewth,' said Dwain. What school did he go to? 'Gimme back me ball.'

Now I can still run. And I outran Dwain who was soon puffing and blowing like the unhealthy PlayStation child he was. I caught up with Jasper but instead of taking the ball away from him, I encouraged the dog to tear off with it again.

'Go get it, boy,' I shouted.

'Gimme b-back . . . me ball,' puffed Dwain, dragging along a way behind.

'Does your father play rugby?' I asked, strolling back.

'Dunno.'

'Haven't you ever asked him?'

He shot a suspicious glance at me as if he was always being interrogated by PIs. Perhaps he was. Perhaps I was the latest in a long line of investigators who Phil Cannon had employed.

'Wotcha wanna know fer?' the boy asked.

'No reason at all,' I said. 'Merely small talk until my dog decides to bring back your ball.'

'That ain't your dawg,' he said. 'That dawg belongs to that batty woman.'

Now I don't mind what people say about me but I object to them being rude about my friends. And Mavis was no way batty. She was a sane and rational person, maybe with a stretched love life and a trifle quick on the sharp draw, but nevertheless perfectly normal.

'She is not batty,' I said indignantly.

He scowled at me as if I was too dim to bother with. 'Fish and chips, fish in batter, batty. Got it?'

He made me feel a hundred years old, then I remembered I could run faster. Jasper came back with the ball, grinning with satisfaction. 'Good boy,' I said, taking the ball from him. It was dripping with saliva. 'I'm afraid you'll have to wash the ball. Sorry.'

Dwain snatched it away from me, not a word of thanks, and turned on a scruffy heel. I was no more nearer deciding whether he looked like Phil Cannon or not. But there was certainly an attitude link. Could you inherit an attitude?

I took Jasper home and he flopped out on the floor too exhausted to climb the stairs to Mavis's flat. 'For heaven's sake, Jasper, have a heart. Do you expect me to carry you?'

'JASPER . . .' At the sound of Mavis's voice, he was up the stairs in a flash, tail thumping with joy. Doggy soulmates.

'Want a cup of tea?' Mavis grinned. 'Thanks for taking him out. Jasper has more energy than all the dogs in Latching.'

'Dawgs,' I said.

'Pardon?'

'That's what they are called. Dawgs.'

'You've been talking to Dwain. I told you he was a charmer.'

Staking out at Mavis's flat was not ideal. Window-watching brought on the cramps. I occasionally caught a glimpse of a lean, fit, bronzed fisherman arriving, all weatherbeaten and sex-starved, and scarpered pretty quick. Not easy when hormones were stirring. Fortunately, there was a back door for refuse bags, milk deliveries etc, and I went out that way.

I looked back and saw Mavis drawing the curtains. She looked happy, face glowing, and I realized how barren my life had become. I wondered when Miguel would be back. There was no point in waiting for DI James to come to his senses and see in me where his future lay.

I might give him one last chance. Like now.

The police station was almost empty. Had the villains gone on holiday? I always got a twinge when I went in, remembering my WPC days, the happy carefree ones, not when I was dismissed to save the skin of an inefficient senior officer who let a rape suspect go free. A scandal I was trying to forget. I should have had counselling. It was not in vogue then.

'May I see DI James?' I asked the new desk sergeant. My friend, Sergeant Rawlings, was not on duty.

'Who shall I say?'

'Ms Lacey.'

I read all the wanted notices while I waited. Obviously not a convenient moment. One down, already.

'So, Jordan. What is it this time?'

My hopes fell. He was annoyed and curt. It was written all over his face, etched with overwork and lack of sleep. The job was killing him. Didn't he ever take any time off? What had happened to rotas and rest and recuperation?

'When's your next day off?' I asked.

He looked at me as if I'd started speaking in a foreign language. Sinhalese? 'Say that again?'

'Day off,' I said, slowly and clearly. 'The kind of day when you do not have to go to work.'

'Not sure.' He leaned closer to inspect my face. 'Are you feeling all right?'

'Would you like to walk the Roman walls of Chichester with me? Third century, one and a half miles. Or watch the tide flood Bosham village, making a guess about Canute's throne? We could visit what's left of the towering ruins of the Benedictine guesthouse at Boxgrove Priory. Courtesy of Henry VIII. It's all free.'

He was making an effort. 'Have you been drinking?'

'Of course. Water, coffee, orange juice.'

'I mean the hard stuff.'

'Hard coffee?'

He ran his hand over the almost non-existent cropped dark hair on his head. 'Jordan. I haven't time for this nonsense. If you want to see me, come to the point.'

'I would like to seduce you,' I said. Was this me speaking? I must be out of my minuscule mind. My knees weakened. 'But first, we ought to go out together and get to know each other.'

There was a sort of stunned silence. A bee was buzzing against a window like a vacuum cleaner. I could hear a phone ringing, unanswered, somewhere, in the distance. Sun rays, of a kind, made a weary effort to lighten the office.

'Jordan, go home. Have a cold shower. Take an aspirin.'

I stood still, ice frosting my veins. What had I said? Was this my answer? Did he know what he was doing? DI James was hovering, anxious to get away now. Was I so completely unattractive that he could not even come halfway to make his refusal palatable, to save my pride?

'James . . .' My voice trailed away.

He was disappearing along the corridor, tucking in his shirt. 'I checked one of those names for you. Nesta Simons. Three convictions for shoplifting. Fined for soliciting. Now will you leave me alone?'

*   *   *

Miguel Cortes had returned from his holiday in South America. He looked well fed, relaxed, at ease, his dark curly hair touched with the sun. His restaurant was full, a well-dressed parade of widows and divorced women who fancied him, who queued for his flashing smile and personal service. But when he saw me standing hesitantly in the doorway, his face lit up. It was like a drug. It immediately lifted my heart and I smiled back.

'*Caro mia*, Jordan, joy of my life, face of an angel. Come in. You have come to eat? Yes? This special table, I have saved for you every evening.'

'Hello, Miguel. Nice to see you. Did you have a nice holiday?'

It might be a polite lie but I did not care. There was a small table in a corner with a red rose in a vase. It had 'Reserved' on a card so he might be telling the truth.

He removed the menu. 'I choose for you. I choose meal and excellent wine. Then, if you permit, I will sit with you and we will talk until the stars fade from sky.'

'Lovely,' I said. 'All the stars?' It might take a long time.

'I have brought you a present, a poncho from my homeland. It will keep this cold heart warm. Very special wool. Red and navy. The colours of passion.'

'Miguel. How kind.'

'That is me, kind all over. But *I* should be keeping you warm, not a poncho.'

It was a superb meal, beautifully cooked by Miguel, hot and spicy, served by Miguel, and eaten with Miguel when he had time to join me. Miguel chose a Chilean red wine and poured me glass after glass. Crushed plum and blackberry, whiff of spice. Then as his restaurant began to empty, he came and sat down, drank from my wine glass like a drowning man.

'I can taste your lips,' he said.

It was heady stuff.

Four

Gill Frazer's house was as boring inside as it looked outside. No wonder her husband was dressing up in women's clothes. Anything to relieve the poverty of imagination in their home.

But surely his work as manager of the Community Shore Theatre brought enough spice into his life without adding earrings and wedgie sandals? I stood on the doorstep and rang the bell. Chimes announced my presence. I cringed at the tune. Some football anthem. What further horrors lay in store?

She opened the door wearing stretch fawn trousers, a green embroidered buttoned cardigan and an apron printed with a pineapple pattern. Hello, trendy fashion icon.

'Hello, Mrs Frazer. I'm Jordan Lacey. Remember me? First Class Investigations. I have a report for you. May I come inside?'

If my colour coordination could manage to come along inside with me, I nearly added. It might refuse.

'Miss Lacey, of course. I didn't expect you so soon. Oh dear, I hope it's not bad news.'

Well, it wasn't bad news like the budgie had died, but it was bad news if it confirmed her suspicions.

She took me through to their back sitting room. There was an austere-looking dining room to the left of the hall, sturdy square table in the centre with four chairs and heavy sideboard. No plants or flowers or prints. Nothing on the sideboard either. Had they sold the family silver?

The sitting room was as bereft of personal input. Not a single book, magazine, newspaper, plant or bag of knitting laying around. Two armchairs were placed regimentally in front of a flat 28-inch television screen. Two cushions in a fascinating shade of fawn were placed at exactly the same angle. A glass-fronted bureau held a small group of trophies but I was not able to see what they were. A coffee table was laid with plain coasters. The faded curtains hung limply, without life or interest in their fate. They were just drawn or undrawn, waiting to be donated to a charity shop or car boot.

'Please sit down,' said Mrs Frazer. 'Would you like some coffee?'

'That would be nice,' I said, following her into the back kitchen. I was intrigued by the lack of character anywhere. The kitchen was the same. Everything was a vague off-beige. Was she colour-blind? The windowsill was bare. I would have grown herbs in pots as it got the morning sun. She took two mugs from a fitted cupboard. They were plain white without adornment. Weird, really. Mugs these days are a fun part of life. Cats, dogs, flowers, crude jokes, traditional, folksy. Jack's mugs, owner of the Pier Amusements, the booming business arcade and flashy Jag, were outrageously jokey. If they had been washed properly, I might have blushed.

'Have you anything new to tell me?' I asked as she filled a kettle with water from the tap. 'Cases like this change all the time.'

'I've hardly seen Brian lately,' she said. 'He works such odd hours. I'm always in bed by the time he comes home. We spend very little time together.'

'Why don't you do some volunteer work at the theatre,' I said, without stopping to think. 'They are always looking for extra help.'

'I couldn't work!' she said indignantly, her tight hair bouncing. 'Besides, my husband is the manager there. It wouldn't be right.'

I put on a noncommittal smile and nodded. 'Of course not. A position to keep and all that. Just a thought. What did you used to do, that is before you married Brian Frazer?'

'I was a nanny,' she said. I wondered if I had imagined the fractional hesitation before she answered. 'A very well paid job. Lovely house. Sweet children. Two boys.'

'How nice,' I said. 'I know very little about children. It must take a lot of patience.'

She was spooning in own brand supermarket instant coffee, not a real bean in sight. Cold milk from the bottle, stirred vigorously. 'Do you take sugar?'

'No, thank you.'

We took the mugs back to the sitting room and sat them on the coasters. Such immense fun. I felt giddy from lack of air. There was not a gin bottle in sight. Gill Frazer was obviously going to weep buckets. Shopping list: travel tissues.

'I'm very sorry to have to tell you, Mrs Frazer, but I have had a definite sighting of your husband wearing women's clothes.'

Her face went white but to her credit, she continued sipping her vile coffee. 'Go on,' she said, taking a deep breath.

I gave her time and place and description of clothes.

'Those are mine,' she said with remarkable composure. 'Even the wedge shoes. I couldn't think where they had gone.'

'Then, Mr Frazer went into a charity shop and upstairs into the bridal room. He spent a quarter of an hour looking at wedding dresses and bridesmaids' dresses.'

Now this shook her. She put down the mug and wiped her hands on the pineapples. 'Wedding dresses? Are you sure? How very extraordinary . . . whatever was he doing that for? We're already married.'

'Has Mr Frazer shown any signs of mental imbalance?' I asked carefully. I did not know how else to put it. I did not know his sexual orientation. It was nothing, these days. Suddenly I had the most appalling thought. My dearest DI James. He never looked at me, touched me, gave me any encouragement . . . but of course not, not a of shred of evidence, not a virile man like him. Surely, not?

Bits of me died. Every inch of James was aggressively masculine and dominant. There were WPCs swooning at his feet from here to Wapping. He just did not fancy me.

'You mean, is he gay?'

Bless her. For the first time I began to like her. I nodded in a sympathic way. 'Is he gay?'

'No. We make love every Friday night. Not very exciting but perfectly normal. What's that position called? You know . . . what everybody does?'

'Missionary?' Every Friday . . . this plain woman was lucky and she didn't know it. I couldn't remember any Friday ever when I had made love in any position, even in my dreams. Perhaps I should email my current batch of admirers and ask what they were doing this Friday.

Possible answers: Joshua – do we eat first? Jack – why wait till Friday? Derek – your place? Miguel – bellisimo, I'll bring roses. DI James – Jordan, are you ill?

Mrs Frazer was still talking. 'Something is seriously wrong with him, of course, but I don't know what it is. I'm very grateful for what you have found out already, but I need to know more. There must be a rational explanation. I mean, I found a magnifying mirror in the bathroom yesterday. It's got flowers round it. I didn't buy it.'

Instant recollection: Brian had bought that mirror at a charity shop. Was he making a statement in this colourless house? What about the traycloth?

'So, you'd like me to carry on?'

'Yes, please. Find out more. There must be a reason for this odd behaviour.' She was not drinking gin or weeping. She was not doing anything. A strange reaction. A non-female type of reaction. Very controlled.

'I've brought an invoice for the last few hours of work.' I handed it to her. It was modest. 'To keep things straight.'

She got up and fetched her handbag from a drawer. It was beige leather. 'Is cash all right?'

'Perfectly,' I said, face immovable.

She put the notes in my hand. They were the only spot of colour in the room. The crisp notes felt good against my skin. Doris, here I come, splashing out on food. More soup and soya.

'May I ask you something?' I said, folding the notes into my back pocket. 'How long have you lived in this house?'

'Three years,' she said. 'Since it was built in the garden of the big house next door.'

'And who lives in the big house? It looks so lovely.'

'Some really snooty people. Made of money. They barely speak to us, but were quick enough to sell off part of their garden. It's not our fault we're here, so close to them. They wanted to raise some capital. It's not fair to take it out on us. They made the profit.'

'And who are they?'

'You've probably heard of them.'

'How do they take it out on you?'

'It's the Fontane family. They own half of Latching, or used to. The family goes back decades, back to the riots in the 1800s. Mostly they sold off to the council so that those two monstrous multistorey car parks could be built. They had a gracious house on the front once. Sold that off, too. Money, money, money. Big block of flats now on the site.'

I knew it. They called it Fontane House. Seven storeys of red brick flats with glassed-in balconies and a hefty maintenance charge. I was not enamoured of the family. But I thought I had read that there had been a bereavement recently.

'Are they nice to Brian?'

I don't know why I asked that. It came out without any prompting.

'Nice? I don't know what you mean. We rarely talk to them. We are not exactly friendly. We don't socialize. They cut us dead when they see us.'

I put the mug down carefully, half drunk. 'Thank you. I must get on. Pretty busy these days. I'll continue to let you know what happens.'

She showed me to the door. 'Goodbye, Miss Lacey.'

I took a sideways wander round the house, hoping she was not looking out of a window. They only had a slice of garden. It had been a rather small plot. The flowerbeds were empty. Just a few weeds looking for a good time and a small clump of parsley. The most colourful thing about the garden were the plastic bags put out for the refuse collectors. As I left I realized that I had not seen Max, the son.

Bin-raiding, that was the answer. I was going to go through people's rubbish for confidential documents. There was no excuse for not shredding with personal shredders selling for around £39.

Bin-raiding might give me a lead. I would have to stay up all night but that was nothing new. I needed new information desperately. Bank statements might tell me that Brian Frazer's finances were in a mess.

This was a positive decision. I looked at the Fontane's old Regency house and garden, spacious and elegant. They let the Frazers have a meagre corner of land on which one could hardly swing a cat. Their bin bags might also be interesting. No harm in having a quick look. They were not exactly my clients but they were connected (loosely) to the Frazers.

The ladybird car did not like the idea of going out at all. A cool midnight and she refused to start. She gave a cough, a revving whine and then a pathetic sigh. It helped a lot when I trudged to a late opening garage with a can, returned with a couple of litres of petrol and poured them in.

I spent the small hours creeping round like a burglar, grabbing black bags from the pavements outside the Frazers' house, the Fontanes' house and, just for luck, Phil Cannon's semi-basement flat in downtown Latching. His lights were still on, watching late-night TV. The paternity case might take on an entirely new dimension if I found a few eye-openers among his confidential documents.

The ladybird was even less happy, bundled up with a dozen or so assorted smelly bags. I had stuck labels on each one just in case. I didn't want the Fontanes' empty caviar tins getting mixed up with Phil's chicken tikka takeaway.

Dawn was breaking through the clouds, streaking light, as I hauled the bags out of my car and stacked them along the wall of the small yard behind my shop. But I didn't have time to look at the approaching rays of light or appreciate their beauty. I tried not to think of the task ahead, stiffling a yawn.

'Two pairs of rubber gloves, please,' I said to Doris as soon as she opened up her shop.

'You've been up all night,' she said. 'I can tell and I hope it was someone nice.' Her eyes spelled Miguel.

'No such luck,' I said, propping open my eyelids. I'd caught a catnap on my office floor and my back was stiff. 'Work and more work. Check my mileage.'

'You look a mess. Go home and have a bath. My shop's got a reputation. I've got to think of my other customers.'

'Don't worry. It's high on my agenda, too.' I put a pound on her counter. Doris looked at it as if the coin smelt bad. 'Is that enough?'

'It'll do,' said Doris. 'I don't want you going through your pockets. Never know what you might find.'

'Thanks.' Doris always made me feel humble.

If I had expected to solve both cases with one bag-raid, I was seriously mistaken. The litter littering my yard was horrendous. It smelt as bad as the council landfill site on the edge of town. I cut down on my breathing.

There was nothing of interest. Just revolting piles of rubbish which had to go back into bags and be disposed of somehow. It made me shudder. Get on with it, I told myself. Don't be such a wimp. This is work. You're getting paid for it.

I did the refilling with my eyes closed. It was like wrapping up Christmas presents. My usual reckless style of packing. Thrown it in any old how, catch the paper, fold and tape. Even the book of one-liners I gave to DI James last Christmas had looked as if a three-legged ostrich had packed it, instead of being wrapped with love (mine) and sealed with kisses (mine also).

There was no energy left for distributing bags around the neighbourhood. I stacked them outside my place. The refuse collectors could think there had been some wild street party.

I was going to spend another night cruising around in my car, picking up bin bags. We'd have to go through a car wash to get rid of the smell. I did not feel guilty. It was their fault for putting rubbish out where it could be stolen. And as for private documents . . . their lawyers should be sacked.

My second trawl was more successful. I stacked the bags in my backyard and leaned on the ladybird, exhausted, eyes drawn and dark. I waited until the dawn arose, half asleep on the floor of my office, stiff-necked and cold. When had I last seen DI James? It seemed like months. I made a lot of coffee but it made me feel sick. Water was the answer but it did not warm the bones.

Time to trawl through bags. It started to rain. In no time I was soggily soaked. The bags were slippery and several had split and spilled their contents.

If only I was still working for the Guilberts, my previous case. I was fast going off this game. There must be easier ways of making a fast buck. I thought with longing of my little black dress and wearing it around Guilbert's store, pretending to be a shop assistant. The dress and shoes were being saved for that date with fate when DI James sought my company socially and carnally.

If ever.

The pieces fell out like confetti, a chuck of torn-up bank statements. I love bank statements. Read this life. I recognized the printout and familiar logo on the heading. Jigsaws are the occupation of residential homes but I guess I could put my mind to it. I might manage to co-join the scraps if the information was riveting enough.

Bottles, bags, yogurt tubs, banana skins, rotting food, torn tights . . . I cringed with disgust. My own rubbish was bad on a good day. And this was the middle of the night. A wet night.

It was time to call it a night. The ladybird stank. I stank. We both needed a carwash, inside and out.

I sat on a crate in the yard, searching for soggy bits of paper. They could belong to the Frazers or the Fontanes, the part with a glimmer of a name was essential. Some people tore off their name and address. Please, no, not this time . . .

A lot of the scraps were stuck to a wet shirt. It was pretty messy. One of the sleeves was half ripped out of the shoulder seam, slashed cut marks. In lust or rage, it had been given a wrench and the stitching had snapped and torn.

Then I smelt the wetness and saw the stain darken. It was not rain. I knew the difference. Rain has a lightness, a sweetness fresh from the clouds.

This was blood. Fresh blood. Human blood. And the man who'd worn the shirt had fought hard. I followed the rents with my eyes and imagined the scene. The cuffs were bloody and torn where he had fended off the knife, fighting for his life, wanting to live, needing a life.

Did I rush back and knock on doors and say, 'Excuse me. Have you got someone who is bleeding to death?'

I didn't want this. No more deaths, please. I'd had enough. The town had its spring face on, the way I liked it. Make it stay that way while I dry my feet. Especially now that my feet were getting better.

* * *

'I had the strangest feeling it was going to be you. A good citizen who shall be nameless, suffering from insomnia, reported a scavenger going through bin bags in the middle of the night. She thought it might be one of the car boot gang who steal from the charity shop bins for resaleable goods.'

'As if I would,' I said.

Detective Inspector James was leaning over the Sussex cobbled wall that flanked my back yard. He was tall enough to do this in comfort. Rain spiked his short hair like pearls on sticks. His lashes would be spiked too only I couldn't see them in the early morning gloom.

'Who else could it be trawling bin bags at dawn, I thought? None other than Latching's intrepid PI. And I can see you are completely unrecognizable in grade four surveillance gear. Well done, Jordan. Like the gloves touch.'

I swallowed the mockery. James was laughing at me. 'They are my own clothes,' I said. But I was still glad to see him, lust rising in my loins at the mere sight of his face. That old black magic, he had me in his spell. And he did not know it. He would never know. He thought I was that slightly mad, always irritating female who blighted his life, on and off duty.

I held up the torn and bloodied shirt. It flapped against my face, leaving a smear on my cheek.

'Know anyone who's been knifed recently?'

The banter slid from his face. He opened the yard gates and strolled in, hands in pockets, wondering what I had for him now to complicate his already overburdened life.

'How do you know it's a knife?' he asked, taking the shirt from me.

'Clean cuts,' I said. 'Nothing else makes straight incisions.'

DI James's face seemed grey and drawn. His expression withdrew as if remembering some scene he did not want me to know about. Sometimes he had an old-fashioned gallantry.

'A circular saw does,' he said. 'An underwater saw that rips up cables from the seabed. And we've just found the body of

a diver who got in the way of one. Not a pretty sight, Jordan.
Especially a body without a shirt. It might just be his shirt.'
He dropped the shirt into a plastic bag. 'Thanks, Jordan.
That's called cooperation.'

Five

Everyone knew the dead diver. Word spread along the shingle faster than a seagull could swoop and fly. The fishing fraternity were shocked, lost for words, weather-beaten faces stony.

'I can't believe it. I just can't believe it,' they said, shaking their heads. 'He was here yesterday, right as rain, working on the beach.'

The victim was the youngest son of a family that had fished off the coast of Latching for over eighty years. They had a string of boats and lockers along the shingle. Dinglewell & Sons was a well known name in the fishing industry. Their burnt orange lockers were a signature marking the coast, blooming like cubic art.

Roy was the youngest son. He was a playboy fisherman, a man that spent as much time sunbathing on the beach, flexing his muscles at the girls, jiving at dance clubs, drinking in pubs, as he did working his boat far out in the Channel, hauling in nets overflowing with bass and pollack, spider crabs and seaweed.

He also dived. That was his other hobby. He liked wrecks, old, submerged, abandoned by man and sea. He spent hours in a wetsuit, mask and flippers, searching the murky depths.

But Roy had gone for his last dive. He'd come ashore sprawled in a trawler's net.

I didn't ask James for details. I did not want to know. It was not my case and all the facts would be in the papers. The nationals took the story to its extremes. No prizes for which paper used which headline:

Sawed Sussex Fisherman In Net

SAW RIPS WRECK DIVER

DIVER DIES IN TREASURE WRECK

NET NETS CORPSE

And how come the shirt, torn and newly bloodied, was in a bin bag? My labelling system had come apart and I no longer knew which bag was from which house. But I could narrow it down. I could still count to four on a good day.

Second thought: was it his shirt? My blood chilled at a third thought. Mavis. Supposing Roy Dinglewell was one of her ardent suitors? Could be. She seemed to have no age barrier in her affairs. Anything with a pulse.

Anyway, who said it was Roy's shirt? That was an assumption. It could have belonged to anyone from the Frazer household, the Fontanes, Phil Cannon or the girly girl Nesta Simons. The options were open. My nightly collections had spread. DI James might have been distracting me from some core truth and he could do that easily. He had only to breath in my direction and I was confused.

I lay back in a lavender oil bath, in easily distracted mode, letting the warm water and the thought of James wash the night's detritus from the pores of my skin. If I closed my eyes, I could almost imagine that he was laying alongside me in the water, hip to hip, legs entwined, toes touching, his arm cradling my head away from the hard slope of enamel. It was an old style bath from the Dark Ages, no hollow plastic shell for me, washboarding in and out.

He had taken the shirt away in a clean plastic bag. Forensic, he said. But a diver would not wear a shirt. He wore a wetsuit. I'd seen the muscular Roy Dinglewell in his wetsuit many times and it left nothing to the imagination. Many females swooned. I was not the swooning type. My emotions were more sensual. I'd seen enough nude males, one way or another, alive and dead.

I dried off, ate muesli and sliced banana, changed the bottom sheet on my bed, walked to my shop, put up the CLOSED FOR LUNCH sign again and went on to Maeve's Cafe. At least it was still open. No signs of protracted grief.

It was nearly empty. A few early tourists were trying a fish and double chips breakfast, one of Mavis's new ideas. She was serving tea and slices of bread, so thick with butter she ought to be prosecuted by a health act.

'Hello, Jordan,' she said. 'Come for a cuppa?'

'Please. It's sunny outside but the wind is lethal.'

'I know. Spring in Latching is an old man's last breath.'

That was colourful but depressing. She'd made it up. I sat at my favourite table for two, sea view, eye on the door. No one came in. Mavis wandered over with a mug of weak tea and honey.

'I ought to charge extra, you know,' she said. 'Honey's dearer than sugar.'

'But you only show it a tea bag. That's a saving. And think of the custom I bring you,' I said, nodding her into the vacant chair opposite. She sat down, mascara immaculate, hair in place. 'I don't know how to say this . . . but are you heartbroken by the latest news from the beach?'

She was obviously a little bit heartbroken, but not your howling, wailing, deeply distressed type of fractured organ. She put up her hand, shielding her eyes for a moment.

'I knew Roy, of course. I've known him for years. Dishy young lad, real one for the girls. But, of course, he was far too young for me. Well, he was too young for me then, but later, I mean, he grew up, didn't he . . . What am I saying? It would have been baby-snatching. I preferred his father.'

'But you did know him?' I probed.

'Yes, of course. A sort of a late-afternoon stand, if you

can forgive the coarseness. He'd come off the beach, dripping with suntan oil and such a glorious colour. We'd nothing else to do. I wanted to make sure he didn't burn.'

My mug of tea cooled. Mavis, Mavis . . . lend me your hormones.

'Ah, yes, naturally. So you knew of him?'

'Carnally, yes. Intimately, yes, gloriously yes. But nothing else. No emotional bond.'

'Mavis, I can't cope with this language at ten o'clock in the morning.'

'Then you ain't going to make no great detective, my girl. You tell that hunky detective friend of yours that it was no accident. There were a lot out to get that boy, mark my words.'

'Why? Who was out to get him? What for?'

'I ain't saying no more.'

'Get him for what? What do you mean?'

Mavis clammed up. She rose, spotting a new customer hovering in the doorway. She could not afford to let anyone get away. On went her counter smile, even if her brain was spinning with memories of an afternoon making sure the boy didn't burn. No one came to me with that sort of problem.

I reeled back. This was not my case, I reminded myself. Finding the shirt had been accidental. I finished my tea, paid for it and went down on to the beach. It was the first time that I had felt brave enough to strip off my trainers. Summer was coming, at least I hoped it was. Not much sign of warmth yet. I tied the laces together and walked barefooted along the wet sand and rivulets of waters. The cool feel was marvellous. My toes tingled with the deliciousness. Gulls wheeled above me, well aware that I had nothing for them. Get going, girl, clear off, they screeched in orchestrated greed, you ain't brought nothing for us.

The tide was washing in, more debris and dead fish swirling with every encroaching wave. The face of the beach was desolation. People threw everything into the sea: bottles, bags, nappies, tampons . . . the sea was becoming the big dump site of the world. Heaven help the fish.

'Help! Help me! Someone help me!'

A very thin voice hung in the air.

I looked around. I could see no one. The empty beach was vast, not a soul, only me and the seagulls. But I had heard a voice.

I went on walking but still the voice was calling. Serious now, I stopped and looked around. A long, long way away I saw a stick figure. Waving. Boy, girl, man, woman . . . no knowing which.

Arms were waving. There was an urgency about the movement. I recognized a degree of panic in the windmill agitation. The hermit's cell I'd been trapped in during a previous case had generated the same panic in me. But there had been no one to see me wave except the spiders.

I changed direction, giving a casual signal back but not hurrying. There did not seem to be anything apparently wrong. We didn't get snakes on Latching beach.

I veered towards the slim figure. It was standing at the end of a long blackened wood groyne. The sea was coming in. I had been wrong about the times. It was racing in, like a horse with long legs. Translucent waves were washing round my feet. I hurried diagonally towards the figure, waved again so that she knew I had heard and was coming. It was a girl and she was frozen with fear.

Then I saw the cause of her panic. She was ankle deep in sand at the end of the groyne. The last post always generates a pool of sea water that sucks itself downwards. A puddle no bigger than a baby's bath but ten times as lethal. In a few minutes the sea would be washing round the post. In twenty it would be halfway up. In thirty, the post would be submerged and half the groyne would have disappeared under the water.

'I'm stuck,' she screamed. 'I can't get out.'

'I'm coming,' I called, not feeling brave.

'Help me! Help me!' the girl screamed again.

As I got closer, I saw her more clearly. She was about eleven or twelve, skinny, wearing shorts and T-shirt, long fair hair. Her face was wet with tears and her ankles were deep in swampy mud and sand at the end of the long wooden groyne. She was sinking deeper with each struggle. Her legs were being sucked under. She was frantic with panic which did not help.

'I can't get out,' she gasped. 'My feet are being sucked in. I can't move.'

'Don't worry,' I said. 'I'll get you out.'

I skirted the pool. No point in both of us getting stuck. The hardest firm sand was two feet further up. I stood there, braced one arm round the post and leaning out as far as I could stretch, hooked my other arm firmly under her elbow.

'Now, both together,' I said. 'One, two, three . . . pull hard on me. Use me as a lever.'

I used muscles I didn't know I had. Her feet surfaced violently like corks out of a fermented bottle. The combined effort was so forceful that she fell over, flat on her face, splashing across the pool. But her feet were free. She was crying again but with relief.

I helped her get up. 'All right, now?'

She nodded a lot, not speaking, covered in sand.

'Are you alone?'

'My father's somewhere.'

But not here obviously. Gone off for a quick one. She seemed embarrassed. Perhaps she had come down on to the beach against his orders.

'OK. Are you sure he's around? You'll go back to him?'

She nodded again, so I left her. She was safe now. I walked out to the edge of the waves, paddling about, deep in thought. The beach was still empty. She could have drowned. The slope of the shingle was steep and people on the promenade might not have seen or heard her cries above the noise of the constant stream of traffic.

A rare philosophical thought emerged. What if I had been put on this planet for this solitary moment of lifesaving? Perhaps this young girl was a rare creature with a high IQ who was destined to discover some immensely valuable cure for human ills. Cancer. Aids. Could be possible. Every genius was once small enough to be stuck in the sand.

I heard her voice again and turned round. The girl was climbing, halfway up the shingle, waving both arms, crossways, over her head.

'Thank you, thank you,' she was calling.

I waved back, hoping it conveyed my pleasure for the now public thank you. Gold star, humane medal, Brownie points.

Both of my cases were at a standstill. I had followed Brian Frazer until I was glazed with boredom. Apart from that one instance, his behaviour was normal, as normal as any theatre manager might be. He worked long hours, going home when he could. There was obviously a shift system because his times varied.

I decided that a different tactic was required on the cards. As yet I did not know what it was. Something moderately drastic but not too dangerous.

Phil Cannon and Nesta Simons were equally unproductive. But I guess that walking Jasper in the hope of seeing something monumental happening was a poor effort.

It was pulling-up socks time.

And my shop was not selling much. Had some sort of recession set in whilst I was otherwise occupied? I laid out the scraps of roughly torn bank statements on the floor and ironed them flat. I had never liked jigsaws and I did not enjoy piecing this lot together. There were too many figures and the picture wasn't up to much. One scrap had 'dolly-bird baby' written on it in poor handwriting. Now which bin had that come from? No idea. I threw it away.

A customer came into my shop, browsing around. No whooping, please or Japanese-style bowing and scraping. I maintained a dignified distance, pretending to sort books into alphabetical order. Fat chance. I had got as far as H for Higgins, when the customer came to the point.

'I want all your jewellery, silver and gold, and be quick about it,' he snapped harshly.

I looked at him in disbelief. He was a very ordinary-looking guy in jeans and Queen T-shirt. He had not bothered with a mask. I suppose he did not have to when a very sharp knife was nestling in his hand.

'You've made a mistake,' I said. 'I don't have any jewellery. I don't buy or sell silver or gold. This is a junk shop. High-class junk, of course.'

'Come off it, missus, who knows what you got out the back there? Be a good girl and go get it. And sharpish. I haven't got all day. And I know how to use this knife. You don't want me carving my initials on your face, do you?'

'Oh, what are your initials?' I asked.

Really, I do have a nerve. It was my WPC tactical training. That same training was sweeping over his features and appearance. But I did not like the look of the knife, or him. There was a gleam of sweat on his skin and his fingers were moving the knife in a restless way, like he was itching for a cut.

'Don't mess with me,' he snarled.

'OK, OK,' I said hurriedly. 'I'll go and fetch it. I've got some stuff out the back.'

I skeltered into my office behind the shop, straight through the scullery and out the back door into the yard. I didn't stop to even catch my breath. Once outside, I began to run round the block. I'd left my mobile phone in the shop on the counter. I ran into Doris's shop.

'I'm being held up,' I gasped. 'Phone . . .'

'Yeah, yeah and I'm Greta Garbo,' said Doris, hardly looking up from her shelf-stacking.

'True! There's a man in my shop with a knife in his hand. He threatened me. He's after anything silver or gold.'

'Well, he obviously picked the wrong shop. Some people have no sense at all.'

'Doris . . .' I collapsed against the counter. My asthma

didn't feel too happy. I started coughing. 'This is not a j-joke. C-can I use your phone?'

Doris looked at my wheezing and decided to humour me. She nodded towards the phone and I clumsily keyed the numbers of the Latching police station. A WPC answered.

I spluttered out the events, briefly, to the point. She said they would send someone round immediately, but there was little hope of the man still being in my shop. Unless he'd started reading a book.

'But he'll be out on the streets somewhere nearby. You can't fail to spot his Queen T-shirt.' My breathing had steadied now.

'Elizabeth or Bohemian Rhapsody?'

'Rhapsody.'

'Don't go back into your shop until we've arrived. Have you a friend with you?'

'Yes, I have a friend.'

I glared at same friend who was still looking at me with hovering disbelief. But she was pouring me out a tumbler of her disgusting cooking sherry. It took a high degree of friendship to drink it. The sweetness was cloying, thick as treacle, the alcohol content near zero.

'Lovely, thank you,' I said, choking.

A flashing police car drew up, all orange and green stripes and cubes. I went out on to the pavement. A tall figure got out of the car and for a moment I fell apart. I could fall apart just at the sound of his name. But it was not DI James. It was Detective Sergeant Ben Evans, his dishy colleague, younger, attractive in an uncomplicated way, always charming.

'Jordan,' he said, smiling. 'Are you all right? Where's this villain, threatening you with a knife? I'll carve him up for you.'

'He's in my shop,' I said, trying to look small and fragile and in desperate need of protection.

He was not in my shop. My shop was empty. He'd gone. My mobile phone had also gone, so had the meagre contents of my cashbox. At this rate of turnover I ought to be buying shares in a phone company. My last mobile got flung into a watermill. I felt in the back pocket of my jeans. At least I still had all my keys and some loose change.

'Wanna jump in the car and tour the streets? See if you can spot him? He can't have gone far.' He held the door open for me and covered my head so I did not bump it. Things were looking up. A DS with manners. 'Feeling well enough?'

'Sure,' I said nonchalantly, settling into the car seat, hoping he couldn't smell the cheap sherry on my breath. Nothing like a free ride with a good-looking policeman. I waved to Doris.

'Thanks for the drink,' I called.

'You're turning into an alkie,' she warned.

We drove around, scanning the streets. They were full of shoppers and early holidaymakers. The robber had disappeared. He could be in any bar, any dive, any joint. I peered out of the window, wondering where he'd got to. Drinking away my money, making calls on my phone. I'd better report it missing before he rang his bookie in New York.

Then I saw him. He was going through the swing doors of the seafront entrance of the Marks & Spencer store. But I stopped myself from calling out. It was like a nut getting caught in my throat.

'He's just gone into M & S,' I croaked.

DS Evans parked instantly, made a quick call for back-up, then ran into the store. But I wasn't watching him.

Brian Frazer was coming out of Marks & Spencer at the same moment in a fetching lilac trouser suit. His head was covered in a flowered scarf. He was wobbling on high-heeled sandals and his toenails were painted a strident red. His taste was appalling. The varnish didn't tone with the lilac. He needed guidance.

I got out of the police car. This was guidance time.

Six

B ut I did not get far. The arm of the law stopped me. Brian tottered off towards the pier, holding on to the scarf. It was blowy. Latching's favourite weather.

'Don't go, Jordan,' Ben said. 'I need you to make a statement. Back-up are at the other store entrance in the pedestrian precinct. They'll get him as he tries to leave.'

I nodded, containing my disappointment. There was no way I could dash off after receding lilac outfit when DS Evans had been so supportive.

He drove me back to the station. No sign of DI James or knife-wielding robber in custody. My friend, Sergeant Rawlings, was on desk duty.

'I could write a book about you,' he said, trying to find a biro that worked. 'We ought to compile a dossier of Jordan Lacey statements.'

'Dossier? That's a long word,' I said. 'I didn't know you knew such long words. It's from the French: to file and Latin: *dorsum*, the back.'

'Watch it, girl. We don't encourage anything intellectual in here. You won't get a fresh cup of tea next time. We have a stewed variety, you know.'

I grinned. I was one of Sergeant Rawlings' favourites. His rugged face always lit up whether I was marched, dragged or carried into the station. We'd known each other a long time.

'Wanna bet, Tiger?'

Making the statement took ages. Now I know how an

author feels. It took an hour to write four pages down in longhand. My recall of his appearance was excellent.

DS Evans took me over to a bank of computers and sat me down. This was new. I looked with interest at the blank screens, grey and winking.

'Like to go through mug shots?' he asked.

'How long have you had this equipment?'

'A few weeks. It's brilliant. We can run through dozens of faces in half the time. Feed in a few basic facts and it eliminates the superfluous, finds a compatible bank. No villain can escape us now.'

'Except the ones that get away,' I murmured.

He keyed in white, twenties, medium height, clean-shaven, thin-faced, pointy nose and dyed blonde hair. Then he deleted dyed blonde hair. It could have been a recent fashion statement.

'He could also have shaved off a recent beard,' I said, observant.

'We'll start with clean-shaven,' he said. 'Now what sort of pointy nose? Big pointy nose or small pointy nose?'

'Medium,' I said. 'Pointed as in downwards.'

Ben keyed in lateral slant. 'Colour of eyes?'

'We weren't into eye contact.'

After the first hundred faces, bleak, blank, lost faces, etched in defiance and despair against a white wall, we were both tiring. Sergeant Rawlings brought me a second mug of sweet tea.

'Gotta keep your strength up,' he said.

'Why don't you leave me to this,' I said, helpful as ever. 'I can see how to work it. I'll give you a call if I spot him. You've probably got better things to do.'

'What a thoughtful girl you are.' Ben Evans grinned, getting up and stretching his lean six feet. He looked clean and wholesome, ironed white shirt, dark tie. Ideal West Sussex CID material. 'Like to come out for a drink this evening? A nice country pub at Findon.'

It was the Findon that clinched it. No way would I be seen drinking with DS Evans in Latching. Word gets around. I did not want DI James to think I was spoken for. But Findon was out in the woods, nestling under the massive hill of Cissbury Ring with its Neolithic flint mineshafts and Iron Age hill fortifications. With all these friendly ghosts around, I should be mentally safe.

'OK.' I nodded. 'About eight, my place? You know the address, don't you?'

'By heart.'

As soon as DS Evans was out of sight, I logged on to a different system, one I was not allowed to access, being an ordinary member of the public. I keyed in Frazer, Brian. Nothing at all. Then Cannon, Phil. It was revealing, some credit card debts and traffic fines. But when I typed in Simons, double-checking on Nesta, it went bananas. She had so many convictions, my pen could not write them down fast enough. I ran out of scrap paper. Mostly soliciting, fraudulent cheques, shoplifting. She had a record.

My luck was holding out but it would not last for long. As a long shot I keyed in Frazer, Gillian. I don't know what made me do it. My heart stopped with a jerk. Manslaughter: two children. Conviction squashed after unsatisfactory evidence was thrown out of court. Nothing more.

I sat back in the chair, sipping cold tea. Manslaughter of two children. It gave me the shivers. That plain beige woman, pillar of society, decent citizen, one supposed . . . well, what was decent these days? I was just about to delve deeper into the case when I recognized the footsteps approaching.

In seconds I was out of that programme and back into mug shots. It was dexterity of the highest order. I had once taken a computer literacy course and it paid off.

'Hi,' I said.

'Looking at mug shots?' said DI James, sitting down beside me. He leaned forward, peering at the screen with interest.

It always took me several seconds to adjust to his nearness.

Delayed madness. If I lost him, I think I would go mad. Lose my grip on life. Every pore of my skin tingled. Without moving an inch, I leaned my body towards him. Quite a trick. The pores of my skin were magnetized by him. He had his usual gritty, sleepless look but was one degree more human. Didn't he ever go home? Where was home? I didn't know but he always seemed pleased enough to come back with me, even if it was only for the home-made soup or excellent coffee.

Cooking dinners was not my style. I couldn't cook a dinner even at gunpoint.

'I got held up, at my shop.'

'So I heard. Running a junk shop is a dangerous business. He had a knife?'

'Yes.'

'What sort?'

'Are there sorts?'

He sighed deeply. 'I'll show you some photographs of knives. It could help. They usually get attached to a certain kind of knife. Steel bonding.'

'I would not want to be attached to this one. It looked lethal.'

'All knives are lethal. Even your average kitchen potato-peeling knife can do a lot of damage.'

I wanted to touch him but I couldn't. He was so close I could smell the Comfort rinse in his creased blue shirt. Who did his washing? I had no idea. Perhaps he had found a Comfort-woman.

The thought was devastating. He might have found someone by now. He was a loner. Loners get lonely. My heart screwed up, imagining a loose-limbed, crazy kind of woman who would take on a man who had lost all normal feeling. Maybe she was divorced too. It wasn't me. But it could have been me. I would have done it.

'Are you living with anyone?' I heard myself asking. It wasn't my voice. This was weird.

'No,' he said. He was bringing up pictures of knives on the next screen. 'Why do you ask?'

'I can smell the Comfort rinse in your shirt.'

'It was a free sample put through the door. I threw it in the wash.'

He did not look committed. He was wearing his normal, tired, distant, out of touchy-touchy face. A man with deep frowns, whose divorce had shredded him of emotion. He did not know that sitting beside him was a smouldering woman, consumed with lust. He probably did not even know how to spell the word. Roll on some pub at Findon.

I shifted over and looked at knives, hundreds of them. This was difficult but I identified the nearest to size, shape, design. James made some notes, waited with me, took a call.

I kept flicking through faces. It was the least I could do. In answer to a prayer, a face came up, younger, unshaven. White-skinned, thin with hunger, pointed with pain, blank eyes. It was etched on my memory.

'Be sharpish,' he'd said to me in the shop.

I saw the face, heard the words and the voice. That's the one. It was him. There was an accent in the echo. North of England?

'This is him,' I said. 'I'm sure. Yes, this is the man.'

'Are you sure?'

'I've just said I'm sure.'

James rolled on the detailed information, did a printout and took it to the desk. 'Circulate this,' he said. 'Miss Lacey is 90 per cent sure that this is the man who threatened her with a knife today. Bert Leech is one of his names. Last known at a Newcastle address. Contact Newcastle. Find out what he's doing down here.'

'Circulate?' I queried. 'But why? You've nicked him, haven't you? Your men were there. He was trapped in M & S in the fruit and veg department.'

'We lost him. He must have doubled back and gone out the way he came in. He probably saw the police car drive off.'

I got up, stiff-kneed, stiff-necked and speechless with fury at their incompetence. What was the time? Was it time to go to Findon? The inside of the station had no windows, no clue as to time of day. It was rows of cheerless rooms, in need of new paint and some decent furniture.

'It's four thirty,' said James, stretching. 'Nearly the end of my shift.'

'Time to go,' I said, signing my statement and everything else in sight. I probably signed for a month's consignment of tea bags. I wanted to go home, have two baths, get rid of the day.

'Like to come out for a drink this evening, Jordan? Police compensation for bungled arrest.'

Was I dreaming? A bit of me sloughed off and died. Was DI James actually asking me out for a drink or was I hearing an instant replay of DS Evans's invitation? After months of nil social life, I get two invites for the same evening.

'Would you mind saying that again?' The words were frosty. I was mad at him. He asks me out for a drink on the one and only night that I already had a date. How could he be so inconsiderate? This was not fair. Some angel was taking a day off.

James was bewildered for a hung second and nothing normally disconcerts him. 'It's only a drink, Jordan. I thought you might need a drink after being held up at knife point. No big deal. A glass of wine at the Bear and Bait, that's all. House red. Sorry, Australian Shiraz.'

'You know I only drink Chilean or Australian,' I flared again. The red in my hair was igniting.

'OK, whatever you like. I'm not an expert. Don't get so het up. I might not even be able to make it. You know how it is here.'

'Yes, I know how it is,' I said, scrambling to my feet. I tried to gather my dignity. I had to scrape together some sort of compensation for my disappointment without letting him know. 'Can I take a rain check?' I muttered.

His face was inscrutable. I couldn't tell if he was mad or
not. He started to walk away, back rigid, hands knotted in a
fist behind him.

'I don't do rain checks.'

Sergeant Rawlings ambled over and collected my empty
mug. 'You didn't handle that very well, Jordan. DI James
never asks anyone out. That was a first.'

'I couldn't go,' I said miserably.

'You should have broken the other date.'

'I can't do that. I don't break dates.'

'Yes, you could. And you still can.'

He was a wise old bird. He winked and patted my arm
paternally. I remembered my father with sudden pain. My
parents' accident had been so sudden, so unexpected. I had
never really allowed myself to grieve. Too much to do.

'Do you think I should?'

'Jordan, I don't have a clue what goes on inside a woman's
head but I sure know naked desire when I see it. I'll get you
DS Evans's mobile number. Put him off. He won't mind.
Say you've got a headache.'

I did not know where to look. Nothing was private in this
place. Naked desire? I ought to wear a yashmak.

'Thank you, sarge.'

I went after James. He'd gone upstairs to his office,
loosened his tie and was immersed in reading a thick file
of papers.

'Changed my mind,' I said brightly. 'Bear and Bait, it is,
James. What time did you say?'

He barely looked up. 'Eight thirty. I might be late.'

'Fine by me. Be as late as you please. I'll pick up some
hunky guy at the bar. No problem. It's always crowded with
hunky guys on the make, mostly firemen.'

'If you are that easily pleased, then you don't need me.'

What could I say? I did need him. I wanted him there more
than anyone else. But I could not say so. Our communication
was dreadful. Wires all crossed. I could not lean over the desk

and touch his hand or kiss his face. Nothing. I'd never kissed him except in my dreams.

'I'd like to meet you there,' I said, trying to sound cool and professional. 'But if you are more than half an hour late, I shall come back here to the station and raise *hell*. Do you hear me? Merry hell. They will hear me from Latching to Brighton. So don't be that late.'

He looked up, a sardonic smile hovering. 'I hear you, Jordan. I may obey, but only in part. Work comes first. You know that.'

I said a fifth-century Anglo-Saxon word and marched out of his office but my heart was singing like the Last Night at the Proms. I phoned DS Evans from a call box and took a rain check on the drink at Findon. He was not bothered. Of course, he was not bothered. He had a string of girlfriends, including Leroy Anderson. He would take her out instead.

Shopping list: get new mobile (again), mascara for fluttering eyelashes, perfume (trial size).

A date with James. Had I eaten at all today? I tried to think back but it was a haze. I ought to eat but I was not hungry. It was only a drink at a pub, for heaven's sake, not a night at the Ritz. No need to go overboard.

I tried to calm down. I wrote up my notes, which was good exercise. The scribbled notes made at the computer desk were not enough. I needed every detail. Dates, times, courts, sentences. I knew a lot more about my clients now. And they were not all Persil squeaky clean. I hoped they were going to pay me. It seemed I was working for a load of crooks.

Although it was late May, our summer had not come. No swanning around Latching in a strappy suntop and sandals. I was still chilled to the bone. My two vests were in the wash. I wore my blue embroidered cowboy shirt, indigo jeans and boots, mascara. My hair went into a plaited rope fixed with an elastic band. No need to overdo the glamour. James didn't expect glamour from me.

He was not there, of course, at the Bear and Bait. I bought my own glass of red, Australian Merlot, leaned against the crowded bar, smiled around, unbuttoned my top button. Men smiled back, expecting to talk. Zero luck.

Eventually I found a seat tucked in a corner and listened to the taped girly music. This was a lesson. Never wait for a dedicated DI. And I could have been in Findon, enjoying myself with the dishy DS Evans admiring my cleavage, holding my hand under the table. When will I ever learn?

The second glass of wine went straight to my head. I had not eaten. I could not visualize even a cheese sandwich. I tried to think about my neglected cases. There was a lot to do now. Especially since I knew so much more about my clients. Ought I to warn Brian Frazer? I had a feeling that he was in danger. Did he know that his wife had been charged with the manslaughter of two children? Were they their children or had she been looking after someone else's children? I remembered that she said she had once been a nanny.

Another sliver of remembered information surfaced: they had been other people's children. So perhaps she had been that family's nanny. This was a gruesome thought.

I was also missing James in a shattering way. No wonder his wife had divorced him. She had never known where he was, what he was doing, when he was coming home. The likelihood of knowing anything about his whereabouts was never open to discussion. The juicy headlines the next day might tell her where he had been. No wonder their marriage had fallen apart.

At least I understood some of it, being a former WPC. But could I cope with such a lifestyle? Could I cope with his psychological quagmire? I was not used to pantomime baddies and goodies. I'd be a loser, proofreading my own wall graffiti. Did he like films, television, books? My knowledge of the man was recklessly insufficient. But my dreams knew all about him. So did my body.

'Jordan? Don't go to sleep. I think you've had too much

to drink and it's far too hot in here. Your face is flushed. You're breathing carbon monoxide by the bucketful. Let's get you outside.' I felt a tug on my arm.

The landlord was loudly ringing the 'Time, gentlemen, please' bell.

'James?'

'Yes?'

'I've been here for a whole year, waiting for you.'

His hand was under my arm, firmly pulling me up and out of the corner seat. It was a tight squeeze.

'Exaggerating as usual. Come along, you need some fresh air. Let's walk the pier.'

'I like the pier. Indeed, I love the pier. It's my habitat, my most favourite place in the whole world.'

'I know. I know.' He nodded.

Detective Inspector James, the sweet, lovable, stiff-lipped detective, heaved me to my feet. Somehow he got me through the door and out into the cool, cooling air of a late spring night. He guided my feet. Above us the stars shone brightly in the black velvet like the galaxy that they were. The air killed off the alcohol. I breathed it in with the gulps of an asthmatic.

'Sorry, James. I was waiting and drinking. It was such a long time.'

'My fault. I was late. An assault case.'

'There will be bouncers at the entrance to the pier. You know, the nightclub at the end of the pier has bouncers. They don't allow anyone on except paying customers. It takes guts to walk the pier late at night.'

'I can deal with bouncers. Jordan, please, I am a police officer. Even off duty.'

We were walking the pier in the dark. It was a different planet. James said a few words to the burly bouncers and they opened the steel gates. The night air cooled my face. The waves were lashing the girders. Planes crossing the sky winked their red and green winglights.

I hung on to his arm, feeling the hardness of his hip against mine, feeling his closeness, listening to the waves that washed around the pier. His body was cleaved to mine but he did not know it.

Seven

Phil Cannon had gone into hiding it seemed, not difficult with his face. I could not contact him anywhere and he still hadn't given me those vital photos. He had vanished into the spring mist. Nesta Simons was swanning around in skimpy items of clothing despite the chilly winds. I tried to log her visitors. If she was on the game, it was not obvious. She looked like a normal young woman with a high-voltage social life.

Her son was doing his usual neighbourhood terrorizing but without police interference. Dwain was addicted to throwing bins and tins, pinching, punching, pulling up flowers, shouting four-lettered words at anyone within listening distance. He was hyperactive, out of control. I could understand why Phil Cannon would refuse to acknowledge paternity, to part from his money.

It was Maggie at the theatre who gave me a clue as to Brian Frazer's afternoon activities. I had steered the conversation round to hobbies.

'He loves trad jazz,' she said. 'I often hear him playing jazz and singing along in one of the rooms at the back of the theatre. You know, those dressing rooms we use when it's a live show.'

I was selling ice cream at a matinee of some mega cartoon film fantasy. It was a kaleidoscope of grotesquely leering animal faces leaping out with gaping mouths and the whole thing gave me the creeps. But the children loved it, screamed and cheered, bought and ate ice cream, crisps and popcorn, all at the same time.

'There's a jazz band playing tomorrow afternoon at Falmer Gardens. We'll be slaving away at the theatre but he'll take the afternoon off and be listening to jazz among the flowers.'

Part of my heart warmed to him. Anyone who loved jazz, even the trad variety, could not be that bad. Gill must be mistaken. Despite this clothes swopping obsession, he seemed an average guy.

Then a bad penny dropped and I didn't like hearing the clang. I'd called in at the station about Bert Leech and someone said tomorrow was DI James's day off and, one in a million, he was taking out an unknown woman. Don't ask me who told me, the station was buzzing with the news. DI James with a member of the female population was a record-breaking, gossip-mongering first. They were going to Falmer Gardens to listen to afternoon jazz.

'Didn't know he had it in him,' a WPC said, straightening her barely black tights. Nor did I, not to listen to jazz, my special love. Both of them. I wished I had not gone into the station to check whether they'd sighted my robber. And I had to get the crime number for my insurance claim. At least I had insurance.

It was not easy in the circumstances. I would be there watching Brian Frazer cruising the talent. DI James would be there with a woman friend. Could I cope with a karate chop straight in the face? I tried a lot of mind-power training. I got my mind to think like an egg but it did not help my heart. Thinking like an egg is a complicated manoeuvre which involves building a mental shell round a problem. Mine was already cracking in several places.

The wind was blowing off the sea, a south-easterly that pierced fabric and chilled skin. Was summer ever coming? I found somewhere to sit on the grass in Falmer Gardens and nibbled an oatmeal and sultana bar. The uncut grass was hung with dews of moisture blown in off the Channel. Half an hour of this and I'd have a damp patch in an embarrassing place.

The afternoon was family orientated. Babies in prams, instant picnics on rugs, kids kicking balls against the trees. No goal posts in this park. Only the grown-ups were lounging about, taking in the music, sipping canned beer. One middle-aged woman was dancing in an oddly buttoned-up orange cardigan and a long caramel skirt flapping round her ankles. She was well away, a resident from one of the residential homes. Still she was having fun, locked in her own world.

It was not my beloved big band jazz or my soaring trumpeter, who could take my spirit flying into outer space. It was a six-piece group from Brighton, banjo strumming dominated. I was beating time but my body was not with it. Lurking in the same gardens was DI James with a woman and I did not know who she was or why they were together. I could not look round in case she was knock-out gorgeous. He did not really like jazz, merely tolerated it for some unknown reason. I'd always thought it was because of me, but I could be mistaken.

Ben Evans threw himself down on the grass beside me, jacket unfastened. That showed stamina. But his hair was blowing over his heavy-rimmed glasses and he brushed it away repeatedly. DI James would not be discomposed. His cropped hair did not blow.

'Are you working, Jordan?' he asked.

'What does it look like?'

He put on a sage look. His attractive masculine profile caught my attention. I can still appreciate male looks.

'It's hard to tell with your variety of disguises. You could be on surveillance. Or you could be taking a well-earned break.'

'A well-earned break is hardly listening to second-rate jazz in a freezing wind. But I am starved of jazz and would listen to almost anything. And this isn't a disguise.' I did not add that DI James was somewhere in the gardens with a strange woman and I dare not look about. If she was blonde and slender, and madly beautiful, I would die of shame. 'I'm following a client's husband.'

'Ah, hanky-panky in the bushes?'

'I doubt it. More like pass the mascara, lovie.'

He looked bemused but did not push me for an explanation. I didn't have one to give him. 'Interesting.'

'And what are you doing here?' I asked.

'Trouble, a gang of youths. We've had word that they are surging down to the seafront, causing trouble en route. They'll pass this way. A whole gang of them, tanked up after some afternoon football match on telly.'

'Shouldn't you be clearing the gardens? There's all these children and people having fun.'

'Not yet, they could take a different direction. No need to panic yet. I'm just keeping my eyes open in case.' He patted his mobile as if expecting it to go off. I wondered if he had a call tune. 'Land of Hope and Glory'?

I nearly asked if DI James was keeping his eyes open too but held my tongue. After all, I was in the company of DS Ben Evans and that couldn't be bad. We were sitting quite close. It might be misconstrued. I smiled at Ben with what I thought could pass for come-on body language and hoped DI James was watching.

'This is great,' he said, his foot tapping. But it was only to the drumbeat. The trumpet and saxaphone were amateurish, a hard sound, all swagger and no feeling. Ben ought to hear my trumpeter. Those ascending notes that sliced the air with brilliance.

'Not bad,' I said, offering him a sesame biscuit from a packet. He looked queerly at the seed-covered biscuit.

'What's this? Left over from your breakfast?'

'Healthy eating,' I added. It was not time to throw him to the wolves. I had to be sociable. I wished I had a younger sister I could pass him on to.

I longed for the deep timbre of James's voice. Then I thought I heard it among all the other sounds. A small quiver of pleasure shot through me. A tingle of awareness. I only had to see the back of his head and my spirits lifted. A day could have a thousand hours and one second of time with him would be enough.

I was seriously round the bend.

'You're looking very happy,' said Ben, wondering if he was the cause. He cleared his throat hopefully. 'Would you like to go out with me sometime? Perhaps a nice meal somewhere. Do you like Chinese?'

He'd asked me out before in some other life and there had been Findon. And I vaguely remember turning him down in the past. But I have a thing about glasses and what they do to a man's face. They give it character. They certainly gave Ben an irresistible something. He was an irresistable accessory.

I shot him a big smile, Goldie Hawn style. 'That would be very nice . . . Ben. When?'

He started hedging. 'Well, er . . . I hadn't actually thought that far. Shifts and everything. Supposing I give you a call?'

'Do that,' I said. 'Do you know my number?'

'Tattooed on my heart.'

'Could be painful.'

He grinned. 'Not the way I do it.' He leaned over and loosely took my fingers. His nails were short and clean. Grimed and bitten nails are a real turn-off. Like socks in bed.

This was getting out of hand and it was time to make a move. I spotted a rustling flamingo pink dress and high-heeled shoes. 'Ah, my prey, I think,' I said. 'I have to go and see what's happening. Time to earn my garlic bread.'

There was something very nice about Ben Evans. A sort of open admiration which had long been missing from my life. It gave my cheeks a faintly warm glow and I hoped it showed. As long as DI James was looking in my direction. I had not seen him yet.

'If you don't like Chinese, I'll take you somewhere posh, one of the big hotels along the front. A slap-up meal, a good wine. I'll book a table. It's what you deserve.'

This was dangerously going to my head. I knew of no one more deserving. And I had that slinky black dress from

Guilbert's store waiting to be worn. Was this the start of something good?

'You've got a lovely smile,' he said. 'One of your front teeth is a little bit crooked. That one.' He touched my mouth. 'I like it.'

I had to move fast. I couldn't cope with a proper invite and all these compliments. It was double-chocolate chip cookie time with a coffee cream filling. Very fattening. I still could not see James.

Brian Frazer was swaying along towards the stage. It was a huge cavernous edifice flanked with mountains of amplification and eddying smoke like it was already November. He was climbing the ramp of steps and the musicians looked at him apprehensively but never missed a note or a beat.

He tottered over to the lead singer, who lowered his hand-held mike and listened. What he heard seemed to amuse him. He was grinning. The group went into a huddle while Brian stood by, his hands preening his bouffant hair, the pink silk and chiffon designer dress blowing in the breeze, his feet squeezed into stilt heels. He was holding on to the folds and the silk roses stretched across his chest. Careful now.

I knew what was going to happen. He was going to sing with the band. I saw it all happening, half heard it before it happened. Brian thought he was the new Danny La Rue, secretly rehearsing at the back of the theatre. Buying pretty things for his new image. This whole charade was a career move. He wanted to look like a woman, sing like a woman. 'Cry Me a River' . . . was that going to be his theme song? Or something Shirley Bassey style. 'Hey, Big Spender'? I looked for glued-on painted silver nails, then hung back from the stage, longing for a straightforward case. Plain theft or harrassment would do.

'Ladies and gentlemen,' the leader announced. 'We have a guest singer. A big hand, folks, for this brave . . . person.'

There was a polite round of applause.

Brian took centre stage, beaming, and began to sing.

Dying a death from embarrassment would have been almost welcome. My senses were paralyzed with shocked disbelief. His sharp, high, belted feminine notes pierced a musical ear; lack of rhythm, wordless nonsense in cadences that did not exist. I wished I was stone deaf. The ground did not open. The chronic amplification made it worse. There was no escape. I clung to the side of the stage like a limpet, hoping it would hold me up till the end. At least DI James would also be suffering, along with his dishy date. That was some slight consolation. Love would not bloom through this catastrophic racket. It was even difficult to breath.

Brian belted out 'Shiny Stockings', even attempting the catchy trumpet notes at the end; then wailed through 'Embraceable You', one of my favourites. Billie Holiday, Nat King Cole, Ella FitzGerald . . . they must have turned.

When the agony ended, I could not look towards the stage. There was a random slow handclap after an eerie silence, more from stunned relief that it had ended. A slight wave of giggling rustled the air. Brian was bowing and beaming, sweat in half-circles under his puffed armpits, the wig askew. The mascara had run. His forehead was a rivulet of perspiration. It dripped off his nose, taking the Max Factor pancake along with the salt.

I heard a woman call out, 'Sing it again, darling.'

My legs began moving. They wanted to go somewhere, anywhere to get away from the man's humiliation. It was a wonder that the muscles still functioned. How could I put this into my report? Would Gill enjoy reading an account of her husband's personal and public disaster? Maybe this experience would cure him of his showbiz ambitions.

'Enjoy that, didya, ducks?' some beer-swigger jeered, grinning, can in hand. 'Should have been shot! Poofter. Needs his head testing.'

'Needed more rehearsal,' I said kindly.

'Rehearsal! You mean referral.'

I saw no one I knew. Both Ben and James seemed to have disappeared. Perhaps the gang of yobs had been frightened off by Brian's debut as a jazz singer. The seat of my jeans were damp. It was time to go home and change. Perhaps to open my shop and start selling a few souvenirs to the first of the holidaymakers. I had not sold anything for days.

The wind had dropped and for the first time that year, it occurred to me that we might get some summer. An early summer with balmy evenings that drew luminous late-night light and were perfect for wine sipped in gardens. Not that I had a garden or a balcony on which to sip wine. Or anyone to sip with. I should be so lucky. Find me a millionaire. Or someone with a passable pension would do.

There was some sort of commotion going on behind the stage. And an odd smell coming from the area. Like burning. There was a lot of noise and shouting and clattering feet. I sidled past, head down. I do not like commotions. Commotions and me do not mix, especially not today.

But it was too late. A girl came flying out, her red dreadlocks swinging round her rouged and distressed face. She caught sight of me and obviously thought I was an A1 sane member of the human race.

'Help! Help!' she screamed, grabbing my arm. 'Come with me. You gotta come.'

'What? Me?' I said stupidly.

'Something's the matter with him,' she gasped. 'He's not breathing.'

She dragged me round to the back of the stage, my feet stumbling over stamped-on beer cans. Sprawled on the steps was a heap of pink silk and chiffon, legs on silver stilts. I recognized that glorious pink with mounting dread. The bouffant wig had fallen off and rolled away on its own lacquer. His eyes were bulging.

And it was obvious why Brian was not breathing. The live radio mike had been jammed down his throat. There was a pale area with a lilac ring round his mouth. His last gasp had gone out to the audience. It was how he would have wished to die. On air.

Eight

Electrocution. Brian Frazer had been electrocuted. Sizzled with alternating current 220 volts. This strength supply is enough to shock, causes the heart muscles to quiver, reduce its pumping and death follows quickly.

The electricity had passed in and out of his body from hand, via head to heart to leg. There was that telltale pale area with a lilac ring round his mouth but no other signs of burning.

The microphone had been a live radio lead. He would not have put it in his own mouth. Someone had tampered with the transformer and jammed it in. In his other hand he clutched what had been a glass of water. Singing jazz can be dry work. The water had spilt and a dark fold of silk was soaking wet.

The girl in dreadlocks was still screaming. One of the band went to remove the mike.

'Don't touch,' I shouted. 'It's live. Don't touch anything.'

He looked at me in disbelief.

'Turn it off at the mains, you idiot,' I said, more politely. 'It's still live. Do you want to die, too?'

It was so quiet without the amplification and yet there was background noise everywhere. The crowd were becoming restless, wondering where the music had gone. People were talking on stage, milling about, crowding round the grotesque figure.

'Is he dead?' The girl was sobering down but shaking. Perhaps she had never seen death before.

'Yes, I'm afraid so,' I said, kicking the mike away from

74

his mouth. His jaws were stiff. I knelt down and felt for a pulse. There was none.

'Oughtn't we to move him?' This was from the leader of the band. They obviously felt the show must go on.

'You can't move him until the police get here,' I said. 'They have to record the scene of the crime. Nothing must be touched or moved. Would you all move away, please.'

'Crime scene?'

'Of course. He has been murdered. He didn't put the mike down his own throat.'

I could sense their thoughts. They did not want that kind of publicity and yet any publicity was good in many ways. They hadn't done anything wrong. This wasn't their fault. They were innocent musicians caught up in a dreadful tragedy. They began to recover and think about themselves and the group's image.

'If we just covered him over a bit, could we start playing again? After all, we've got our audience to think of. We don't want all those kids upset and tramping all over the place. We can't exactly announce that there's been a murder on stage.'

The young leader of the band was waxing eloquent. He could see now that he was on to a good thing. But the band kept playing. A touch of the *Titanic*.

'I've got a mobile,' said the girl. And I hadn't, being between mobiles. 'I'll call the police.'

'All right,' I said, almost agreeing. 'You can phone the police. They'll be here soon enough. There's several officers around.'

'I'm here now,' said Detective Inspector James coming up on to the stage with a bound. Time well spent at the gym? He was without his lady companion. But he was too busy to look at me. This was serious. He was down on his knees by the body of Brian Frazer. 'What happened?'

Everyone started talking at once. Then he glanced up at

me for assistance. He'd never asked me for help before and I savoured the moment. 'Jordan?'

'He'd been singing with the band. Then he was found with a live radio mike jammed down his throat,' I said. 'I think that's how he died. He'd been singing on the stage right before that. A couple of lively numbers.'

'I heard him,' said James without comment. He was looking at every aspect of the scene but not touching anything. 'Move back, please. Don't touch anything!'

'I imagine he was having a drink of water. No one has said if they saw anything or anyone around. He obviously didn't push it down his own throat.'

'Nor is a microphone live unless it's tampered with. There are several ways of doing it. The transformer for a start.'

DI James was on his phone to CID. He was snapping out orders. Then he switched off his mobile and got to his feet. 'I want a list of everyone here. No one is to leave. You can cover him with a sheet or something light if you are upset by his appearance. Does anyone know who the man is?'

Me again. Informant Number One. I nodded. 'His name is Brian Frazer. He's the new manager of the Community Shore Theatre. He's the husband of a current client of mine, Mrs Gill Frazer. That's why I'm here.'

'Husband of your client?' DI James' face was a picture. He looked incredulous. It was as if he'd been told by the Chief Constable of West Sussex that Latching was about to be annihilated by an asteroid. 'Jordan . . . are you sure?'

I bristled. 'I do know my own clients. And I've been following him for days.'

'I sometimes wonder about you,' he groaned. 'And why has Mrs Frazer employed your services?'

'I never disclose private details of a case,' I said.

'I suppose it couldn't be something to do with this fetching outfit,' he said. He'd spotted the wig, taken in the high heels and mascara.

'This is, I believe, a stage outfit,' I said, not wanting to say anything before I'd seen Mrs Frazer. Was she going to be upset? I could not work out how much she cared for the man. Poor Brian Frazer. He'd had such fun, singing with the trad band. Perhaps it was not a bad way to go out. I could die listening to my trumpeter. His music would soothe my way into the next world. If there was a way. I was never quite sure.

'Will you stay here, Jordan? See that nothing is touched while I scout round a bit? The men in white with their tape will be here in a few minutes. We'll need everyone's fingerprints. Someone obviously fixed the mike. Do you mind?'

Did I mind? I no longer worked for the West Sussex Police so asking me was in fact an imposition. Yet I could be called upon as a citizen of the realm to assist in a police matter. And as for being asked by DI James to do something . . . he did not know I would walk burning coals for him.

'What about your lady friend?' I asked sweetly. I could not resist the dig. 'Do you want me to look after her as well?'

He looked at me closely, half-squinting, wondering if I was clairvoyant. 'My what?'

'Crystal ball,' I explained.

'She's gone for a cup of tea at the pier cafe,' he said.

'Very wise.'

It was only then that I noticed he was in his black casual gear. The same gear that he had worn to Cleo's house-warming party. Black sweatshirt and black jeans. Very jazzish and a night to remember. We had danced on the landing in half-light without speaking. I expect he'd forgotten it.

Soon James was lost to sight in the crowds, gathering witnesses. I let them put a black stage curtain over Brian Frazer's body. The leader got the band together and moved them to the far end of the stage. Within minutes they were strumming out their New Orleans jazz, without amplification, to an appreciative roar from the crowd. I think it was called 'Green Dolphin Street Blues', a classic.

Brian Frazer would have loved it. He was still on stage. He was part of the act. They were playing him out. And on the other side, maybe there was another jazz band waiting, rocking the rock, to welcome him home.

Everyone forgot me. I was stiff with sitting. The police team arrived. Out came the scene of crime tape, the cameras, the fingerprint experts, the medics, the police surgeon, the men in white taking samples of everything. DI James ignored me. I thought I could go home.

'Don't go,' he bawled at me. 'You are an important witness. I shall want a statement.'

'I did not see anything. I merely arrived after the event. I am not a witness and I'm not wasting another two hours at the station making a statement.'

'Now, now, Jordan, that's not a nice attitude to take. You did find the body.'

'No, I didn't. The girl with the long red dreadlocks found the body. I don't know who she is. Part of the group.'

'She says she didn't. She says it was you.'

'So who are you going to believe? Me or Miss Airhead? I only went up on to the stage because she was screaming fit to burst a blood vessel.'

'You told them to turn off the mains.'

'Of course, I did. They would have touched the body and got a shock. We didn't want a mass electrocution of the entire band however sub-standard their performance.'

James had withdrawn into his usual grim ice-palace attitude, drawbridge up and bolted. Humour did not reach him. I suppose it was the second violent death in Latching in a short space of time. There was the diver/fisherman trawled up from the seabed. And the bloodied shirt. Now this. Nothing was safe. Even hobbies were lethal. You could get stabbed with a knitting needle.

'I'd like to pop home first and then I'll come around to the station, if that's all right with you?' I said this in my most innocent, pleasant, cooperative voice. But James was barely listening. He nodded, making notes. DS Evans would not have been taken in.

I was not going straight home. I was going round to Gill Frazer's colourless home, number three St Michael's Road. Her initial reaction was important and I wanted to see it. She'd been acquitted of the two manslaughter charges but only through lack of evidence. It was not a nice thought. I felt she was quite capable of unscrewing a microphone and crossing the wires of a transformer if that's how it was done. I'm not an expert on electrocution.

It was a long walk even taking short cuts and I was out of breath by the time I got there. My asthma wheezed, protesting at the pace. My feet hurt.

The garden was still as cheerless as the house. You would have thought they could afford a few spring bedding plants, say tulips. Instant gardening. My favourite outdoor pursuit. I once had two window boxes but they fell down. Nobody sued.

I knocked and rang. It was some time before anyone answered the chimes although I was aware that someone was moving about indoors. Gill Frazer eventually opened the door. She was in her taupe suit, the one she'd worn when she first came to see me.

'Sorry, I was in the bathroom.'

'That's OK,' I said. 'We all have to go.'

She looked momentarily shocked. Perhaps it had never occurred to her. It brings people down to size. The Queen, Tony Blair, Madonna.

'May I come in?'

'I've just been shopping.'

I went into the hallway, not a carrier bag in sight. It had been a mini-shop, maybe a few safety pins or a bargain roll of Sellotape. I was in a prickly mood. Brian Frazer's death had affected me. It seemed so unfair. He had not been doing any harm, except to the nation's eardrums.

'Have you seen your husband this afternoon?' I asked.

She shook her head. 'No. He went out, not long after lunch.'

'Did he say where he was going?'

'No. I assumed he was going to the theatre. A matinee or something. He never tells me anything.'

'He never said anything about going to the jazz concert in Falmer Gardens?'

'Heavens, no. He doesn't even like jazz music. He'd never go to a concert. Falmer Gardens . . . that's down near the seafront, isn't it? Where all the down-and-outs and winos hang about. Not Brian's scene at all.'

She bustled around, moving things, not exactly achieving anything. I had the feeling she wanted me to leave but I was not going. No offer of coffee this time. Perhaps they had run out of instant.

'Would you like to sit down, Mrs Frazer? I have some bad news for you.'

I was not exactly sure of the legal position on this. There's nothing that says that only the police had the right to inform next of kin of a death. Take a volcanic eruption or earthquake. Surely then all sorts of categories of people rush about with information on fatalities.

She sat down, arranging her skirt. She was quite composed. 'I don't understand. What do you mean?'

'I have to tell you that your husband, Brian Frazer, died this afternoon. It was a bizarre accident involving a live radio mike. I expect the police will be around to see you soon. They'll need to ask a few questions.'

'Dead? Are you sure?' She said this in a strange, stiffled voice. It was weird. 'This afternoon, you say?'

'Yes, I am quite sure. I saw him myself.'

'And he's dead?'

'I'm so sorry. Yes, he is.'

'At the theatre?'

'No, at Falmer Gardens. He was at the jazz concert.'

'But he doesn't like jazz.'

'He was there.'

I waited for her reaction to his death. There was absolutely none. I could have been telling her that Guilbert's store had closed, or that a neighbour had moved. She unbuttoned her jacket without fumbling. The toning taupe shirt was wrinkled and not tucked into her skirt. One of the buttons was hanging by a thread.

'Oh dear, what will the theatre do? They'll have to get a new manager now, won't they? Though I suppose Maggie can run it for a few weeks. Then they'll have to advertise, won't they?'

It's wrong to judge people too harshly. Maybe she was in delayed shock. It happens. I'd seen it many times in my WPC days. People carry on, making cups of tea, talking naturally until the truth hits them. Until the reality comes home and shock sets in. It is not a pleasant sight.

'Would you like me to stay until the police come?'

She looked surprised. 'No, thank you. There's no need. And of course, I shall not be needing your services any longer. You can send me your final bill and a report.'

'I certainly have a report to give you,' I said, rising. 'A very interesting one. It will reassure you in many ways about what Brian was doing.'

'Thank you. That's all I need. Some reassurance that there was a reason, I suppose.'

'Again, I really am very sorry.'

She was showing me to the door before I had even finished talking. I was out before I had drawn another breath. The door closed on me. Was she going to sob her heart out, take Valium, pour out a double gin? I had no idea of her reaction.

Nothing prepared me for what happened next.

I was halfway down St Michael's Road when I suddenly heard a piercing scream. My spine chilled at the harrowing sound. It was demonic, not of this world. I had no doubt it was Gill Frazer but I was not going back to help her. She could scream the house down. And probably would.

This was one for DI James.

Maggie was in tears when I turned up that evening for an adult film. Tom Cruise on track. Action man. Could that boy run down a straight street. Legs in motion.

'Mr Frazer was such a nice man,' she sobbed. 'It's awful. And to be murdered in Falmer Gardens, of all places. All those lovely flowers. Who would do that? Some awful tramp on beer or drugs, I suppose. The management have said we have got to carry on, but the theatre will be closed on the day of the funeral. OK?'

I nodded sympathetically. At least someone was showing the proper respect. She did not seem to know the actual details of death and it was not up to me to tell her. The *Latching Gazette* would carry the official version.

I patted her arm. 'I really am very sorry. I never actually knew Brian Frazer but everyone seemed to like him.'

I had only been following him for several weeks, dodged his steps, copied his swaying walk, a shadow on his path, admired wedding dresses alongside him, yet I did not know him. Yet I did seem to know him. There was some sort of acquaintanceship.

'Shall I do the same as usual, tickets and ices?' I asked. Maggie seemed incapable of deciding what to do. She really had liked Brian Frazer.

She nodded vaguely, mopping her eyes. 'Carry on, Jordan. I know I can leave it to you to know the routine. I'd better fix my eyes before the customers arrive.'

I ate a choc ice in the ladies' loo. I'd forgotten to eat again. Murder does take away the appetite. Shopping list: anything organic that Doris has on her shelves. Caviar, mussels, Brie, avocados.

The cinema-goers started to arrive. All seats were booked in advance so I had to tear tickets, show them to their seats. I

did this with flair and style. It was the expensive skirt. I hoped
they had a lovely evening. I often wished I had someone to
go to the cinema with. Sitting in the dark with DI James by
my side would blow my mind. I could not image the joy, the
closeness, the togetherness. He might even hold my hand,
stroke my fingers. I did not know if he liked films.

'Jordan! My dear, I didn't realize you were working here.'
The voice was familiar. It was Francis Guilbert, the owner of
the biggest department store in Latching. He looked older but
as always, debonair and dapper in well-pressed fawn trousers
and a navy blazer. I smiled at him in the fading darkness.

'This is voluntary,' I whispered.

'There's always a job for you at Guilbert's,' he said.

'I know,' I said. 'But I was only temporary seasonal
help.'

'When are you coming round to see me?' he asked. 'You
never come to see me now. You know my house has an open
door as far as you are concerned.'

The longing in his voice hit me hard. But how could I
encourage him, give him ideas? We were decades apart.
Yet I was fond of him. If only it could stay that way. But
I knew that he would try to move things on into a different
relationship. Like Miguel, like Jack. Dear me, I was getting
quite a list. I hoped I wasn't getting a reputation, too.

'I'll see you in the interval,' I went on. 'Enjoy the film.
It's a long one but very exciting.'

'As long as you promise to explain the plot,' said Francis.
But he looked better already, a sort of lifting of the spirit. Did
I really have that effect on some men?

But never the right man.

The right man was pacing outside the theatre. As soon as
he saw me in the foyer, he came in. He was fuming but in
control. As always. If only he would lose control one day.
Sweep me off my feet, make mad, passionate love to me in a
patrol car, on the beach, mind the seat belts or the pebbles.

'You went to see Mrs Frazer,' he said coldly.

'That's right. She was my client, remember?'

'Uniformed police inform a homicide's next of kin. You had no right. You were totally out of form. And as a former WPC you should have known that.'

'That's exactly the point. I am a *former* WPC. None of the rules apply to me now. So I went round to see her. My case had involved following Brian Frazer and that's what I had been doing, following her husband. That he got murdered this afternoon in Falmer Gardens was not connected to my surveillance but certainly an event I should report.'

DI James was cooling down. He'd stopped pacing and took in the long skirt, the pristine white shirt, the hair piled up in a tawny top knot. He had never seen me with this classy look. The mascara went unnoticed.

'How do you know he was murdered?'

'No one sticks a mike down their own throats. Of course, he was murdered. Anyone could see that. It doesn't take rank to spot that one.'

He swallowed the rank jibe and he deserved it. 'So what can you tell me, Jordan?'

'Brian Frazer was leading some sort of double life. I think he really wanted to be a woman, inside himself. You know, one of those people locked in the wrong body. And he wanted to be a jazz singer. His wife had noticed her clothes disappearing. They were about the same size. I spotted him, several times, in women's clothes, in charity shops, buying feminine things, image building. And I think that lately he had been looking for something glamorous in which to make his debut as a singer.'

'The pink creation?'

'Not a brilliant choice but it was expensive. But then he had no one to advise him.'

DI James sighed. 'Thank you. I'm sorry to have interrupted your new theatrical career.'

'It's voluntary,' I said again for that evening.

'Will you come round to the station later and make a statement?'

'I beg your pardon.' I waited for the word that my mother had taught me.

'Please.'

'OK,' I said, 'but not tonight. I have a date after the film.'

'Enjoy your date.' He turned on his heel. I dare not watch him go for fear of disintegrating. I had almost told the truth. It was only a guess about the date.

When the film finished, Francis did ask me to go back to his Edwardian villa where we downed a bottle of good red Merlot and some Stilton, slices of apple and grapes. It made a very pleasant change and the conversation was stimulating. I liked his house and his company. We talked about everything except work.

'Thank you, Francis. Lovely late supper.'

'Don't leave it so long before you come again,' he said.

I kissed his cheek a soft goodnight and went back to my two bedsits.

How could I be so devious? I don't know. It came natural.

Nine

Nesta Simons knew something was up even if she was not sure what was up. She came storming out of her house the moment I appeared with Jasper and marched straight over to me. I knew trouble was coming.

''Ere you. What do you think you're doing? I've seen you, day after day, walking that stupid dog, talking to my son. Are you one of those queer people? After children and the likes. I'll get the police on to you, I will. They'll put your photo up to warn people off.'

'Heavens, no,' I said, trying to sound like a normal dog lover. 'I'm not doing anything to be alarmed about. No need to call the police. I'm only trying to train Jasper for a friend of mine. She's hopeless with dogs.'

The untrainable Jasper leaped about as if to back up my point. He successfully put muddy pawprints on Nesta's white jeans. She backed off.

'Down! Sit!' I ordered. Jasper looked at me with tongue-lolling adoration. He loved being ordered about. He loved disobeying. It was all such fun.

'Why do you keep talking to my boy, then? I've seen you,' said Nesta dubiously. She took a packet of cigarettes out of her pocket, shook one out and lit up. She blew the smoke straight into my face.

'He's a friendly sort of boy,' I coughed. 'He likes throwing a ball for Jasper to fetch.' Slight exaggeration of circumstances.

She scowled at me. Nesta was older than I had first

thought. There were frown lines under her blonde fringe and the first fan of wrinkles were framing her heavily made-up eyes. Her nails were red talons, several broken, two fingers nicotine-stained. Her body was wiry but not fit, no strength in her scrawny arms. Bangles jangled.

'Well, you mind it. I'll be watching you, just you remember.'

'Perhaps I could speak to your son's father, just to reassure you,' I said. It was a random thought. 'That ought to put your mind at rest.'

'He's not around at the moment,' she said, inhaling deeply. 'Working abroad. Better dosh.'

'How interesting,' I said. 'Whereabouts is he? Somewhere nice and warm, I hope. One of the oil fields? We haven't had much summer yet, have we?'

Working abroad, was he? Well, Phil Cannon still worked in the UK. He'd offered to fix something at the shop. Exactly what escaped me . . . nothing much worked. Oh yes, the bell.

'No,' she said, almost sulkily. 'He ain't in that class. He's cooking at some holiday camp, one of those club things in the Med.'

Oh dear, then she had plenty to worry about. Those club things in the Med were friendly places, very friendly. Lots of free booze and warm, sultry nights and unattached females on the make for a good time.

'You must be lonely without him,' I said, remembering the stream of visitors to her house. 'Perhaps you'd like to come out for a drink one evening. My treat. Crack a few jokes. I expect you've got a favourite pub.'

She looked at me with suspicion but the thought of being treated to drinks began working. A muscle relaxed. She stubbed out the cigarette on a gate post.

'I'd rather go to your favourite pub,' she said, sensing fresh ground and fresh conquests.

'Oh, I don't have one,' I laughed merrily. 'They are all my favourites. Show me a pub and I'm in it.'

I groaned inwardly. I was behaving like the idiot I could be at times. She was not coming to my Bear and Bait. That was strictly off limits. The last place I'd take her. She could flutter her falsies at some other watering joint.

'How about tonight?' I rattled on, caution thrown. 'Nine o'clock at The Cyprus Tree in the old high street?'

The Cyprus Tree was spanking new and flashy. I had not been there but had noticed the burly bouncers in black on the door and the flock of mini-skirted girlies that streamed in late at night. It was laid out in areas for drinking, eating, dancing to disco, playing the fruit machines. A few double vodkas and Nesta might tell me more about Dwain's daddy.

'Yeah, I'd like that,' she capitulated, zipping through her wardrobe. 'A bit fancy, isn't it?'

'Well, why not?' I said, leaning against the tug of Jasper on the lead. 'Enjoy ourselves while we can, eh?'

She was mine already. We were mates.

'See yer, then. Nine o'clock.'

She flounced back to her house, already planning hair-do. Was there time for highlights? She might meet someone. What gear? Black and silver shimmer? Backless white halter and jeans? Shorts and string top?

I staggered round the pond with Jasper. The ducks flew off in desperation. The conversation had exhausted me but I felt I was earning my pay. Phil would certainly be charged for all the drinks.

I was trying to put Brian Frazer out of my mind. I knew nothing yet. No one did. It was a mystery how he got the mike slammed down his throat.

Oddly I had heard something at the gardens, soon after he sang 'Embraceable You'. Like the wind carried it. A voice saying seductively, 'Sing it again, darling.' I'd got Casablanca on the brain.

Jasper only got half a walk. He'd played his part admirably. I returned him to doting owner.

'Don't ask me what we've achieved,' I said to Mavis. 'But I may tell you tomorrow if I'm still standing.'

'Where are you going?' She was worried.

'The Cyprus Tree.'

'Heaven help you, girl. Wear your bulletproof vest.'

Anyone would have thought I had a date with DI James. The bath foam, the shampoo, the nail varnish (blue glitter). I had no fab girly clothes. I wore my oldest threadbare jeans, a bit torn and tore them some more, and a faded red shirt that was too tight, half unbuttoned, and I tied the front ends into a waist-high knot. Pretty cool.

Hair. What could I do with this mass of tawny stuff? Bunches. I tied each bunch with several coloured ribbons. I looked about fifteen. Perhaps they would not let me in. I added heavy lash-building mascara. That put on a few years.

There was just time to eat. A quick salad and tuna sandwich. I needed the fish oil for my joints. I wrote up detailed notes at the same time as eating. The page got spotted with mayonnaise.

Nine was a late start. I filled in an hour with a seafront walk. It was still light. Four youths whistled at me. It was the gear, the bare waist, the swanky sway, the fluttering ribbons. Perhaps I had been following the wrong track all along.

'Where are you going, darling?' they shouted.

'None of your business,' I swaggered.

'Give us a call if he doesn't turn up.'

'He'll turn up,' I said.

'We got better equipment,' one of them shouted back.

I did not reply.

I went into the amusement arcade on the pier. Jack was in his booth, counting the money, wearing his usual jeans and once white T-shirt. He put the packets of coins into buckets. He had buckets of money. It was unbelievable. He was rolling in the stuff.

'Strewth, Jordan,' he said, his look steaming through the window of his booth. I could read his lips. 'What are you dressed up like that for? Is it a vicars and tarts party?'

I swallowed my hurt and knocked on the window. He keyed the code to open the door. He was protected from the world by every gadget invented.

'I'm working,' I said. 'This is work gear.'

'Well, you'd better be damned careful, my girl. You don't look safe. I'm coming with you,' he decided immediately. 'Where are you going? I'll shut the arcade.'

'No, you won't,' I said firmly. 'Don't be stupid. You've hours of custom yet. I'm only having a drink at some new trendy place and I've got to look the part.'

'And I'm looking at your waist. I ain't seen your waist before. It looks a treat. Nice bit of skin. Can I touch? Or is it out of bounds?'

The sea air had gone to his head. I recoiled instinctively which was sad because Jack was a good man. Mental but nice.

'Strictly out of bounds,' I said lightly.

'I'd marry you.'

Heavens, this was going from bad to worse.

'Nobody marries me,' I said, trying to make it into a joke.

He got up and took my arms quite roughly. I was stunned by the swiftness of his action, unable to move. Jack was his usual slob self, but the hold was strong and forceful. His nails were stained, bitten.

'Anybody touch you and I'll kill them,' he said.

Somehow I got myself out of his grip, not wanting to hurt his feelings. He was so vulnerable.

'I'll be all right. I can take care of myself. It's only a drink and perhaps some information. Nothing dangerous.'

He calmed down. 'You got your mobile?'

'Er . . . no. My last one was stolen from the shop.'

He handed me one straightaway, as if he had a drawer full

of spares. 'Use this,' he growled, 'if you get into trouble. Anything, any time. I'll be down there like a shot, to sort them out. And I mean it.'

'I don't know your number.'

'Ring zero, zero, one, zero. That's me fast emergency number. I'll keep it open all night. Don't you know how much I could go for you? If they touch you, I'll kill them.'

I was humbled by his passion. He'd never stood a chance with me and yet he would do anything. It was sobering. Jack had always waved a banner for me since I floored a robber in his arcade. It was a year back now but nothing had changed. I liked him immensely but it could never be anything else. His flashy blue metallic Jaguar would not change my mind. I even drank his awful coffee.

'Don't worry,' I said, smiling. 'I'll ring you to say everything's fine. Then you can go home.'

'Promise?'

I had no idea where his home was. It was probably as chaotic as his booth. A bedsit somewhere, full of unwashed mugs and fast food boxes. Jack was not convinced. His stubborn bristles were bristling.

'Look, Jack, I'm going now. This was just a courtesy call. Now I have to work. I will call you. Thank you for the loan of a phone.'

'Keep it.'

'I'll bring it back tomorrow.'

But I didn't. I forgot.

The Cyprus Tree was full to bursting point and the noise was deafening. There was hardly room to buy a drink. The pub was far more spacious than I had thought from outside but each area was full of seething bodies. The decor was modern, airy, wood and brass, posters and adverts, what you could see of it. There were even a couple of sofas, already occupied by coupling couples. The disco was blaring out dance music, competing with the staccato ringing of the fruit machines working at top speed. Not your normal Latching country pub.

I wondered how long I would last.

But Nesta was there, no drink in hand yet, waiting for me. I gave her a big smile. It took courage to come in here on her own but it was the kind of thing she could do without thinking.

'Hi,' I said. 'You look gorgeous. What would you like to drink, if I ever get near the bar. Grab those two seats quick. I'll be back. What do you want?'

'Vodka and passion fruit,' she said. 'A double.'

It took me ten minutes of pushing and waving to get the order through to the barman. I was drinking orange juice. I had to keep my head on straight.

I weaved my way back to the two seats Nesta was keeping. I put the long drink down in front of her. It was lethal looking, turquoise in colour, served straight in a bottle. At least I hoped it was lethal. My own modest juice would have to last. That body jungle, three-deep at the bar, was intimidating.

'You look great,' I said, at last taking in what there was of her outfit. It was an economical lurex front. Her back was bare with narrow crossed straps. Her shoulder bones jutted out like wings. They were tanned but the tanning was fake and streaked. Her legs were encased in skintight black trousers. Her feet were in heels so high, I would have fallen over.

'This is fun,' she said, flashing a smile. Her eyelids were sparkling with more glitter stuff. I was learning a lot.

'Love the place,' I said. 'Seriously classy.'

'Wow,' she said. 'And look at those hunky men.'

I had not noticed them but now that Nesta pointed them out, they were rugged with a capital 'R'. Rugby players? Was this where the talent of Latching went at nights? I'd been missing out.

'Cool Jacks,' I said.

Not that any of the men came up to my standard. The DI James standard. But they were young, well built, had

gleaming teeth and I could only guess at their virility. They
seemed to please Nesta. She was glowing with anticipation.
My hand closed round Jack's mobile, just in case.

'Happy days,' she said, raising the rim of the bottle to her
mouth. My juice was in a glass.

'Happy days.' I would second that.

'What are you drinking?' She looked scornfully at my
juice.

'Orange juice with a brandy chaser,' I lied. 'A double.'

'Oh, that's all right then. I thought perhaps you were a
teetotal git. Brandy'll rot your guts fast enough.'

We talked about men, Dwain, men, Dwain, in that order.
She was obsessed by her son. He was a born angel in her eyes.
He did nothing wrong. The complaining neighbours were all
senile and should be put away in homes. Mavis was a stuck-up
fish fryer. I tried to get the conversation round to his father.

'But what does his father think of all these complaints?
Surely he's concerned?'

'He's never around. He never gets the flack like what I
do. Sometimes I say to him, look, buddy, if you didn't
keep flying off, we might get something sorted out.' She
was on her third turquoise vodka, looking flushed but not
turquoise.

'Buddy? Is that his name?'

'No, his name is Tone. Tony, Anthony, y'know.' Her
face fell for a moment as if remembering a decade of the
wandering Tone that had become too much to bear.

'Never mind,' I soothed. 'He'll be back soon.'

'Will he?' she gulped. 'Will he? I never know where he
is, the bastard. I'd like to get rid of him.'

I pushed a fourth vodka in her direction. I was into bulk
buying at the bar. My skin was taking on an orange tinge.
I was overdosing on vitamin C.

'If he's got any sense he'll be back,' I said. 'Lovely home,
lovely woman, wonderful son.' I was a creep.

'Lovely home, that's what he's got. He left me once

before,' she wept. 'Walked out on me and I was pregnant. But he came back, like I knew he would.'

'When was that?'

She was passed being able to give me an exact date. But it was almost what I wanted to know. Tony had gone off during the early months of her pregnancy. Of course, thinking herself abandoned, she began clutching at straws, and Phil Cannon had been the most available straw.

There was some kind of brawl going on round the bar. I wanted nothing to do with it but Nesta was craning her neck, eyes alight.

'Hey, what's going on?' She stood up to get a better view. 'Jeepers, it's a fight. Look, a real fight. Blimey, what a punch-up. Bottles and all.'

The noise was rising. It was alarming. I wanted to get out but how? The exit route was blocked. I would have left Nesta to fend for herself but I felt responsible. She'd have to come with me but she was enjoying herself, reluctant to leave.

'We ought to go,' I said. 'This could get nasty.'

'Don't be an old spoilsport. Cor, look at that! It's terrific. Go on, beat him up!' she yelled.

My fingers curled round the phone. I did not want to call Jack but I would, if the situation worsened. Someone jerked back and knocked against us. My juice spilled on the table.

''Ere mind out,' Nesta shouted. 'Mind yer manners, you louts! Wotcha think you're doing?'

I tried to keep her quiet but she was determined to speak her mind. I couldn't leave her but I could shut her up.

'Don't say anything to irritate them, Nesta,' I said in a low, cool voice. 'If you don't shut up, I'll knock you out cold. Now shut up and keep quiet.

She looked at me with astonishment.

'Blimey,' she said, sitting down.

The bouncers, those burly men in black, were pushing their way in, getting hold of the struggling men, heaving them out by their shirts without putting a hand on them. People sued these days. I kept my head down. It was more difficult to restrain Nesta. She was excited with vodka and the rising temperature in the pub. It was unbearably hot. Sweat was running down my back. Nesta's make-up was streaked and smudged.

'I think we ought to go,' I said. 'We could get out now.'

'But it's still early!'

'I'm going,' I said. 'If you stay, you stay on your own.'

Her face went into sulky mode. I didn't care any more. It was out of here for me. I'd had enough of The Cyprus Tree. I pushed a fiver towards her.

'Enjoy the rest of the evening,' I said. 'See yourself home. Take a taxi with this and that's an order.'

I didn't wait for any argument or protests. I just wanted to go. I struggled through the crowd out on to the street. There were so many people about. Where had they all come from? I was nearly pushed into the roadway, a bit frightened. Yet I'd coped with crowds, some worse than this, when I was a WPC. Where had my nerve gone or had the situations worsened?

I staggered out into the night air. It hit my bare waist like a cold hand. Which way was the way home?

'Have you been drinking? Don't you know it's against the law to drive when you've been drinking?'

DI James pulled me to one side and pushed me against a wall, out of the way of the milling, chanting crowd. The bricks were rough against my skin and I arched away from it.

'Smell my breath. Juice of the orange. Not a drop, I swear it, officer sir.'

He came close, almost to my mouth and it was unbearable. He was like a breath of mountain air even when he was tired and grim and not particularly affectionate. But he was pushing me against a wall and that was a start.

'What are you doing here?' he snapped.

'Working.'

'Jordan. What a load of cobblers. Tell me the truth.'

'Cross my heart. This is work. I've been interrogating a

possible lead. Took her for a couple of drinks to loosen her up. She loosened up all right.'

'In that gear? I don't believe this rubbish. You're asking for trouble. And there is trouble inside. I've just sent in a couple of heavies.'

'I didn't get any. Not until now. And you're pushing me against a stone wall. Does it mean something personal or could I sue for harassment?'

He relaxed his grip on my arms and I leaned forward, rubbing my sore back. It was time to unknot the knot and let the creased hem of the shirt hang down. It looked like a rag. I wanted to go home, wash the smell of cigarette smoke out of my hair.

'I've a car here. We'll take you home.' He could read some of my thoughts. Briefly. Not the right thoughts.

He pushed me into a waiting patrol car. I fell into the passenger seat. But he was not coming with me. Someone else was driving. I stared into the windscreen, seeing a dim white face staring back. Mine.

'Hello,' said DS Ben Evans, turning in the glow from the street lights. His face was handsome and grinning, his glasses reflecting light. 'I'll take you home, Jordan. You look beat. Time for bed.'

But not with him.

Ten

G ill Frazer had to be sedated and was eventually taken to a nursing home where she could be looked after. She was screaming for hours. The neighbours called an ambulance. It would make visiting rather more difficult for me. Ben Evans told me that her mental breakdown was genuine but she would recover in time.

'She's completely devastated, utterly inconsolable. She simply fell apart. The doctors are concerned for her mental health.'

'Oh dear.' And I had thought Gill Frazer was suspect number one. The police must surely know about the manslaughter charge.

'At least with Mrs Frazer safely in a nursing home, we know where she is,' said Ben. He was telling me something without telling me. Did they think she might make a run for it?

'Do you think she has something to do with Brian Frazer's death?'

'Jordan, we really cannot have this conversation.'

'We are not. I am merely commenting. You can either agree or disagree.'

'I shall do neither.'

'Then I suggest you take me home and I can get my beauty sleep.'

'You don't need any,' said Ben, giving my hand a squeeze.

My reaction was mixed. I was feeling relaxed now but it was a result of all that pushing by James against a wall, and

97

his fresh breath fanning my hot face. Not Ben Evans or his expert driving. He was a smooth driver but he wasn't coming down my street.

'And you've got killer legs,' he said, his hand moving to my knee. I froze. He flexed the flesh like he was kneading bread. I moved his hand back to the wheel.

'One-handed driving is against the law,' I reminded him. 'Like mobile phones.'

'Who's watching?'

'There are speed cameras everywhere.'

He was looking confident, humming under his breath. I suppose he thought it was invite in for cosy coffee time, that I would have a big sofa, an even bigger bouncy bed. Little did he know of my spartan style of living. But I was feeling lonely. Perhaps a dose of seduction was what I needed.

'I hear you make excellent coffee,' he said, drawing up to the kerb near my bedsits and putting on the brake. 'You have a reputation.'

'But only for making coffee. I'm not an empty vessel.' It was a good line. I was not sure what it meant or where it came from, but the words sounded enigmatic.

'Come on, Jordan. Take pity on a weary Detective Sergeant. Two murders to be solved, villains everywhere. I'm worn out. And it's not even the holiday season.'

'You're saying that the fisherman diver was murdered?'

'Maybe. The neck of his suit was cut. The water rushed in, filling the suit and he drowned. The suits have tight neckbands, wristbands and anklebands. At some point or place, the neckband had been ripped open.'

'That's awful. Who could have done that underwater?'

He didn't answer straightaway. 'An awful way to die, choking underwater, being dragged down and knowing what was happening.'

'What does forensic say?'

'You know better than to ask me that.' Ben got out of the car, came round and opened the door for me. He was expecting an invitation. He would wait a long time, I decided. He pulled me roughly to him. I hoped no one was watching.

'You're lovely,' he said huskily, his face against my hair. 'You're beautiful.'

His mouth came down on mine. His lips were soft and moist and seeking. It was a pleasant feeling but did nothing for me. My body was still. I tried to respond but it was not real. It was pretending, being friendly and trying to make something out of nothing. What a fraud.

'Shall I come in?' he asked.

'Not this time,' I said, stalling. 'It's been a long day. But thank you for bringing me home.'

I let him kiss me again. A pressing session. It was the least I could do.

Once safely indoors, I phoned Jack on zero, zero, one, zero.

'I'm home,' I said.

'About time,' he growled.

A nursing home is hardly the place to send an invoice for services rendered. It looked like I would not get paid again. I thought of Francis Guilbert's generous payments with fondness. Thank goodness I had a small nest egg. Quail size. It was a tempting thought to take up his offer of regular employment but I did not see myself as a nine-to-five shop assistant.

And drinking wine with the boss would not go down well with the rest of the staff. I rather liked the au pair evenings and suppers with Francis. He was almost like a father to me although I'm sure that was not how he saw himself.

I typed out an invoice for Phil Cannon and another report. He owed me. He had not paid a penny yet and it was time. I could not work on air. I added up the expenses for The Cyprus Tree. He might argue with me over the high consumption of vodkas but they were legitimate. I did not charge for my juice. I'd got approximate dates and a name. Tone, Tony. I couldn't charge expenses for walking Jasper or muddied jeans. Shopping list: biological washing powder and floral-scented rinse.

Four hours of walking Jasper. I owe him a new lead.

The jigsaw puzzle bank statements were of little use to me now that Brian Frazer was dead. But one bank page was different, nothing to do with my client. It was addressed to Mrs Lydia Fontane, who lived in the big house next to the Frazers. The family who had sold off a sliver of their garden as a building site. Perhaps the postman delivered it to the wrong house.

I should not really have read it but I have this uncontrollable curiosity. Like we all read cornflakes packets at the breakfast table. The eyes need something to do. I read any piece of paper put in front of me. And Mrs Fontane had been careless enough to lose it in the first place. I mean, who puts bank statements in the dustbin?

She had quite a tidy sum in the bank, several thousands, and it was a current account. No second mortgage needed here. It was a elegant villa and the family had several businesses around the town. I was not sure what they were but the name was synonymous with Latching and old money. She was a generous woman with several standing orders to charities.

Then I spotted a standing order that had nothing to do with charity, or did it? Mrs Fontane was paying £250 a month to a Mrs G. Frazer. Gill Frazer? Possibly the woman who lived next door and who was at present supine in a nursing home under sedation?

It was so extraordinary. I was not imagining it. There it was, in cold print. She paid £250 on the first of each month to a Mrs G. Frazer. Surely it was not just a coincidence?

I was on to the bank immediately. I turned on a Mrs Fontane-type voice, Mrs Lydia Fontane if you please, quoted the account number correctly. The cashier suspected nothing.

'And how can I help you, Mrs Fontane?' she said.

'It's nothing special. Just this silly brain of mine,' I apologized in a slightly senile way. 'I'll forget my own name next. I simply cannot remember how long I've been paying this monthly standing order to Mrs Frazer.' I quoted the standing order reference number. I was impressed by my efficiency.

'I'll go through your records,' said the cashier. 'If you wouldn't mind waiting a few moments, Mrs Fontane.'

'Of course. Not at all.'

I heard computer keys clicking. My hearing is exceptional. The cashier came back on the phone, clearing her throat.

'It's over ten years now, Mrs Fontane. You began the standing order payments in March 1992.'

'Is it as long as that?' I fluttered on. 'My, my, how time flies. Thank you so much for looking it up. Is there any current address for Mrs Frazer?'

'No, just her account number at a different bank.' The obliging girl quoted it to me.

'Thank you so much,' I said, aligning the numbers with the other jigsaw bank statements I'd put together. They were the same. The same Mrs G. Frazer. Gill of the mud-coloured clothes.

'Not at all, Mrs Fontane. Any time.'

My maths are not top of the class but even I could work out that a payment of more than £30,000 in total had been payed to Mrs Fontane. Not exactly over-the-hedge pocket money. And she had been paying it long before the Frazers moved to next door.

Someone was rapping on the counter of my shop. I really ought to get the bell fixed.

'Anybody there?' a voice called out. 'I warn you, I might start shoplifting any moment now.'

I hurried out. I'd been so engrossed in the bank statement I had forgotten that I'd opened up the shop. A man was standing nonchalantly against the counter. He had a rucksack on his back, but a smart one with lots of pockets and zips. He turned and smiled at me. It was devastating. He had those mature, what's-his-name film star looks, the whiter than white teeth, blonde hair streaked with grey, tanned skin . . . and an American accent.

'I hope I didn't call you away from something special, ma'am,' he said, his eyes sweeping over me. I love the way Americans call you 'ma'am'.

'Just some bookkeeping,' I said, hoping I'd got my own voice back. This was not the time for early senility. 'Can I help you?'

'You sure can. Those two old maps of Sussex. Are they for sale?'

I could have said something witty, like yes, this is a shop. But I did not want to frighten him away. He was just too gorgeous. I hoped Doris was watching.

'Yes,' I said. Brilliant response.

'I'm on a touring holiday of Sussex and these maps look so interesting. All the ancient names of farms and paths and woodland. Very historic.'

'You'd get lost if you followed them.'

He obviously thought this was really bright, because he laughed, showing a lot of teeth. All perfectly aligned. He'd got a good dentist.

'That's for sure, ma'am. I don't intend to use them. Just get them framed and hang them on the wall when I get home. A really nice souvenir of my visit to the south of England, don't you think?'

I nodded. Any moment now, a super-slim blonde would walk through the door, matching rucksack, designer jeans, tuck her arm through his and say, 'Come on, honey, haven't you finished looking at those old maps yet?'

'Ideal,' I croaked.

'How much are they?'

I would have given them to him, but sanity returned in time. 'Six pounds each.'

'Worth every penny,' he said. 'I'll take both of them. Could you roll them and wrap them for me? I'm going to mail them on ahead.'

I had one of those postal tube things. He was impressed, so was I. I dug out my cleanest wrapping paper and Sellotape. I even gave him a label.

'This is very kind, ma'am,' he said, printing out his address on the label. I couldn't read it upside down.

'Are you walking around Latching?' I asked. It was the best I could do. Where had the fluent conversationalist gone?

'No, ma'am, I've done Latching. I'm planning to move on to Shoreham tonight. Didn't Prince Charles escape from Shoreham port after the Battle of Worcester?'

'Prince Charles?' I was confused.

'In 1651. He eluded the Parliamentarians and escaped to France. He was disguised as a servant of a Colonel Gunter, leading his horse. I love your history.'

Offer the man some coffee. Be polite, hands across the pond stuff, talk more history. He was taking the money out of his wallet, handling the notes carefully like a foreigner. He added two coins and put them on the counter. They were both bright, golden new from the bank.

'Twelve pounds,' he said.

'Thank you. Do you need a receipt?' I added. Had I gone completely mad? He looked at me curiously.

'For customs, or anything.'

'Oh no, I don't think it's necessary, ma'am. I believe I only have to declare the value of the contents on the outside of the package.'

He was leaving. The shop already seemed darker and empty. He flashed me a smile from the doorway. Robert Redford, that was the name I was looking for.

'Goodbye, ma'am, and thank you.'

'Goodbye. Enjoy the rest of your holiday.'

I stood with the money in my hand. I felt I ought to frame the two golden coins as a remembrance of bright magical moments.

Doris appeared in the doorway, slightly out of breath. She grinned.

'I sent him round to you,' she said, all chirpy. 'Do I get a commission?'

It took a while to get my head screwed back on. Mrs Lydia Fontane. I decided to pay her a visit. No one had asked for my assistance. But I felt I owed Brian Frazer something extra. A decent departure perhaps.

Lucy Locket was due for an airing. Her appearance and occupation might change but I was getting used to the name. I found some interesting clothes in my charity box. A multi-flowered skirt, green shirt, clumpy shoes, and faded denim jacket. Ms Locket was about to become a social worker.

I lifted the polished brass knocker of the front door of the big house. It was called The Limes although I could not see a lime in sight. Perhaps they had been cut down to make way for building the new house.

Mrs Lydia Fontane opened the door. She was tall and skinny, all sparrow bones, a limp mauve chiffon dress wrapped round her body, feet in narrow leather shoes. I'd seen her several times at mayoral functions in my days as a WPC. She would not recognize me now.

'Mrs Fontane? It is Mrs Fontane, isn't it? I'm Lucy Locket with West Sussex Social Services,' I said in a soft Irish drawl. 'May I ask you a few questions in connection with the illness of Mrs Frazer who lives next door?' I had rehearsed the lines a few times.

'Yes, of course. Poor soul. She's very upset and not surprising considering what has happened to her husband. How can I help you?'

'It is a very sad situation but it's her son that I am enquiring about. Max Frazer. No one seems to know where he is and I have to find that young man.'

'Oh, Max. But he's twenty-one,' said Mrs Fontane. 'Surely that's old enough to look after himself?'

'Er, yes,' I floundered, thrown. 'Social Services are involved indirectly. Do you know if he has a lot of friends?'

'I'm sure he has the normal number of friends of any young man of that age.'

'Do you know Mrs Frazer well?'

'No, I'm afraid I hardly know her at all. She is not a sociable type of person.'

'But she is your neighbour. Isn't their house built in your garden?'

A fleeting smile crossed her thin face. 'That doesn't mean that I have to make her a bosom pal. It's hardly obligatory with the transfer of land.'

'Of course not, but neighbours usually talk.'

'I'm not exactly the kind of person to waste time gossiping over a garden hedge,' said Mrs Fontone, slightly ruffled. 'Now, if you have any more questions, Miss Locket, I'm rather busy. I have several committee meetings scheduled today.'

Ah yes, a busy committee-type lady. It fitted.

'No, of course not. I won't take up any more of your time. It is just that I need to contact Max now that his father has died and his mother is ill.'

'I expect he's staying with friends.'

'That's probably the answer. But if you do see him . . .'

'I'll give you a ring. Please give me your number at work.' Mrs Fontane produced a notebook and pencil.

Ah. 'Unfortunately all our phones are down at the moment. Serious structural engineering work. I'll give you a ring tomorrow if that's OK with you.'

'Perfectly. Goodbye, Miss Locket.'

We did the required nodding and shaking hands and I went down the drive, liking the airy feel of material swirling round my legs. It was a long time since I had worn a skirt like this. Quite different to the slim black number I wore at the theatre.

Something made me look back. It was that tingle one

sometimes gets at the back of the neck. I looked up at the house, at the upstairs bay windows and gabled attic, and glimpsed a white face. A youth was peering from the top window, half in the shade, spiky hair. He drew back suddenly.

I went home along the shore. There was a brisk wind and the surfers were out on their boards, skimming the water like butterflies. Summer was definitely on its way. It was lazy days ahead, rearranging pebbles to ease the bones, shedding tops to tan, forgetting problems as the sun heated the skin. I love summer.

There were quite a few people strolling on the beach. They had also felt the stirring of good days ahead. I said hello to dogs. I always say hello so that they will not attack me. I don't mind muddy paws but I object to teeth marks.

I saw him before he saw me. DI James was slithering down the shingle, scuffing his nice black loafers. He walked over the wet sand towards me.

'Jordan,' he said. It was more a command than a hello.

'What have I done now?'

'Neither the death of the diver nor the electrocution of Brian Frazer are anything to do with you.'

'I know,' I said, all innocence. 'Nothing at all to do with me. And I have done nothing.'

'So what's this about a social worker visiting Mrs Fontane at The Limes?'

'What a suspicious lady,' I said, astonished. The skirt was getting splashed. My legs looked pale and wintery.

'She said some social worker came calling asking about young Max Frazer. Her description was a bit like you.'

'Am I the only woman in Latching with reddish hair? It's not even totally red. More mixed up rust and brown. And what about today's dyed hair? Everybody wears a colourant. It's deep plum and mahogany red this season.'

James looked confused. He had never strolled the hair dye counters of Superdrug.

'I don't know what you are talking about. She said the woman wore a flowered skirt.'

I jumped in immediately, totally defensive. 'Since when is it against the law to wear a flowered skirt? Dozens of women are wearing long skirts today. Go on, count them. Perfectly acceptable on a warm day when the sun is coming out and summer's on the way.'

'You look like a kindergarten teacher,' he said.

'That's a racist remark,' I snapped back.

I did not want him to go. He had taken off his jacket and flung it over a shoulder, the other hand in his pocket. No free hand to hold mine. Still, one could not have everything.

'Your shoes are getting wet,' I added.

'So are yours,' he said. 'I have to talk to you.'

Eleven

Phil Cannon was not pleased. He was clutching my invoice in one hand and waving the other in a fist at me. His face was tight with fury.

'And what do you mean by this?' he demanded.

'It means I would like to be paid for the work I have done, Mr Cannon,' I said. 'You will see by the enclosed report that my investigations have been pretty successful.'

'Tone! Tony!' He almost spat the name out. 'I could have told you that.'

'But you didn't,' I said. 'Nor did you produce the photographs which I asked you to get.'

'And what's all this drink for? Sounds like a hen night out. I'm not paying for you going out drinking.'

'It is itemised as entertaining Nesta Simons and it was my chance to get her to relax. As you know, she likes her vodka. She became very friendly and was quite happy to tell me a lot of things, including the name of her long-time boyfriend and various information about his times of working abroad.'

'I told you he was abroad when we met and had this sordid weekend. That's nothing new.'

The morning had not started well. It was becoming hot and sultry with a haze over the horizon. The sky stretched azure blue and a few fluffy white clouds hung about as if they had lost their way. I had too many clothes on. I still thought it was spring. Time to ban the vest. It was hard to trust this changeable weather.

Phil Cannon could not see or would not see what I had

achieved. I thought I'd done well, considering the circumstances. I had not mentioned Nesta's various charges held on
the police computer. He'd not asked me for a moral report.

'As I said before, there is a simple answer. A DNA test
would settle paternity, once and for all.'

'She'd never agree to it,' he growled, starting to roll a
cigarette. It was stick thin. He was mean with tobacco
as well.

'Have you asked her?'

'I told you, I don't speak to her, never have, never will.'

'Would you like me to approach her on the subject? If she
is so sure that you are the father of Dwain, then she won't
object. She'd be nailing you to the wall.'

He went white round the gills. For the first time, I wondered
if indeed he was the father of the dear boy. I'd believed
his innocence, given him room for doubt. But there was
something about his face that I did not trust, a slender
filament of caution.

'And the NHS won't cough up for it?'

'No, you have to pay privately. I can get the address of a
clinic for you.'

'I'm not paying,' he said, his clenched fist coming down
with a thud on my desk. 'And no one is going to make me.'

'Well, you either pay now for the DNA test or you go on
paying support for Dwain for another six or eight years. You
make a choice. It seems obvious to me which is the course
to take.'

'I don't intend to pay for nothing.'

I sighed. The man was difficult and as tight as superglue.
I wondered if Sergeant Rawlings could talk any sense into
him. He was stubborn to the point of lunacy. And was he,
or was he not, going to pay me?

'I'd be glad if you would kindly pay my invoice. It is very
modest for the number of hours I have put in. You wouldn't
like it if your customers didn't pay their bills.'

He was shuffling in his pocket and brought out a wad of

notes as thick as a triple hamburger. Business was obviously blooming. He peeled off a few grubby tenners, smoke spiralling from his ciggie. I wished I'd asked for more. You never can tell in this work.

'I don't think you've earned it,' he said with his usual charm. He reluctantly put the notes on my desk. I put a glass paperweight on them immediately in case he changed his mind and whisked them back. I trusted him as far as I would trust worn out elastic.

'Do you want me to continue working on this case?' I asked, without much interest. He was my least favourite client.

'Well . . . if it won't take long. A couple more hours wouldn't hurt. See what you can come up with.'

He was asking a lot. I'd found out everything that there was to know. What did he expect? A signed confession from Nesta that she was already pregnant before their wild weekend?

I made out a receipt. He took it without thanking me. I hoped he would go before I said something I would regret.

'I'll get another report, won't I?' he said.

'Of course.'

He grunted as he went out of the door. It was a sort of repressed, obliged noise. The best he could do. He went out of the door but did not close it.

I put the money away and wondered what else I could do. No way was I going to pay for the tests. Perhaps Nesta might. She would have Dwain's interests at heart. It was to her advantage to prove that Phil was the biological father, but she would lose out if he was not. But if I suggested it to her, then I'd have to admit my part in the investigation and that was not what I wanted. It was best that she did not know my role in the charade.

I knew who I wanted to talk to. Dr Williams. He was the retired doctor who collected old medicine bottles and was one of my best customers. I had an inkling he had something to do with the demolition of the bowling pavilion in the winter. He was not the obvious type to wear a baseball cap and drive a JCB over those precious greens, but I just had that feeling he might have been involved.

He did voluntary work down at the Salvation Army Centre. Cruising therapy of some sort, talking to the down-and-outs and the homeless who inhabited the seafront shelters in Latching, mostly drinking and sleeping. He could not practise now, but he gave good advice or pointed them in the right direction.

It was a lucky guess. He was sitting at a plain wooden table on a grey plastic chair, having a cup of tea with a very large woman. The chair looked hard and the tea strong. The woman was wearing a dozen layers of coats and jumpers despite the sunny day. No one could relieve her of them. They were her insurance against cold nights.

'Hello, Miss Lacey,' he said, rising. 'Have you found me any more medicine bottles?'

'No, I'm sorry, I haven't. But I do have some interesting glass in at the moment. It's a mixed bunch but they have funny stems.'

'Twist, spirals or corkscrew?'

'Heavens, I'm not sure. But something like that. Perhaps you'd like to take a look at them sometime?'

'My pleasure. I know a bit about glass.' He nodded towards the mountain of rags sitting opposite and nodded politely. 'Have you met Gracie? She is one of Latching's well known seafront inhabitants.'

Yes, I knew Gracie. I had once attempted to help her cross the shore road in the pouring rain. She had to be helped because she was trying to ferry five laden supermarket trolleys to the other side. As soon as one trolley was safely across, she went back for the next one. A bit like a mother cat and her kittens. It was a hazardous business as Gracie took no notice of the traffic. All the trolleys were piled high with carrier bags and bin bags, stuffed to bursting point. Her moving household.

Gracie apparently thought I had cunning designs on her precious possessions that day, for she brushed me aside and quite pointedly told me where to go. I went, but not to the place she suggested.

'Hello, Gracie,' I said.

She grunted and took a noisy gulp of her tea. Her hair hung in grease-locked corkscrews. The skin of her face was grimed with weeks of unwashing. It was one way to get a tan.

'Dr Williams,' I said, turning away from the smell. It was making me feel sick. 'I wonder if I could ask you something privately.'

'Of course. Would you excuse us for a moment, Gracie?'

Gracie grunted again and helped herself to a ginger biscuit, dunked it in the tea. His manners were perfect. Dr Williams was a such a gentleman.

'How can I help you?' he went on, from the other side of the crowded refreshment room. 'You're not ill, are you?'

'Oh no, nothing like that. I need information on DNA tests. Are you able to tell me anything?'

'Well, I may be a little out of date. They are constantly researching DNA profiling. It's a highly complicated procedure as there are something like three million bases in a DNA molecule. And it seems there are no two people exactly alike. They look like a bit like barcodes.'

'My query is about establishing parentage.'

'Yes, half come from the mother and half from the father.'

'And do you have to get a blood sample?'

'No, that's a fallacy. Blood, semen, saliva, a fragment of rooted hair or bone. A lot of different samples can be used. You can get a sample off a cigarette end. It's an intelligent tool.'

My brain went on red alert. Both Nesta and Phil Cannon smoked. But Dwain didn't. Or did he? Kids tried everything these days. Or could his sample be something different?

'Interesting,' I said. 'And a DNA test has to be paid for?'

'Privately, yes, but not when it's a police procedure. The

police have set up a national DNA register. It's a matter of routine now. Every crime leaves a signature of the criminal. Did you know that identical twins share the same DNA but have different fingerprints?'

'That's fascinating. Thank you, Dr Williams. You've been a great help.'

'I'll go back to Gracie. I'm trying to get her to see a dentist before her teeth fall out. Heaven help the dentist.'

I hurried back to my shop. Phil Cannon had left a cigarette, stubbed out in an ashtray that was on a shelf for sale. I hoped I had not thrown it away in a moment of distracted housekeeping.

But it was still there, like a thin brown worm. I tipped it into a specimen bag and sealed the top, labelling it. Very methodical. DI James would have been impressed.

It's amazing how often DI James appears when I am thinking of him, or is it that I am always thinking of him? He came into the shop and filled the doorway with his presence. He was wearing an open-necked, short-sleeved shirt and black jeans. It was one of those ex-RAF pilot's shirts with tabs on the shoulders. I was not sure if I liked the gear, but it suited him. The vee of the open neck revealed a crinkle of dark hair. My craving to touch became a pain, clenching my muscles to my side.

'Would you like some coffee?' I fell back on my old stand-by.

'I thought you'd never ask. I'm sorry about the other day on the beach. I wanted to talk but there wasn't time. A mobile is like a damned chain and manacle.'

He followed me through into my office. I made the coffee fresh from fresh beans. The aroma immediately filled the room. He always got the best.

James slumped on to the edge of my desk, hands clasped between his knees. He was watching me closely.

'Been out drinking recently?' he asked.

'What a thing to ask,' I said coolly. 'I suppose your spies have been out in case I repeated my binge at The Cyprus Tree.'

'Something like that. Your friend had to be thrown out for causing a fight at the bar.'

'Nothing to do with me. She's not my friend and I'd already left that night. I went home to my solitary bed. DS Evans gave me a lift, remember?'

He did not comment on the solitary bed. 'She had an argument with someone and it ended up in a fight. The other woman got a black eye and some hair torn out.'

'Oh dear.'

'How come you were out with Nesta Simons? She is not one of Latching's angels. You say she's not a friend.'

'I was working on a case. And you know better than to ask me who, what, why and when. My client information is private, like a doctor.'

'Is Nesta your client?'

'No.'

'Her boy, Dwight, is always in trouble.'

'Dwain.' Ouch. He'd caught me. It was too late to bite the word back.

'So you know her son as well?'

'Is this an interrogation? I thought you came in for a coffee.'

'The best in Latching,' he said rewarding me with the merest glimmer of a smile. 'I'd tell everyone except I want to keep you to myself.'

I could have taken that remark the wrong way, basked and lazed in happiness for several days, but I knew James did not mean it. It was the Columbian beans. Still, I could dream. I could suggest a picnic on the beach, tuna and salad sandwiches, Pringles sour cream and chives flavour, home-made sausage rolls (surely I could buy some somewhere), cold beer or yogurt smoothie. I'd bring a rug to soften the pebbles and we'd lay in the sun, not too close but close enough for skin breathing, eyes closed to the brightness of the sky, both dreaming our own dreams.

'Wake up, Jordan. I've just asked you if you'll be seeing Nesta again.'

I jolted myself back to Mother Earth. 'I guess so. The case isn't finished, though I wish it was. My client is the most difficult man.'

'Most men are difficult.'

'You're telling me. Find me a group of single, straight, emotionally-stable, money-wise, intelligent men and it'll be an empty room.'

'Jordan, that sounds bitter.' He shot me a fast look. 'Has someone hurt you?'

This, coming from James? Hurt me? I did not know how to answer. I was not exactly ready to open my heart to him. Maybe, one day. But he would have to make the first move. My pulse was racing. I took a few deep breaths to steady it. There was a nasty lump in my throat, like a swallow that has gone wrong.

'Me? Never. I'm much too independent. Sure, I hope to meet the right man, one day, someone devastating, but in the meantime, life is for living, not for washing up and ironing.' The light voice was right. I'd not been cast in school plays for nothing.

'I agree with you. No commitments. No involvements. Keep one's freedom to the last. Wait until Calista Flockhart is heart free.'

'To freedom,' I said, raising the mug in a toast.

James raised his and the rims touched briefly. It was awkward and contrived. 'Agreed.'

He took a sip of coffee and went on as if nothing had happened. 'We'd like to know more about Nesta Simons' activities and I wondered if you could tell us anything of interest.'

'It'll cost you a lunch or a supper.'

'I think that could be arranged,' he said smoothly.

It was too easy. For a second I did not trust him. He'd said that it could be arranged, not that he would be taking me himself. He'd send Ben Evans as a stand-in or slip me a fiver. No, thank you.

'You tell me about Nesta and I'll tell you what we've found out about the dead fisherman, Roy Dinglewell.'

There had to be a catch. I was being baited. He knew that Mavis and I were friends, that I would do almost anything for her since she got beaten up.

'Tell me.'

James was not sure about me either, I could see that, but he decided to risk it. He poured himself out a second cup of coffee and helped himself to a chocolate chip cookie. He'd forgotten breakfast, if he ever had any.

'At first we thought it was a tragic accident, that something had gone wrong underwater. His diving suit had got ripped round the neck. They were diving round a wreck and he could have got caught on some sharp bit of machinery.'

I said nothing about the bloodied shirt which I had found, the shirt that I thought had smelt strongly of fish. The smell could have come from adjacent fish pieces and it could have belonged to anyone. Although the fishing fleet from Latching had diminished over the years, they did still exist and sell their fish daily from the beach.

'Yes.' I nodded.

'But forensic have come up with something else. It will appeal to you, with all your healthy food and herbal stuff.'

'Appeal to me?'

'At first, they were somewhat confused. After all, they are trained to find the normal poisonous substances but this was something different.'

'He was poisoned?'

'Don't interrupt. They found traces of a narcotic drug called hyoscine, which was once used medically, but today morphine and codeine are prescribed.'

'It's a plant called Henbane,' I said. 'It's a very poisonous and coarse-looking plant with sticky, hairy leaves and white flowers. It has a foul smell.'

'Ah, you know . . . ?'

'And I know that it grows around here near Latching, in the south, near the sea. You'll find it on sandy soil, on the cliffs, in farmyards. Anyone could pick it, if you know what it is.'

'Go on.' For once I had caught his attention. His ocean-bright eyes were willing me to continue. 'Please . . .'

'It disturbs the nervous system, stops the brain from functioning properly. A kind of mania sets in. You need to find out how Roy was behaving before the dive . . . if he was agitated or quarrelsome or nervous. The bladder gets paralyzed.'

'How do you know all this?'

'Books. I buy books, read books. I've got a shop full of them. I've got a reference book on plants. Do you want to buy it?'

James got up, stretched, looking long and tall and lean. I melted. He'd forgotten about Nesta. The dead fisherman was more important and rightly so.

'We'll follow it up. Nothing is straightforward with this one.'

'And Brian Frazer?'

'Going nowhere.'

'Pity. He did not deserve to die. Dreadful singing is not a motive.'

'My mother thought he was brave to get up and even try. She gave him two out of ten for the songs. Ten out of ten for courage.'

'Your mother?'

'Making one of her rare visits. Thank you for the coffee. Just what I needed. And the sane conversation. I owe you a lunch, Jordan. And soon, I won't forget.'

He went out, closing the door. My office was bereft. His mother. He had taken his mother to the trad jazz in Falmer Gardens.

Shopping list: buy trendy clinging skimpy top, cleavage revealing, tiny straps. On second thoughts, shopping list: new snow-white T-shirt, small sleeves, best quality.

Twelve

It was like going round and round in circles. I needed a new case and a paying one. Phil Cannon was only good for a couple more hours. Mrs Gill Frazer was in a nursing home and the investigation into her husband's strange habits had come to a halt. A definite demise. DI James was not paying me, only with a meal. But I had to support various habits, like eating regularly. At this rate I would be signing on for unemployment.

I was busy making my shop look nice. It had been neglected of late. Takings were down. Stock was low, no medals or top quality stuff. People did not shop so much in the summer. They were on holiday, sunning themselves on the beach, eating Italian ice cream in twenty flavours.

Holiday? I couldn't remember when I had last had a holiday. What did people do on holiday? Eat, drink, make love, get sunburned. I would scour the beach for fossils or crabs that needed up-ending.

A woman came into the shop. I recognized her but did not say anything. This time she was wearing a natural linen dress down to her ankles. Leather sandals and a gold ankle chain. Interesting effect.

'Miss Lacey?' she said. 'The private investigator?'

'Yes.'

'Have we met before?'

She was thinking of Lucy Locket, erstwhile social worker, a recent caller at her house. I tried to sound older and look different with a firm stance, clipped voice. 'No, I don't think so. Can I help you?'

'Is there somewhere we can talk privately?'

'Of course, would you like to come through into my office?'

The Victorian button-back and the Persian rug worked their invisible magic. She sat down and crossed her legs, relaxed. On went the coffee.

'How can I help you?'

'My name is Lydia Fontane. I live at The Limes in St Michael's Road. I want you to find out who murdered my two children.'

The words hung in the air in a block. As blunt as that. I was stunned. It was like a stab in the heart. I did not have children but that did not mean I could not feel some emotion. I took out a clean sheet of paper, tried to look detached, efficient. It was not easy.

'I know this must be difficult for you, Mrs Fontane,' I said slowly, picking my words. 'But I shall need to know all the circumstances. Are you able to tell me everything?'

'Not everything, but as much as you need to know.'

'Please, go ahead. Begin in your own time.'

I was shattered. There was within me some dormant maternal feeling for children, like that girl on the beach, toddlers exploring pools, plump babies asleep in buggies. I could imagine, almost, the complete devastation of losing children, and much worse, to murder. The blood drained from my face. I felt sick.

'It was ten years ago but sometimes it seems like yesterday. I had two children, Ben aged two and Izzy aged three. Izzy was short for Isidore. I know it sounds lame now, but I was busy, helping my husband with his various businesses. He had a lot of interests in the area and was overworked. We employed a nanny. She was good and reliable, we thought. We trusted her. She came with good references and the boys liked her.'

'And her name?'

'Gill. She was an unmarried mother with a son called Max. We took Max into the family. He was a nice boy and the right age to be a help with my children – about eight years older. We all got on really well. It seemed an ideal arrangement.'

She was beginning to look pale. It was painful for her. I did not know what to do. Double child slaughter was not something I came across every day. I wanted another lost tortoise.

'And your husband?'

'He died a year ago. A heart attack. I'm a widow.'

'I'm sorry. Please go on.' I did not know that. I didn't remember Mr Fontane dying or reading about it in the papers. 'And the children?'

'My husband and I went out one evening to the Mayor's Charity Ball. It was a white tie affair and the tickets were expensive. You know the kind of thing. I had a lovely dress, I remember, a heavy antique lace in a champagne colour.'

I murmured, not knowing that kind of thing at all.

'It was held at the Pier Pavilion and everyone who was any-one in Latching was there. All the councillors, the aldermen, the mayor and his wife, the town clerk, our local MP and his wife. It was a glittering evening. Buffet supper and dancing to a good band. It raised a lot of money for charity.'

She paused. It was obviously hard for her to go on.

'And you left the children with their nanny,' I said, carefully leading her back. 'She would give them their supper and put them to bed.'

'Yes, that's what she did, then she watched television and went to bed herself at some time, I suppose.'

I waited, not wanting to watch her.

'I thought it was strange the next morning that the children did not come running in to me. That's what they always did. They usually came into my bedroom, making lots of noise, not too old to climb into bed with me. They always used to do that, climb in beside me for a story.'

Lydia Fontane was making huge demands on herself. I

could see her throat tightening, her hands clenched against her knees to stop them from trembling.

'When I went into their bedroom, they were still in their beds. They looked so quiet. I thought at first they were ill. There was a meningitis scare about at the time, but then I realized it was worse than that. It was awful. They were both dead, quite dead. They had been suffocated.'

What could I say? Sorry was inadequate. I ought to learn some more words. I said nothing but gave Mrs Fontane time to recover. No wonder she was thin. I guess she lived on air and grief.

'Gill, the nanny, was charged and stood trial. But she insisted on her innocence all along. She said someone must have broken in and murdered the boys. But there was no trace of a break-in. They reduced the charge to manslaughter. Then the case got thrown out of court for insufficient evidence. The police have never come up with another suspect.'

I was even more confused now. The same Gill, now Mrs Gill Frazer, was living next door to her. And the same Gill Frazer had been receiving monthly payments from Mrs Fontane for years. How could she bear to have Gill Frazer anywhere near her? It did not make any sense.

'And you want me to find out who really killed your sons?' I asked. 'It's a pretty cold trail.'

Hardly a tactful remark but it had to be said. Mrs Fontane wore a lot of rings, mostly emeralds in gold settings. The stones winked at me, semaphoring their collective value. They helped me to make up my mind. I was not proud of myself.

'I want you to try. The police closed the case, of course. It's no use going to them. But I can't rest until I know what really happened to Ben and Izzy. My boys . . .'

Shopping list: more tissues. I'd run out, but Lydia had a beautiful lawn handkerchief, edged with fragile French lace, perfectly white. I waited until she had dried her tears. There was nothing I could do except give it my best.

I leaned forward and took her hand. Her skin felt like paper. 'I will try, Mrs Fontane, but I can't promise any results. It's so long ago.'

She smiled. 'Thank you, Miss Lacey. I feel better now, knowing that I am doing something for them. I understand that you are quite successful.'

I did not tell her it was mostly luck. I got out a client form. 'There are a few formalities,' I said, smoothing a page. 'Sorry to be so businesslike.'

'I understand. My husband was a businessman and I know everything has to be written down and signed for. Even detective work.'

I looked at my notes when Mrs Fontane left leaving a heady whiff of Joy perfume behind. I'd written reams. A visit to Mrs Gill Frazer was number one on my list, even if I was not quite sure what it would achieve. Her mind might still be unbalanced. But a break-in . . . it seemed unlikely and the police had found no trace.

Would DI James let me look at the police records? After all it was a long time ago. Hardly breaking any law, surely? Number two on my list was the local newspaper office. I had to read everything in print. And see Sergeant Rawlings. Now, he might remember something. My favourite sergeant might let slip a few nuggets of information.

But there was a lot more to this. Why was Gill Frazer living next door? Why was she receiving monthly payments from Lydia Fontane? There was an iceberg somewhere beneath all this information. Mrs Fontane was not telling me the whole story. But that was nothing unusual. Clients rarely told me everything. They always kept some truth close to themselves.

The local office of the *Sussex Record* did not have copies of newspapers going back ten years. Not surprising. They'd need far bigger premises than their present cramped accomodation. Hardly room to put in a small ad.

'Our head office in Brighton will have them,' said the girl

at the counter. 'If you make an appointment, they'll let you see them.'

'Thanks. It looks as if I'll be making a visit to the big B in the very near future.'

Or sooner. I got into my ladybird, glad to be behind the wheel of her again. She had not been used of late. She sprang to life at a touch and I wheeled her out on to the A27 towards the great fantasy seaport of the south. I put my foot down carefully, not too fast. There were speed cameras everywhere. The speed-hogs overtook everything, mostly BMWs and Mercedes. Let them get caught and fined.

The problems began in Brighton. Where to park? I wasted fuel circling and circling, trying to save money by finding a vacant slot in a side street. Waste of time. I gave up and put her in a multi-storey. I could tell she did not like it. All those strange cars around her, bigger and flashier. Still, she had spots.

I cheered up when I realized that Mrs Fontane would pay the exorbitant charge for parking. The *Sussex Record* office was in a new tower block. It was almost impossible to find a way into the building. It even had an escalator to the first floor and trees planted in the foyer. There was a big area given over to public searches. You gave the year and edition you wanted to the girl behind the desk and she came back with heavy wads of paper pinned to a wooden slat. She could hardly carry them.

'These ought to be on microfilm,' I said. 'That's what they do these days.'

'In your dreams,' she said. 'Trees in the foyer first priority. Never mind, I'm getting muscles.'

The Fontane story made the headlines for weeks. There were photos of the boys, fresh-faced and innocent-eyed. Another photo was of a younger Gill Norton, as she was named then. Her hair was frizzed and home permed and she wore glasses. She was not looking at the camera, but looking down at the ground as if she could not face the world.

Those were not the days of TV interviews of the bereaved parents or rows of wrapped flowers in sympathy. It was more private, more low-key but just as shocking. There were a lot of photos of the parents taken at earlier events, but not too close, nothing intrusive. A greenfly was crawling over the page. I brushed him off, gave him a chance to find his way home. Perhaps he lived on an indoor tree.

The court case made columns. The court reporter was paid on lineage. Gill Norton protested her innocence. She had been asleep all night. She knew nothing of the boys' death until she awoke in the morning. Her story of intruders breaking-in was discounted by the police evidence. There was no sign of any break-in.

> SUSSEX nanny, Gill Norton, 27, today denied in court that she had suffocated her two charges, Benjamin (two) and Isidore (three).
>
> Her employers, Mr and Mrs Edgar Fontane, had been at the Mayor's Charity Ball that evening, and returned late. It was morning before Mrs Lydia Fontane found her sons dead. "I am innocent," Miss Norton protested. "I was asleep all night. No way would I hurt those two little boys." Police evidence ruled out any possibility of a break-in. Detective Sergeant Spring said there was no sign of any breaking and entering. It was an inside job.

And then the case was thrown out of court and Gill was never proved guilty. It happens all the time.

The photocopying machine in the corner was humming. I had plenty of loose change so could copy as many pages as I wanted at ten pence a copy. It saved making notes.

I took the heavy newspapers back to the girl. 'The Fontane murders,' I said. 'An awful case.'

She nodded though she was too young to have remembered it. 'Are you writing a book?' she went on.

'No.'

'We get dozens of people in here every day. Half of them are writing books. God help the libraries. Do you want anything else?'

'No, thank you. You've been most helpful,' I murmured on my way out. I said hello to the trees. Not much fun for them either.

I walked the pier, the famous Brighton pier. It was so different to our home-grown Latching pier, bigger, longer, brighter, brasher. The far end was being rebuilt after the fire. Funfairs, sideshows, jumpy castles, food and drink, fortune telling, candyfloss and rock . . . It was Blackpool on legs, scaled down. Not a bit like Latching pier. We had only Jack's amusement arcade and the anglers. They were a bundle of fun on a windy day.

I was getting homesick for the wide empty stretch of Latching beach. Brighton sea did not go out so far. And it was crowded. There was even a nudist beach somewhere. I'd not found it yet. It was almost impossible to look sideways while walking ahead.

Then I had a big problem. I'd forgotten in which car park I had left the ladybird. There were several multi-storey car parks and a variety of entrances. They all looked the same. My time was running out. You cannot run on crowded pavements. It was a kind of run, hop, jog, walk, hunt about.

My car had to be somewhere. I ran up and down sordid stairs, walls covered in obscene graffiti. I'd be able to spot her spots but she was dwarfed by the monsters parked around her.

I searched for an hour. But it was fruitless. My car had vanished. My legs were hollow with all the walking and climbing.

She must have been stolen. She was unique. Some collector would pay a good price for her extraordinary appearance. No wonder I could not find her. And in Brighton of all places.

I sat down on a church wall, desolate, and tried to formulate a plan. Should I phone the Brighton police? Surely they would be able to find her? And I wanted her back. She was part of me, part of my life.

My new mobile went off. I used a unique style of call sign, a phone ringing. No pop songs or football anthems for me.

'Hello,' I said, half-choked.

'Jordan?'

'Yes, it's me.'

'I never know for sure. You are always losing your phones.'

'They are always being stolen. You know, the police are too busy stalking motorists parked on yellow lines or checking speed cameras. The public ought to complain. Get the mobile robbers, I say.'

I knew who it was. He knew who it was. We were playing the same old game. Still, if it amused him . . . I relaxed slightly into the sound of his voice. His face came into my mind, every line, every touch of grey in his dark crew cut. James James.

'Have you lost your car?' he asked.

'Yes,' I said. 'I can't find her. I parked her in a multi-storey and she's gone. She's been stolen.'

'Where are you?'

'In Brighton. How do you know I've lost her?'

'Because we've just found your car, halfway to Hastings. Abandoned on the side of the road. Run out of petrol.'

'Meant to fill her up,' I said.

'Just as well you didn't. There's no damage, you'll be pleased to hear, except one broken door lock. A couple of joyriders.'

'Hastings.' I said it as if Hastings was the other side of the Strait of Dover. 'How do I get there?'

'Don't worry. We'll fingerprint the car and then return it to you in Latching. You can pick it up.'

'How do I get home?'

I heard his sigh. 'Ever heard of the train, Jordan? They run on lines. You go to a station and buy a ticket.'

In time I remembered my manners. 'Thank you for finding the ladybird. I was going mad, looking for her. You've no idea.'

'OK. Relax, go home and write up your notes. I take it you were working on something?'

'Sure. Always working. Thank you again.'

James rang off. I got off the church wall, stiff and disorientated, suddenly chilled even though it was hot. Where was the railway station? I found it in time after a long uphill walk, a great Gothic, echoing place. I bought a ticket, sat on a slow stopping train and rattled home to Latching, glad when I saw the flat silvery water of the river Adur flowing under the bridge at Shoreham.

A police car was waiting outside the station, no flashing lights. I peered in, force of habit. DI James was in the driver's seat, huddled into a light jacket, reading a paper. There was a faint, enigmatic smile on his face.

'You took your time,' he said, leaning over and opening the passenger door. 'You look shattered.'

'Not exactly a fun day,' I said, sliding in. 'Melancholy research.'

'Do you need cheering up?'

'Desperately.'

'Fancy a drink at The Gun?'

'Shoot me,' I said.

Thirteen

I would never forget that drink in The Gun. It's an old pub out at Findon, a bit smoky, low ceilings with wood beams, old brass and as atmospheric as Nelson's *Victory*. Close your eyes and it rocked.

We sat in a quiet corner. James bought the best red they had behind the counter. He had to duck his head at the bar. It was not my Chilean or an Australian Shiraz. But I forgave him. I'd have drunk any old plonk to be with him. It was Italian and rather good, a serious red with a taste of black cherry and bitter plum.

He was drinking juice because he was driving. Bless his matching black socks. I sensed he was longing for something 40 per cent stronger. A straight whiskey, a dram and a half. He had that taut, haunted look.

'What's the matter?' I asked, biting back the words.

'We've got two murders, remember? And we are no nearer to solving either of them. Hell, we don't know anything. Any moment now they'll send down the big guns from London, and boy, do we love them interfering.'

I wanted to say: I've got two murders, too.

James was staring at the panelled walls, not at me. I yearned to touch him, put my hand on his, show that I understood. But I'd never done that, touched him. Our courtship was so slow it was like a snail going backwards. If it was a courtship . . . How would I ever know?

'Can I help you?' I asked, uncertainly.

'You do . . . help me,' he said unexpectedly, turning round

to face me. 'You are funny, Jordan, crazy, an idiot. It does me good just to talk to you. It brings me down to earth, settles me in an odd way. While people like you exist, the world can't be that bad.'

I did not know what to do, what to say. I did not take kindly to being called an idiot. Was this an upside-down compliment or not? I decided to accept whatever it was, weird or wonderful. It was better than nothing. James could call me an idiot. It was only a small word.

I gave him one of my best smiles, eyes sparkling, sidled an inch nearer. Who'd notice? He didn't. 'And it's always fun to talk to you, buster, even when you are telling me off. And you do tell me off for no good reason. Sometimes you make me feel less than three feet tall.'

'I thought you were three feet tall. I'm sorry.'

He leaned over my way and cupped round my hand. I was holding the wine glass at the time so I could not respond. But I could feel his skin and the warmth coming from his fingers. His nails were scrubbed clean. This was the nearest we had ever been. I could have died in the moment. He was my man. I had never heard such tenderness from him. I was confused, lost, bemused. If I said the wrong thing, it could all disappear sideways.

'I accept your sorrowing,' I said, like some Victorian maiden in an Edith Wharton novel. 'Occasionally share your thoughts with me.'

He had barely told me anything about himself. I knew he was divorced, that it still hurt, that he had no real place he could call home. He had not made anywhere a home. And that was about all. It was not enough for any normal relationship.

'You would not want to hear my thoughts, Jordan. Sometimes they are so strange, they'd frighten you out of your best boots. Not for public consumption.'

'I'm not public. Try me.' This was brave.

'OK, Ms Lacey. Tell me this. What do you think of a man

whose thoughts are so black that sometimes he can't even see through his own darkness?'

What could I say? His voice was twisted with some internal agony and his eyes clouded over. The ocean blue pigment dulled like a day of storm and tempest when the sky was bruised and swirling. He was telling me something without telling me.

'Well, Mr Detective Inspector,' I said, playing for time. At such moments my brain is incredibly slow. 'I think we all have black thoughts. It's how we deal with them that makes each of us different. I go for walks on the beach, on the pier, watch the sea. I play jazz. Sometimes a trumpet will cleanse my thoughts with the sheer magic of soaring notes.'

'Ah . . . your trumpeter. The mysterious man dressed in black. I have no one like that. Though I do walk the pier, watch the sea.'

He'd noticed. I did not realize that. But James was perceptive. He would have seen the rapt look on my face when my trumpeter last played, that evening at the Bear and Bait. The last time I had seen the famous musician, whom I cherish to distraction but in a totally different way.

He was married, happily. I knew it. He knew it. There was nothing to be done except to enjoy the infrequent times that he played in Latching for the sheer joy of playing. No money involved. Only a goodnight kiss and murmured endearments. He always had the sweetest things to say. Just words, lyrics from songs.

'My trumpeter,' I said, forlorn.

'You care about him?'

'Oh yes. Very much. But he's married so that's the end of that. Full stop. Draw a double line. It's only his music that's allowed to fire me.'

'But if you had met him earlier, before he married?'

'I don't know. How can I answer that?' I said, making my feelings dormant. 'We are a decade or more apart. You are asking me something that I can't answer. I'm not the sort of person who would follow a band around the world like a groupie.'

'But you might have followed him?'

I shook my head. 'It's impossible to say. It didn't happen. We are a million miles apart. He's famous, flies over to Los Angeles to do soundtracks for films, the James Bond films and others. I recognize his sound, that top F. Who am I? Just an adoring fan, that he sometimes sees in this sleepy seaside town. I'm like a herbal sleeping tablet. One to be taken when required.'

There was a silence. James did not know how to accept this. He had never heard me talk of my inner feelings before. There was nothing more to tell him. My trumpeter and I had shared nothing more than warm hugs and a goodnight kiss. James had never kissed me. He knew nothing about how it would feel to hold me close. How my body would cleave. It was his loss. A sudden coldness touched me.

'Would you like another drink?' he said, picking up my empty wine glass.

If I had another, I would be treading cloud nine. And when DI James left me, as he always did, it would be an empty cloud.

'No, thank you,' I said. 'It's been lovely but I'd like to go home.' I still had some sense left.

It took me some time to stabilize after that evening with James in The Gun. It was the closest we had ever got in our brief relationship. Such surprising togetherness. Still, summer was on its way and there were the hot and sultry evenings ahead. I was working winter out of my body. Soon I would meet up with him on the seafront, as he went after the muggers, the robbers, the rapists. What fun.

There were a lot of summer thugs about. Several women had been robbed and knocked about. The *Sussex Record* regularly had photos of elderly ladies with blackened eyes. If they caught the yobbos, they were often too young to be prosecuted.

I packed away my woolly clothes and got out the T-shirts and cut-off jeans. My feet, now healed, needed an airing, so I painted my toe nails Royal Red and slipped on some sandals.

My last two cases, although not concluded, had been reasonably successful. Perhaps I was improving, getting more experienced. I had found out why Brian Frazer dressed in women's clothes: he wanted to be another Danny La Rue. But I did not know who murdered him and it was not my case. And it was pretty obvious that Phil Cannon could not have been Dwain's father and that Nesta had taken him for a ride. It was up to him now to have a DNA test and prove it once and for all. I couldn't force him.

James had two murders on his hands and I had an old double one. The trail had gone so cold it was practically moribund. That was not funny. Wrong word. Two small children had died.

The monthly payments to Gill Frazer puzzled me. I could not understand why Mrs Fontane was paying money to the woman who had been accused of murdering her children. There must be a good reason.

Shopping list: flowers, fresh cut, box of chocolates. I was going sick visiting.

I got a shock when I reached The Laurels Nursing Home in Lansfold Avenue. It was the same solid, double-fronted house that had once belonged to the nun, that I had broken into last year, searching for clues, where I found fragments of burnt war-time bank notes in a grate.

A developer had bought the house, added a new wing at the back of the garden, turned it into a nursing home. It looked smart and clean, meeting all current health and safety requirements. I wondered what had happened to the old air-raid shelter that had figured in the dispute. Demolished, probably, along with all the ghosts.

I rang the bell in the porch. The porch was filled with hanging baskets with trailing lobelia and geraniums. A bee was buzzing around, cruising the nectar. I had trouble keeping my head out of the way of both bee and baskets.

A woman came to the door wearing a trim nurse's outfit. It was pale blue with navy touches. She was wearing minimum make-up and her short brown hair was flicked back behind her ears. She smiled cautiously. 'Yes?'

'Hello,' I said. 'I'd like to visit Mrs Gill Frazer. Would that be possible? Just for a few minutes. I'm an old friend.'

I waggled the bunch of mixed carnation sprays as evidence of our old friendship.

'Well, I don't know . . .'

'I do realize how ill she has been and I won't stay long. I'm sure it'll cheer her up to have a visitor.'

I tried to look terribly cheerful and the perfect visitor.

'Just a minute, please. I'll ask the doctor. What's your name, please.'

It took a second to sort out who I was at that moment. I checked my clothes. Clean jeans, clean plain white T-shirt, hair tied back with a bobble band. I was not being Lucy Locket. The T-shirt had 'dream boat' embroidered discreetly on the left hip. I covered the words with my arm.

'Jordan Lacey,' I said. It would mean nothing to her. She disappeared along a corridor and I peered into the hallway. I hardly recognized the place. It looked as if the house had been gutted and the downstairs was now redivided into waiting rooms and consulting rooms. The stairs were the same although the wood was newly polished and the carpet was a thick mushroom pile.

'The doctor says you may see Mrs Frazer for five minutes,' said the nurse on her return.

'Thank you,' I said, following her up the stairs. She opened a firedoor that led to the new wing. Gill Frazer was in room six on the first floor.

'Mrs Frazer, you have a visitor. Miss Jordan Lacey.'

It was a pleasant room, light and airy, with pine furniture and floral curtains that matched the counterpane on the bed.

Gill Frazer was sitting in an armchair, half asleep, a magazine unopened on her lap. It did not smell or look like a sick room. There were no personal belongings around apart from a camel coloured dressing gown hanging behind the door.

'Hello, Gill,' I said softly. 'It's me, Jordan. I've brought you some flowers. Look, spray carnations. And chocolates.'

Gill blinked. She seemed quite heavily sedated but I did not really know, nor could I ask. But she managed a smile.

'Jordan? Oh yes, Jordan, I remember you. Come in and sit down. Sorry, no chair.'

'I'll perch on the end of the bed. I'm not staying long, only five minutes. It's nice to see you looking better.'

The nurse left us which was a relief. I could not maintain friend-type conversation for long. It was going to be tricky. If she was still disturbed, then I must not do or say anything to alarm or agitate her. She took the flowers from me and stared down at the the peachy buds.

'Brian never brought me flowers,' she said. She sounded quite calm. 'I'm glad to see you. I haven't got anyone to talk to here and they won't tell me anything.'

'I suppose they don't want to upset you.'

'It's more upsetting not to be told anything. Brian was my husband. I have a right to know what happened.' There was a certain intentness in her eyes. She was fighting off the sedation.

'I don't think they know much yet. Your husband was electrocuted by some means, when he was holding the microphone. He'd been singing with the band. He sang . . . two songs. It could have been accidental but it's more likely to have been deliberate, someone tampering with the tranformer.'

'You mean he was murdered?'

'They are not sure but it is possible. It's a bit difficult for a transformer to get its wiring mixed up accidentally.'

'You say he was singing? I didn't know he liked singing. What were the songs called?'

Gill looked across at me with a glimmer of disbelief. Surely he sang around the house? Apparently not. I remember the office marked Private at the theatre. He probably practised in the theatre when everyone had gone home and he was left to lock up. The perfect place to rehearse and, dammit, I'd never checked the timing.

'First he sang "Shiny Stockings" and then he sang "Embraceable You", a really good classic,' I said. It sounded tacky. I wished I could have said he had sung some famous piece from the Marriage of Figaro.

'Was he any good?' This was unexpected.

And it was not easy to answer. 'No, not really. But it was a good try and people clapped a lot.'

'I guess he would have liked the clapping.'

I wondered if my five minutes were up. The nurse would be back any second now, whip in hand.

'Mrs Fontane sends her best wishes,' I said casually.

'Really? I hardly know the woman.'

Did I go for the jugular? She might start screaming or have a heart attack. She had put the flowers on the windowsill and her hands were loosely clasped. No twitching.

'Hardly know her? But she's your neighbour. They sold you the piece of garden on which your house is built. Mrs Fontane lives next door at The Limes.'

'Oh yes. That's right. She lives in the big house.'

'I'm surprised that you say you hardly know her. I thought you worked for her some years ago, as a nanny for her two children, two little boys.'

There was the slightest movement as if a nerve jerked. But she made no sound. It was uncanny. I wondered if she had heard me.

'You were their nanny, weren't you?'

The nod was so slight, I nearly missed it. 'Yes, for several years. It was a long time ago. Then I left to get married.' She heaved a big sigh as if to say she was glad to get shift of the job. 'They were difficult children. Very spoilt. But then, Mrs

Fontane was never at home. She was always out. That's why I said I hardly knew her.'

'Busy helping her husband with all his businesses.'

'You could call it that.'

I got up, straightened my T-shirt, in leaving mode. 'Anyway, lovely to see you, Gill. You'll soon be home.'

'Where's Max, my son?' she said suddenly. 'Is he at home? He hasn't been to see me.'

'Max? I don't know. Do you want me to find out? I could call in on my way back.'

'Would you, please? I'm worried. I know he's old enough to look after himself, but not to hear anything . . .' It was the first time I had seen any genuine emotion on her face.

I could hear footsteps coming along the corridor, relentless and determined. I had about twenty seconds left and I had not got round to the monthly payments.

'This place must be pretty expensive,' I said.

'It is. Fortunately my health insurance covers it.' I walked home slowly. The ladybird needed a carwash and a repair job after her last traumatic experience. Mrs Fontane would not be paying for the spray carnations, even though I could call them expenses. I was no nearer the truth but at least Gill Frazer was recovering and might soon be home.

Did Mrs Fontane really want to know who had killed her children? The coroner, according to the newspaper reports, ruled that both children had been smothered and the forensic evidence found pillow debris in their nostrils.

But if it was the nanny, then why had Mrs Fontane been paying out £250 a month for the last ten years to Gill Frazer? This was giving me a headache.

A striped green and yellow car slowed down beside me. The driver leaned over and opened the passenger door.

'Want a lift anywhere, Jordan?'

'I don't want my friends to see me getting into a patrol car again,' I said.

'Stop arguing and get in.'

It was DS Ben Evans. He smiled his usual grin, his glasses steaming up slightly. It was a hot evening. I liked the look of his profile as he drove, keeping his eyes on the road. It was definitely Clark Kent with longer hair and not quite so tall. Well, the nose and the glasses were the same.

'Working on a case, Jordan?'

'A double murder, only it's ten years old.'

'Not a chance,' he said. 'Trail gone cold.'

'Don't I know it.'

'Isn't this a bit out of your usual remit? I thought you were into lost tortoises and vandalized WI stands?'

'Thank you for the vote of confidence,' I said, watching the coming speed camera. I wasn't going to warn him. 'My experience has broadened. I get all sorts of cases now.'

'Sorry. Have I upset you? I detect a slight frostiness.' He slowed down at the camera site.

'I don't expect the West Sussex Police Force to be trained in tact and conciliation. Catch the muggers and sling 'em in a cell. Leave me to deal with the really emotional cases.'

'Now, that isn't fair, Jordan. How much time do we have to tread softly, softly? I rarely have time to shower.'

'You smell all right,' I assured him.

'And you smell wonderful,' he said, suddenly stopping the car and unfastening his seatbelt with the speed of light. His arms were round me and he kissed me with what I can only describe as the wildest of unleashed passion. I was riveted to the seat.

'You are beautiful, darling,' he said, all husky and masculine, the slightest of new bristles brushing my chin. No one had ever said that to me before. I wanted it in writing.

'I must get back to work,' I said, coming up for air.

'My shift has just finished.'

'Lucky you. I don't work shifts. My life is one long shift.'

'I could change all that for you,' he said vaguely.

I had no idea what he meant.

Fourteen

This was the first time that anyone had actively cleared my mind of thoughts of DI James. Not completely cleared, but momentarily. Ben's kisses were nice, competent, acceptable in these days of famine.

'Hey,' I said. 'What's all this about?' I managed to extract myself from his arms.

'Jordan,' he groaned. 'When were you born? In the Middle Ages? I'm crazy about you, don't you know that?'

I looked passed the lamp lights in the empty street and gazed, bemused, at the moon. He was crazy about me. And he was normal, straight, unmarried, unattached and completely on line. It was almost too good to be true. Doris would be over same moon, dancing a jig.

'I'm very flattered,' I murmured like some Austen heroine. 'But you hardly know me.'

'I know all I want to know,' he said huskily. 'You're sweet, funny, clever, honest and above all you have the most delicious nose.'

Ben then kissed delicious nose and sent his glasses askew. He took them off impatiently and put them some place on top of the dashboard. This was obviously a sign for the kissing to begin in earnest and he gathered me into his arms as easily as if he had been doing it all his life.

I somehow lost track of what was happening. Reality got mixed up with that beach dream I once had. 'Can you see Venus?' James had asked then. Nor was I sure who I was kissing. Ben was so like James in many ways, without the weariness. I closed my eyes and let the comfort wash over me. Comfort kissing. The phrase could have come from a television ad.

His hands were not wandering, which was reassuring. Gold star, Ben. They stayed firmly round my back, occasionally massaging a shoulder or easing down my spine. My hands crept round his neck, my fingers went deep into his hair. It was crisp and wiry, feeling good to the touch.

It was awkward, kissing in a car, especially a striped patrol car. Any moment now someone might tap on the window and say, 'Excuse me, officer . . .'

Our knees were clashing. That damned gear lever was in the way. His way. My way. Car designers have a lot to answer for. I was getting a nasty crick in the neck. My surge of passion was dwindling and all I wanted was to get indoors to a quiet life and a cup of cocoa.

'I must go,' I said weakly.

'Can I come in for a few moments?' Ben asked.

I shook my head. 'No . . . not this time.' Then I added by way of consolation. 'Another time.'

He kissed me again with a fierceness that was quite alarming. Again I could feel the stubble prickles under his lower lip. 'I can't wait that long,' he said.

'I'm afraid you'll have to,' I said, without a clue what I meant. I was saying words plucked from the air, trying to get out of the car, out of his arms, hoping not to be too brusque or unkind. I liked him and did not want to hurt him.

The extraction complete, I wished Ben farewell in a meaningful way and escaped to my bedsits. The car sat outside in the street for a while. Perhaps he thought I might change my mind and come rushing out to drag him indoors.

Eventually the car started up and I heard him drive away. I leaned against the door, thankful that I had got away, my body intact if not my brain. Whatever had I been doing? Kissing the man like the world was due for imminent extinction. Supposing James had seen me?

I went cold at the thought. My blood almost froze over. It would have been the end. James would have flung up the drawbridge, armour clanging, visor down, never again to eat chips with me in Maeve's cafe.

I looked at my face in the mirror. It was the same face. Nothing had changed. Cheeks a bit flushed, eyes twinkling. I couldn't think why he liked my nose.

Next morning I resolved to put the lapse firmly behind me. It had not been a one-night stand. More a one-evening sit. The non-kissing DI James had no right to impose restrictions on me. I am free and kissable with a delicious nose.

Well, Ben said it was.

My visit to Gill Frazer had not been all that helpful but there was definitely more to this mystery. I went through all the newspaper cuttings that I had photocopied from the Brighton office. Again and again the police evidence was that there had been no sign of a break-in. Gill Frazer had said that she thought she heard something, but she did not investigate. Why not? She was supposed to be looking after the two boys. She should have got up.

No break-in, so if someone had come into the house in the night, that person had a key. And how many people had had keys? Both Mr and Mrs Fontane, obviously. Gill maybe – but she was already in the house, half asleep.

I phoned Mrs Fontane. 'Hello, Mrs Fontane. This is Jordan Lacey, First Class Investigations.'

'Hello, Miss Lacey. Have you any news for me?'

'It's beginning to come together,' I said with more conviction than I felt. 'But one more little thing. Can you remember how many people had keys to The Limes in those days? I know it may be difficult to remember.'

'I have an excellent memory. We had four sets. One for my husband, one for myself, one for the nanny and a spare set which was hidden in the garden, for emergencies.'

'And is the key in the garden still hidden there?'

'I've no idea,' she said sharply. 'I've never bothered to look. Is that all? I'm on my way out to an appointment.'

'No, that's all. Thank you. You've been very helpful.'

She put the phone down.

I got out my trusty mountain bike and cycled round towards her house at the speed of light, parking the bike in a nearby twitten, remembering to secure the chain. Bikes can be stolen even from the fisherman's ancient twittens. I was in time.

Mrs Fontane was indeed going out, glasses on, and she was late. Her car shot out of the garage as I arrived. It was a glossy black BMW. I ducked back. I did not want to be caught snooping.

After her car disappeared down the road, I went up to the door and rang the bell. She might have left a cleaner indoors, some trustworthy pensioner in a flowered pinny looking for specks of dust.

But there was no answer. I rang again to make sure. The old dear might be deaf. I wandered round the side of the house as if inspecting the damp course.

'Council business,' I would say, flashing defunct inspection card appropriated some years ago from careless council worker.

The Fontane side of the fence was still a big garden, neatly laid out with lawns and matching flowerbeds. A stone bird table stood in the middle of the lawn, empty. No water for the sparrows to splash about in. Not such a good memory after all.

I went round the garden lifting rockery rocks, the smaller ones first, flower pots, watering can, brushing earth off my fingers. Nothing. The garden shed was tidy, two lawn mowers parked side by side, clean tools hanging from hooks. Not a cobweb in sight. Nor any keys hanging under eaves. Closing my eyes, I tried to think myself into this woman's mind. Where might a fastidious Fontane-type woman hide a key? She would not want to get dirt on her fingers.

Somewhere in full sight of everyone. I looked up at the

back of the house, at big bay windows with draped damask curtains. Such a substantial house, weathering the years with grace. I thought I saw a shadow move but maybe it was my imagination. The walls were hung with creeper, frail blue wisteria and a white clematis with showy waxen flowers.

My gaze went to the bird table in the middle of the lawn. I wandered over, peering round it for a crevice, feeling under the edges of the base. I thought I felt a movement, a slight rocking. Gripping the edges of the bowl, I lifted it an inch. The stone was a ton weight. I was near to dropping the damn thing on my feet.

A rusty old Yale key was buried in a moss covered indent. Very clever hiding place. I put the bowl down on the grass, whipped out the key, and lifted the bowl back on top of the pedestal. Then I thought I heard a car returning and fled. In a second I had scrambled over the dividing fence, a feat of dexterity beyond my normal ability.

I was not sure why I had taken the key. It seemed useful. I was not planning to do a walkabout in Mrs Fontane's home. Anything of interest would have been removed in the intervening years. There had been time to obliterate every trace of whatever I might be looking for. And that was vague enough.

Now I was in the Frazer's garden. It was as bare as the house. No one had taken any trouble with the ground. There were a few tomatoes in growbags, some geraniums in pots, sad-looking herbs. Brian or Gill? The grass was raggedly cut, the edges ignored.

I wondered if Max was at home. I went up to the front door and set the chimes chiming and knocked on everything in sight. I shouted his name through the letterbox. There was silence. And I could see a scattering of unopened post. Nobody at home. He had probably gone to stay over with friends. Young men did that kind of thing.

But something was wrong. The day seemed the wrong shape. It was unnerving me.

I went slowly back to unchain my bike and cycle home. I was missing James, feeling guilty, wanting to see him to explain or not to explain. He meant nothing to me and yet he was everything. I was in a muddle. Time to eat.

Maeve's Cafe was full of chomping families. It was the height of the season. Lots of holidaymakers and day tourists were discovering the pleasures of the Sussex coast. Coaches were parked in orderly lines along the front. Many carried flotillas of wheelchair visitors for their annual sight of the sea.

My favourite window seat had gone. Mavis ought to put a reserved notice on it. After all, we ate there all year round. I was a regular. We were regulars.

James waved me over. There was room for me to eat on the end of his table. 'Bring a chair,' he ordered, moving his plate up.

I carried over a spare chair. Men's manners these days were appalling. I put it down with a clatter, not looking at him, not wanting to see why I loved him.

'Look at all that fat,' I said. 'Sausages, eggs and chips. Swimming in fat. You'll die young.'

'Join me in an early death?' he asked, offering a glistening sausage on his fork.

'No, thank you,' I said, squeezing myself into the space available. 'I'd like to live to a good old age.'

'You're getting there,' he said, dipping the sausage into a pool of tomato sauce. 'Watch the high life, though. Several more wrinkles are threatening to appear.'

'I haven't seen you for ages,' I commented. 'Where have you been?'

'I had a day off. And I took it.' My head went into a spin. Cells surfaced and jetted into the heart of chaos, splitting the storm into several systems.

He had a day off. Another day off. This was unheard of laxity. There'd been that jazz afternoon off with his mother. But you didn't phone me, I almost said. 'What did you do?'

'I walked from Cissbury Ring to Chanctonbury, along the top ridge of the Downs. All the old paths. It was very peaceful and beautiful. A few other walkers around, even a guided llama walk. The animals were carrying the rucksacks. I took some sandwiches and had a picnic in a quiet spot with wonderful views. All on my own.'

'I once found a flint axehead on that path,' I said. 'Probably Iron Age.' I was aching with envy and disappointment. I would have liked to walk with him, would have contributed fruit and wholemeal rolls filled with three cheeses, Stilton, Brie and Cheddar, topped with honey and mustard dressing. Delicious.

'Do you think my nose is delicious?' I went on.

James looked at me with incredulity, his blue eyes glinting like sapphires. A chip was halfway to his mouth. His teeth were strong and even. Not a filling in sight. Egg yolk dripped off the chip, back on to the plate. He did not notice.

'I know it's getting warm, Jordan. Are you feeling the heat? Shall I get you a glass of water?'

'I'm perfectly all right. It was a joke question. But it woke you up, didn't it? Ha, ha.'

'I was unaware that I was asleep,' he said, eating the chip, then another. They were disappearing. 'I was certainly awake a few moments ago when I came into the cafe. Of course, I may have fallen asleep since. I need stimulating company. That's why I called you over. It could have been a mistake.'

'How's work?'

'Stalemate. Can't get anywhere. It's frustrating. Nothing is happening about the diver, Roy Dinglewell, or the electrocuted singer. Caught the muggers, though. Couple of local baby bullies. Under age.' Every sentence was punctuated with a chip. 'Aren't you eating?'

'I think Mavis is too busy to serve me. Perhaps I ought to go and help her.'

'Can you cook?'

144

'No.'

'Then keep out of the way. She knows what she's doing. Have one of my chips to keep you going.'

I took a succulent chip and chewed it slowly. Yes, I was hungry. Surveillance and searching gardens is exhausting. I was also emotionally exhausted. The hormones had been shaken up. And I was not used to it.

'I'm trying to solve a ten-year-old mystery.'

'Ah, the babes in bed murder.'

The man knew everything. I wondered if he knew about DS Ben Evans and me in the patrol car. Maybe the good sergeant had gone into the station bragging about a new conquest. I'd skin him alive if he had. I was not gossip fodder.

'They never found out who did it,' James went on. 'Weird case. Not a sign of anything. Not a clue. Nothing. The house was as clean as a pin. Even the carpets had been vacuumed.'

'You don't think the nanny did it then?'

'No, too convenient. I think she was asleep when it happened. She said she was and stuck to her story.'

It seemed a good moment to tell him. 'That nanny you're talking about, the nanny to the Fontane children . . . Do you know where she is now?'

'No.'

'Well, I do. She's a patient in The Laurels Nursing Home. She's Mrs Gill Frazer, wife of the electrocuted Brian Frazer, he of the talented singing fame. Now that's woken you up, hasn't it?'

It had indeed. DI James was all attention. I didn't tell him about finding the key, or about the regular standing order into Mrs Frazer's account. No need for him to know about that. He let out a low whistle.

'Very fishy, Jordan.'

'But the trail is colder than a polar bear's posterior.'

He half smiled. 'A vivid metaphor. You can always be relied on to colour the English language.'

Mavis came over. Her face was flushed and her hair straggling down. It was a new colour, not exactly flattering. 'I haven't time to do a honey tea,' she said. 'Sorry. I'm really pushed, Jordan. Can't complain though. It's good business.'

'I'll eat anything,' I said. 'When you've got time. I don't really care.'

She was back in a mega-moment with a glass of chocolate milk and a roll and an apple. 'Perfect,' I said. I made myself an apple and chip sandwich. It was different.

'Fancy a few of my chips?' James said, watching the last of them disappear.

It was time to do some real work. So I cleaned out my shop, rearranged the window displays, checked the empty till, made fresh coffee, sat at my desk writing up recent notes and waited for customers to arrive.

Nesta came in. She was furious. She slammed her canvas bag down on the counter, her barely covered 32B bosom heaving. She was wearing a strappy cotton top of dubious dimensions.

'You're a bloody detective,' she shouted.

'It's not my fault. That's my job,' I said.

'You were bloody investigating me and my Dwain.'

I didn't know what to say. She might have a knife. She had been happy to drink all the free vodka.

'It was for the good of your son,' I said. 'You want everything to be right for Dwain, don't you? It's his future.'

She calmed down, marginally, basic street-walking fury on hold. I thought of the bouncers at The Cyprus Tree and longed for their support. This was nothing like WI wedding stand trashing or Joey wandering about looking for a long-lost love. For a two-second moment, I was frightened. No one gave me a bulletproof vest. Who would mourn a slashed small-town PI?

'So,' I said. 'What are you going to do? Have the DNA test or spend the rest of your life wondering?'

She clearly did not understand the options. I did not care
to explain. Their squalid sexual passion meant nothing to
me. I did not care who was the father of Dwain. It was their
problem. They could sort it out themselves. I'd send in my
last invoice soon and leave it to them to work out.

'What's he trying to do?' she asked suspiciously, teetering
on absurd heels, hip thrust out.

'My client does not believe he is the father of your son.
He's been paying maintenance all these years for a child
that's not his.'

'Dwain is his,' she shouted. 'I ought to know, shouldn't
I? I'm his mother.'

'But you did have another boyfriend at the same time. You
told me so. He'd gone away to do some work.'

'He's a chef. But, yeah, he'd gone off and I wasn't pregnant
when he went. I know that. I know my dates. You may think
I look stupid, but I ain't.'

Was she telling me that she'd had a period between
the two lovers, if you could call the weekend's drunken
romp anything to do with love. Nesta was nodding vigorously.

'That's it, Miss Clever Clogs. The full works. Eve's curse.
I ought to know, shouldn't I?'

'Yes, you ought to know.' She could be lying. How could
anyone ever prove to the contrary?

'So, will you tell that low-down buster to stuff his
investigation and keep the dosh coming? Dwain needs
new football boots by the weekend.'

'Football boots.'

'And the shirt. He's gotta have the shirt. Arsenal.'

'You tell him,' I said. 'He won't like it.'

'Don't I know him. Tight-ass.'

She was wandering round my shop, picking things up,
putting them down. She picked up an album on football
stars and thumbed through the pages.

'How much is this?'

'Six pounds, but you can have it for free,' I said, suddenly overcome with ridiculous generosity. 'If it's for Dwain.'

'Ta. He'd like it a lot. Football mad.'

She sauntered out, then looked back over her shoulder. 'I suppose I owe you a drink after the other night.'

'That's a date,' I said.

There was the oddest look on her face, a boldness and an audacity. I wanted to paint that look but I couldn't paint. Thinking back, that glimpse told me something. But I didn't understand.

Fifteen

I'd had the feeling before, that the day was the wrong shape. I was getting it again and it was not pleasant. Perhaps it was my head. Ben had unsettled me and now I was getting the feedback.

It was difficult to know where I was with Ben. James did not care about me so what was I losing? Nothing. Man in hand, not exactly in a bush, is surely worth two out chasing villains.

The solicitors in Chichester, where Cleo worked, had sent me a Process Serving. It was my bread and butter. I was more than a glorified postman. I had to make sure that the person concerned actually received the document. I had to be disciplined and efficient. The family owed over £600 for electrical equipment, ordered, delivered and never paid for. I had to give them sufficient warning of an impending court appearance. It had to be served in person. Always tricky. These people seemed to be able to spot a server a mile off.

I put on a distressed check shirt, i.e. creased, old jeans and trainers, pulled my hair into an elastic band, knowing I would pay for it with split ends when I tried to take it out. What could I carry? No baby to borrow, no dog (Jasper in training), leaflets (no election), forms (no census). Find a street map. That's it, I would be lost in Latching. I checked all the documents and the letter of instruction. There were a lot of rules. I was the legal go-between.

It was a run-down street in the back of Latching near the main line station. Cars were double parked. Many of the terraced houses were boarded up with 'For Sale' signs propped up in the rubbish-strewn front yards. Number twelve's yard was littered with boxes filled with junk, old engine parts, sinks, microwaves, sewing machines. Perhaps they ran a secondhand business. My curiosity was growing. After all, First Class Junk exists on other people's throwaways. This was an intermediary stage.

The front door was open so I did not have to knock or ring. It lead straight into a sitting room, although as far as I could see there was nowhere to sit. The room was packed from floor to ceiling with boxes and cartons and piles of stuff. Somewhere, submerged under the junk, were a sofa and a couple of padded armchairs. I could see only that much sagging structure. There was no floor space, only a narrow walkway between the door and a television set perched unsteadily on several boxes.

'Hello,' I called. 'Is anyone at home?'

There was no answer.

'Hi there . . . can you help me?'

A woman came through from the outback. One of those built-on kitchen extensions. She was towelling a tumble of wet hair. She was small, stout and blonde but a weathered blonde. The kind of blonde whose hair is daily tormented with undiluted peroxide.

'Yes?'

'I'm sorry to bother you but I saw the open door. It looked so friendly.'

'What do you want?' she said, not friendly at all.

'I'm lost.' I waved the street map. 'I'm trying to find Beech Lane.'

'Dunno. Never heard of it.'

'OK. So could you show me where I am now on this map? That would be a start.'

She peered at the map but the lines meant nothing to her.

She could not read a map any way round. It's wonder she could read the small print on a hair dye bottle.

'I'll get Reg,' she said, wandering off somewhere back along a corridor of more piled-up junk.

My eyes glazed over. I had never seen a room so packed with stuff. There was no obvious reason for it all. This was not a mania for collecting books or videos or sporting trophies, which I could understand. The mania was for stuff itself. Object mania. I saw bits of wood, iron, metal, plastic . . . old, new, clean, filthy. Debris from a dozen takeaway meals, empty bottles, beer cans, chocolate wrappers, and strewn clothes littered the floor. No carpet visible. My bedsits were a serene floor of Buckingham Palace compared to this chaos. How could this woman, any woman, live here?

Reg appeared. He was short and stocky too, a sort of double of the woman, in torn oil-stained clothes, swigging beer from a can. He stood in the doorway, swinging the can from one hand.

'What do ya want?'

'I'm sorry to disturb you,' I said, accelerating the lost and wavering vibes. 'But I'm not sure where I am. Could you just look at this map and tell me where I am now?'

I stepped inside the room. It was a positive step. My hand closed on the order in my pocket which I had to serve. The papers were folded in two and out of sight. No envelope. He peered over my shoulder at the map and I could smell his breath. His bald head was sweating ribbons of sweat. A few hairs sprouted from his ears.

'Mr Reginald Gibson?' I said. I had to identify the right person. I had a description and a photograph.

He looked surprised. His uncombed hairs twitched.

'Yes? Howja know me name?'

'I have officially to serve this order on you from the county court,' I said, putting the papers into his hand. 'An outstanding debt, I believe, for electrical goods.'

He dropped the papers as if they burned his fingers.

151

'Sorry, but it's been served,' I said. 'You have legally received it. You should see a solicitor if you are unaware of what you should do. Goodbye and thank you.'

''Ere! Where are you going?'

'I've done my job, so I'm off.'

'That's what you think. Not on your nelly, missus.'

He was like lightning, quick for a heavy man. He slammed the front door shut and flung across the bolt. His wife was on me in a flash, pushing me down on three inches of sagging sofa. My head hit the corner of a box.

'Let me go,' I shouted. 'I'm only the server. I'm nothing to do with this.' I had no time to dodge or walk away.

'You ain't going nowhere,' he said, with some satisfaction. He picked up the papers and tore them in half, then half again. 'That's what I think of your county court, missus.'

'Tearing them up doesn't mean anything,' I said, struggling to get up. 'They are legal and they have been properly served.'

'Who says so? Who says they saw you coming here? No one. No one saw you come in here and no one will see you go out.'

'Masses of people know,' I said, trying to think of masses. 'The solicitors for a start. They instructed me. And my husband,' I added valiantly. 'He knows.'

'You ain't wearing no ring,' said Mrs Gibson, sniffing. 'You ain't married.'

'People don't always wear rings these days,' I gasped.

'Married people do.'

I was being pinned down in the most awkward way. Space was non-existent. Sharp corners were sticking into my ribs and the back of my neck. I had to get myself out of this fast. It was not funny. The papers were laying on the floor but they had been touched.

'Look,' I said. 'Please be reasonable, Mr Gibson. This isn't going to work. Let me go and I'll say nothing about it.'

'You ain't going to say nuffing anyway.'

'Let's get her upstairs. Someone might come in.'

The pair of them were strong. There were muscles in them there arms. They started dragging me towards a staircase at the back but I was struggling like mad. It was one of those narrow, straight-up staircases, made even narrower because every tread had boxes sitting on it. If I kicked out enough, the whole lot would come tumbling down.

I began pushing like a tormented dervish. I had grown four extra arms and legs and several elbows which I put to good use. But the pair were not gentle. They were cuffing my head and the woman winded me with a vicious punch to the chest. I gasped with shock.

But it made me even madder.

'Hey, you're not supposed to attack me. You won't get away with this,' I shouted, wasting good breath. 'This is ridiculous. The summons will still go ahead, whatever you do. You'll see. I'm totally independent. I'm simply doing a job.'

'Get her in here,' Reg wheezed.

They dragged me into an upstairs room. It could hardly be called a bedroom. I couldn't see any bed. It was full of boxes and crates and bulging bin bags. I was thrown down on to the floor. My head hit a hard edge of iron. The pain tore down the back of my neck, scraped the roots of my teeth, lodging somewhere across my right eye. I hoped I still had the eye.

'Now, don't you move,' said my charming host. 'We'll be back to see that you don't.'

'And while you're here, you can have Bonzo to keep you company. He's a nice, gentle soul as long as you don't move.'

Mrs Gibson cackled with laughter. Out of my good eye I could see why. Bonzo was a huge bull mastiff, saliva dripping from his jaws, sweat glistening on his short brown-black coat. He growled with evil.

'Nice dog,' I said faintly.

I had no intention of moving while Sirius, the dog from hell, was watching me with malevolence. Bonzo stood squarely on his four thick legs, planted wide as if they were rods of iron. How had they trained him or did it come naturally? Blood was trickling down my face. I hoped he didn't have a taste for blood.

I lay where they had left me and tried to focus on recovering my energy, of thinking of a way out, of trying to outwit canine guard. The ceiling was miles away, stained with nicotine fumes, cracks like old eggs zagging across from the window. There was a window and it was barred.

Whoever would think of putting iron bars across a window in the back bedroom of a small terrace house? Why? A stately home, maybe. A museum. A bank. But a two up, two down terraced house? They must have something to protect.

The room was waist high with boxes. It was like a warehouse. Many were unopened, with stencilled information on the outer lids. They were goods of some sort. Could be they were electrical goods like the £600 worth the Gibsons had not paid for. Or was this part of a bigger scam, buying goods, not paying for them, selling them off?

Or was it a mental illness? I had read of people who collected things for the sake of collecting, with no intention of using, selling or disposing of same. It probably had a long Latin name. Collectusphobia?

Cramp was attacking my legs. I'd have to move soon.

'Nice Bonzo,' I said, shifting a foot a few centimetres at the same time. Spiteful barbs bored into my muscles.

The dog lunged forward and stood over me, growling, wet dripping from his drooling mouth, his bloodshot eyes telling me he was only an inch off clamping his jaws on my arm or ankle.

'Hello, gorgeous doggy,' I said softly. 'Who has got beautiful bloodshot eyes?'

Bonzo looked suspicious. He was mystified by prone idiot human talking sweet nothings. He was more used to kicks and screaming oaths and howls of anguish. He backed off, not trusting me.

'I think you and I could get along really well if you would just get over this negative attitude,' I said. Bonzo was growling under his breath. I could see his massive throat throbbing. I wondered what I had in my pockets that might be a doggy treat. Bull mastiffs were not likely to be addicted to polo mints.

I knew nothing about dog psychology. I had no idea how to reach his mind, peanut-sized as it might be. At least the low tone of my voice seemed to have him perplexed.

'Shall we go walkies?' I offered seductively. 'I know a lovely pond where there are hundreds of stupid ducks to chase. You'd like that, wouldn't you? Lots and lots of ducks?'

Not a tail or ear twitched at the word walkies. I guess he did not get taken for many walks. Who'd want to walk him? He was probably under a house arrest civil rights order.

'I think that's a real shame,' I sympathized, appealing to his better nature. 'All dogs should be walked regularly. Seagulls are great fun to chase, too. And up on the Downs there are rabbits everywhere. Hundreds of them.'

Nothing reached him. He did not know rabbits. He led a restricted life. He was as much a prisoner as I was.

'Poor baby,' I said. 'Don't they ever let you out? What a shame. And you are going to put on weight, if you haven't already. Extra weight is not good for the heart, especially doggy hearts.'

He sank down onto all fours, bored by this meaningless babbling. It was mesmeric. The non-activity was tiresome. His heavy lids lowered over his eyes, shutting out the light. It was the first time I had ever bored anyone to sleep.

I waited, hardly daring to breathe, moving my legs with caution. Bonzo began a hearty snore. It was a sand-blasting vibration.

This was fast-thinking time. There was no way I was going to get out of a window that was barred. My only escape was the door and down the stairs. And Bonzo was laying across the doorway. I began scrutinizing the room and its contents, inch by inch. There must be something I could use. Like a sledgehammer.

But I would not be able to use it, not even on a dog as revolting and threatening as Bonzo. No way could I brain a dog. He had life immunity as far as I was concerned. And it wasn't his good looks.

There was an abundance of black dustbin liners, those big bags made of heavy-weight plastic. Very useful for bodies. Might be useful for a dog.

Bonzo was sound asleep, lost in the land of doggy dreams. I checked by moving slightly and there was not a twitch of canine muscles. I double-checked with a few silent leg stretches to ease the cramp. Not a rumble.

A nearby black bin bag seemed to have little in it. My hand explored in slow motion and brought out a hairdryer. New, price label still attached. I put the item aside and opened up the bag, cursing each crackling sound.

It was now or never. Stay and die or jump and run. I did not trust the Gibsons. I struggled to my feet and rushed towards the door, the bin bag held wide open at knee height.

Bonzo was galvanized into action. He leaped towards me, head low, growling like a demon. He was truly magnificent, except that he did not look where he was going. He went head first into the bag, the rest of him propelled by force. The moment he was halfway inside, I tipped the bag up. The weight was horrendous, almost pulling my arms out of their sockets. Five stone of mastiff. I nearly let go but knew I dare not.

A thrashing leg ripped a hole in the bag and clawed nails slashed my arm.

Bonzo was struggling like fury. I tied the top into a vicious knot, the end of his tail sticking out like a stubby rope. It would only hold him for moments but I knew I could use those moments.

I dropped the bag and was out of the doorway in a flash,

making sure the door closed behind me. I hoped Bonzo was not clever enough to open the door. The only room certain to have a lock was the bathroom. She'd been washing her hair. An open door led me to the towel-sodden hole.

The bolt on the door worked. I slammed it fast. I could hear voices as the couple were charging upstairs. I did not have long, but long enough to notice a box of brand new top-brand electric toothbrushes on the floor. I tucked one into the waistband of my jeans. I put down the lavatory lid and climbed on to the narrow windowsill. The window opened outwards and there was just enough room for me to get my legs out and then turn on to my hip.

It looked an awful long way down. I knew how to do a fireman's drop. Hanging on by your fingertips meant you were extended the five foot plus of your height already. No jumping.

But I did not want to risk a broken ankle by landing on the concrete yard below. Bathrooms always have drains. I transferred my grip to the nearby drainpipe, my knees and toes turned inwards. There wasn't time to think. I had no option.

I slithered downwards, the rusty pipe creaking and protesting. Then it gave way and pipe and I fell in an ungainly heap at the bottom. A shower of brick dust added to the fallout, plus a gallon of dirty water.

Coughing and choking, I got to my feet. The Gibsons were leaning out of the bathroom window, shaking their fists and yelling at me. I heard a distant Bonzo barking. They would be letting him out in seconds.

I was over the back wall using a pile of dumped stuff as a climbing frame. My heart was pounding, sweat in my hair, blood dripping from my arm, covered in sticky brick dust. The twitten at the back of the terrace was empty. I chose the quickest route back to civilization. They could hardly set Bonzo on me in a pedestrian shopping street.

My homing instinct took me towards Latching police station. Several people looked at me in disgust. I suppose

I looked as if I'd been in a brawl or drinking. A stitch pierced my side and I doubled over in pain.

'You ought to be ashamed of yourself,' a woman said, thinking I was going to vomit on the pavement. She walked on, stiff-necked with indignation.

I made myself limp on despite the pain, clutching my side, barely able to see for the dust and sweat in my eyes. I was going to charge damages to that firm of solicitors. My best old jeans were ruined.

A gang of spiky-haired youths were loitering outside the police station, hands in pockets, kicking air. They began to jeer at me.

'Come on, granny. You'll make it.'

'The cops'll find you a nice comfortable cell.'

'On the meths again, are you, gran?'

'Give us a kiss, if you can remember how.'

'Lost yer hearing aid?'

Sometimes I really hate the very young. What I needed was a helping hand, not this bawdy barracking. I pushed my way between them. Wait till they needed my help. I had a good memory for faces.

I groped my way into the station. It was like coming home even though it was a long time now since I'd worked there. The colour of the walls was the same, a dull magnolia. The floor was the same, dull washed-over wood. The desk sergeant was also the same, my dear friend, Sergeant Tiger Rawlings. Not dull at all. He glanced up, expecting trouble, seeing me.

'Jordan,' he said in despair. 'You always come in here looking a wreck. What's happened now?'

'I fell down a drainpipe.'

'Breaking and entering, I suppose.'

'Not this time. More like being held prisoner by force and intimidated by massive and ferocious bull mastiff.'

I held out my arm. The long gash was oozing blood, starting to clot.

'Nasty,' he said. 'We'd better see to that. When did you last have a tetanus?'

'Sorry, I don't remember.'

'Do you want the station doc to look at you or would you like a lift to the hospital? I can arrange either.'

'I'd really like to speak to someone in CID.'

I meant DI James. The man himself. I wanted to see him more than anyone. I needed to tell him about my experience, to be fussed over, to have a little tender loving care. TLC. Maybe it was not in his vocabulary.

There were footsteps coming along the corridor and of course I knew them. I was so keyed into his persona that I would know him in a crowd of hundreds. Note I don't say thousands. I do not exaggerate.

'Jordan, whatever have you been doing?' said DI James. He pulled up a chair for me, a cheap, grey plastic stackable chair. 'Sit down before you pass out. Do you want a drink?'

I nodded. 'Please.'

He brought me water in a plastic beaker. I wish I could say that it tasted like champagne, but it tasted like piped water. He stood over me while I drank the water and then he pushed the hair out of my eyes. The elastic band had disintegrated along the way.

'You look a right mess,' he said, peering down. 'And you're bleeding.' He put a pad of handkerchief on my arm.

I nodded again, past speaking.

'Anything to tell me?'

I handed him the expensive electric toothbrush, still swinging a price tag. I got my breath back.

'Found a house full of stuff. A lot new, a lot of junk. There was a box of these in the bathroom. At least a dozen toothbrushes. I want to make a statement.'

'You had to go to the bathroom?'

'To avoid being eaten alive by a bull mastiff.'

'Do you have the address?'

I started coughing and wheezing. My asthma does not like

stress and this had been stress in bucketfuls. My inhaler was at home. Any minute now someone would take me to hospital to be nebulized. I could see it coming. I would spend hours on a trolley in A & E when all I wanted was to go home.

'I'll . . . write it down.' It was a struggle, trying to control my breathing. 'Mr and Mrs Reginald Gibson. I was Process Serving a debt demand.'

'You ought to be in hospital. Your arm is bleeding. Is your tetanus up to date?'

It's quite difficult to lie to the man you love. But lie I did. I've been in enough hospitals to last a lifetime. I wanted my own bed and my own bathroom, my own cranberry juice and my own Napoleon brandy. I just hoped Bonzo had clean nails.

'Sure.'

'I'll take Jordan home.'

DS Ben Evans had arrived, coming down the corridor on his white charger, exhaling steam. A knight in shining armour. I could not believe it. He was soon beside me, tall and good-looking, eyes full of concern, the kind of concern I wanted to see on DI James's face but which was never there.

DI James shot a withering look at his Detective Sergeant. He did not seem too pleased. His blue eyes glowed an unusual shade of green. 'OK, Evans. You take Jordan home if you are free. I'm too busy with that break-in at the off-licence. Come and make a statement tomorrow, Jordan.'

It was a lot like dying. There's an Ella Fitzgerald song which says, 'Everytime we say goodbye, I die a little.' I died a lot then. Bits of me curled up and fragmented.

I remember Sergeant Rawlings wrapping a wet antiseptic bandage round my arm and it stinging. I remember Ben Evans driving me home in a white patrol car, no lights flashing, silence plugging my ears. He took my keys out of my back pocket and I remember him steering me upstairs, taking off my clothes and putting me to bed. The sheets were cold. I don't remember anything else.

Sixteen

It was the longest sleep I'd had for months. Something like twelve hours. When I awoke, I was not sure whether it was night or day. Did it matter? I was not going anywhere.

My damp, brick-dusted clothes were on the floor but I was decently clad in a long T-shirt and some skimpy panties. Across the front of the T-shirt were two cuddly bears entwined, saying, 'We need friends'. DS Ben Evans had been my friend. I knew that much. DI James had been too busy.

I ought to take a course in speed yearning. Then I could do a year's longing for him in ten minutes.

I stood in a warm shower, washing out the brick dust, hoping my blood had cleansed the wound on my arm. It did not look too inflamed, only a bit pink. I was exhausted by everything, could hardly remember where I'd got to in the cases I was supposed to be working on. What had happened to this famous note-making? Any minute now I'd need a one-to-one interview with myself.

The sea would change that. I needed recharging. The tide timetable gave me bad news. Then I remembered. It had been in the newspapers. A tide of seven metres was expected at 1.17 p.m. It was the highest tide of the year. Red alert all along the coast. The council had dragged up a shelf of shingle to make a barrier, placed huge rocks where a diagonal current was expected, issued sandbags to seafront houses and pubs. It was serious.

If the wind was off-sea, then the tide would surge over

the promenade. Fishing boats, those fragile shells, would be flung from their moorings, dragged over shifting shingle. Pebbles would litter the roads as waves encroached on the land, swirling towards doorsteps.

I hurried down to the front, wind blowing into my face, cooling my skin. Huge waves were surging up the shingle, each one eating into the carefully piled defences. The pebbles slid down into the sea, leaving gaping holes. The next wave made for that gap, swirling over the promenade, catching careless feet.

Crowds were gathering with cameras and videos. A TV crew was bustling about. It would be on Meridian news.

The sound was ferocious as tons of stones shifted and crashed together under the weight of water. The deafening music of the sea. A hundred-piece improvised jazz concerto. I stood listening and watching. This video was in my head.

Jazz never sleeps in my mind. Any doctor listening to my heart would be alarmed by the primitive beat. An ECG would record the rhythm of 'Call Me Irresponsible' laced with 'Shiny Stockings', the vocalist echoing the high brass.

I had not heard my jazz trumpeter for months. This was not good news. I needed his kind of music. Classic jazz. There was no way I could find out where he was or what was happening. His wife, or his agent, would not appreciate it if I called. It was only when he played locally that he came into my life. But he was always so caring, so affectionate. He knew our special kind of what might have been.

Sometimes he played at the Bear and Bait. He turned up and of course, because he was an international star, they loved him and asked him to dust down his trumpet and play.

If I was lucky, I might be there. It was always crowded on jazz nights so then I sat on the floor. I can curl up small, back against a pillar, making sure no one steps on my juice.

As I stood watching the sea, I made a mental list of what I had to do, superwoman style:

1. Resolve paternity case of Phil Cannon.

2. Find out who electrocuted Brian Frazer.

3. Find out who suffocated two small children.

It was a chilling list. Nos. 2 and 3 were not really my responsibility, though Mrs Fontane was paying me for No. 3. I did not seek fatalities but they kept coming like I was a one-woman Samaritan. Was half of Latching bumping off the other half? They belonged to DI James, the bastard, the man who let someone else take me home, let someone else put me to bed. I don't remember any wandering hands, thank goodness. What was the matter with James? That divorce must have been a hell of a bad news day, but what else? Perhaps I ought to find out what happened then I might understand him.

There was something not quite right. I cried for a bit, like a depressed teenager. James did not understand me or perhaps he understood me too well. It was like a vast beach with no one on it. The whole world was an empty space. I could hear that music playing solefully, a man and a woman, it tore me apart. I'd seen the film, a long time ago. I could barely remember the story, only that haunting tune.

Housework was a sure way to wake myself up so I went home to retrain my dusting arm. I cleaned in monumental disgust at the debris and dust. I need glasses. How could I live in such chaos? It took me two hours. By the end, my wrists were aching. I had repetitive dust strain syndrome. Pass me the blue elastic wrist wrappers.

Statement to make. I inched towards the police station, dragging one foot at a time, brain intact but body strangely aching. The wind was still south-easterly. It was a different sergeant on duty at the desk. This fresh-faced youngster, straight from a training course, took me seriously. He showed me into an interview room. The one glossy magazine was the same one. Hello, look at me, I'm a bride.

'Would you mind waiting? I'll find someone to take your statement.'

A WPC took my statement. She had lank hair and needed

to lose weight and fast. The buckle on her trouser belt was straining over a bulge, but she was nice despite the discomfort round her middle. Did she drink after hours with my DI James? Did they spend evenings in some corner nook at the Bear and Bait? All the uniformed liked the Bear and Bait. It was convenient. They would not run into any villains. Well, not many.

It sounded pretty tame by the time she had laboriously written down my account. How could I have been scared of a dog? Even a big, drooling mastiff.

'I'm sorry to have wasted your time,' I said, getting up stiffly. 'It was obviously nothing much.'

'It was not nothing much,' she said. 'There's the injury to your arm. I'll get it photographed. How is it this morning?'

'I don't know. A bit hot.'

She insisted on looking, hitching lank hair out of her eyes. I would not have allowed such untidiness if I had been in charge of the station. She should tie it back. An area of skin on my arm was swollen, red, inflamed, pulsing with multiplying bacteria.

'That bull mastiff was a nasty brute,' she said, peering. 'You ought to get to Latching hospital immediately and have that seen to. You could lose your arm,' she said, hoping to comfort me.

'One less arm to wash,' I said. 'I'll pop along.'

'No, not good enough. I'll make sure you get there.'

She phoned for an ambulance, photographed wound, in colour, gave me some water to drink. At some point I read and signed my statement. I was starting to feel odd.

An ambulance arrived and I was loaded aboard. I refused to lay down. I sat up, chatting with the paramedics, clutching my arm which was throbbing. I was light-headed by now, some sort of fever setting in. It was so hot inside the ambulance. We talked about local politics and councillors who did nothing but collect their expenses. I was trying to make sense of their computer system.

'I need to update my word processor.' Then I remembered that I did not have one. I had to get one. I had to get email.

I was not sure where I was going. The A & E department looked different even though I was a regular visitor. A sort of vibrating sound was washing round me. They put me on a trolley and I did not protest which was unusual. Darling trumpeter, come and play for me. James, please . . . come and talk to me. But no one came.

I washed in and out of the feel of the place. The overhead lights hurt my eyes. The trolley scratched. They rolled me into a ward and on to a hard bed. I wanted to go home. But where was home? I wondered if I would ever see it again. Someone had to come and get me. They stabbed injections into my arm and installed a drip. The ceiling wavered like the inside of a washing machine. The smell of old ladies in wet beds was overwhelming.

'Jordan? Wotcha doing here? Hey, baby, wake up, don't go AWOL on me. You ain't supposed to be dying yet. Where's yer doc? I'll speak to him.'

I was not sure who it was, but I knew the voice. Was it Jack from the amusement arcade? Yes, of course, it was Jack. The lingering, uncouth owner of the arcade who made thousands from the punters, could afford a blue Jaguar. How did he find out I was here? Or was it Miguel? No, Miguel had a different accent. He was smoother. His Mexican restaurant was classy and expensive. It was not Miguel. My mind was wandering again.

'Is it Jack?' I said, fighting for a voice. 'Go away, please. I'm too ill for visitors. Don't hang around. It's a waste of time. It might even be catching. They don't know what they are doing. Half the doctors are off duty. They are going to let me die.'

'Not now, they ain't,' he said ferociously, scratching his stubble. 'I'll make 'em come and see you. You ain't just nobody. I'm on your side, baby. Hang on there.'

Jack went off, striding down the ward pulling down his

T-shirt, ready to fight anyone. If I had the strength I would have smiled. He wanted to care for me, for better or worse. But how could I agree to that? It was too complicated to sort out now. Yet Jack was the kindest man around. And generous. None of this counting the change, working out the least possible tip. He knew how to give a girl a good time. But it couldn't be me. Never. I wasn't his girl.

'Stay there. I'll find somebody,' he called back.

I hardly had a choice.

Some time later Jack was back with a young man in a flapping white coat. He took my temperature with some handy new-fangled gadget.

'Yeah, sure. Her temperature's coming down. She can be moved to a private nursing home.'

I did not recognize the voice. I'd never seen this doctor before. He was in the normal white coat with a stethoscope slung round his neck. He looked as if he had qualified about yesterday.

'Do you know my name?' I asked, struggling to sit up. 'Have you read my notes? What's the matter with me?'

'You're looking much better,' he said. 'Do you feel well enough to cope with a move?'

'You mean you want the bed?'

'We are short of beds. I'll give you a course of antibiotics to take. Remember to finish the course. The results of your blood tests will be back tomorrow.'

'I think I'll get better quicker out of here. I don't want to catch any germs.'

The doctor detached the drip. 'Drink plenty of water,' he said cheerfully.

It took twenty minutes to find my clothes. They were in a different locker. Jack was getting hot under the collar but still in charge. He was like a volcano about to explode.

'You ought to have private health care,' he growled. 'Ain't you in BUPA?'

'On what I earn?' I said, pulling my clothes over the

paper hospital nightgown. 'I can barely afford a packet of aspirins.'

'You'd have everything you want if you'd marry me,' he went on, holding my good arm at the elbow. I actually needed his support. It was fine getting out of hospital, but I realized I was not well. It was easier to pretend I had not heard him.

His blue Jaguar was parked in the visitors' bay. It unlocked automatically. Jack opened the passenger door and lowered me into the seat. Then he leaned over, too near for comfort, and did up the belt.

'We'll get you looked after,' he said, sliding in the other side of me. He drove carefully, not too fast for once. He was probably worried that I might be sick all over his beautiful car.

'I'll be all right at home,' I said, closing my eyes, wishing the world wasn't spinning.

The car stopped and I opened my eyes. We were in a road that had big houses and trees. 'I don't live here,' I said.

'Right on the ball. Jordan, now I don't want no arguing,' said Jack. 'You're going to stay here and be looked after properly. I'm paying. Then if you're all right temorrer, OK, you can go home.'

For a blind moment of panic, I thought he had brought me to his home, that he lived in one of these expensive houses and had satin sheets on a king-sized bed. Nothing would have surprised me about Jack. But then I recognized one of the houses and the beech trees. This was Lansfold Avenue and we had stopped outside the newly converted nursing home called The Laurels. He'd brought me to the nursing home where Gill Frazer was recuperating in room six. We were going to be under the same roof.

It was the same reception nurse. She did not seem to recognize me, pale and wan model. I was taken to a small comfortable bedroom overlooking the back lawn, similar to Gill's. In no time, they had filled in a chart, made notes, taken my prescription for antibiotics off me, and tucked me into bed. They tut-tutted at the hospital regulation paper gown and found me a pretty cotton one covered in forget-me-nots.

'I have a friend staying here,' I said, sinking back on to the pillow. 'Gill Frazer.'

'Mrs Frazer isn't allowed any visitors,' said the nurse. 'You have a good sleep. I'll look in with a tray of tea in about an hour.'

'How lovely,' I said. Tea served on a tray. What luxury.

'There you are, my girl,' said Jack, putting his head round the door. 'I'm off now. Business to look after. Are you all right? You look really comfortable.'

'I am. Thank you for everything.'

'I might slip in and join you after dark,' he said cheekily.

'I'm not allowed visitors,' I said. I meant to thank him again but he had already gone. I could always pop round to the arcade when I was better. I did owe him now.

When I awoke I really did feel a lot better. It was such a luxury, waiting in bed for my tray of tea. Might as well enjoy being pampered. But I decided that I would not recover too soon. I needed to see Gill Frazer again before I signed myself out. The dressing on my wound did not feel so hot. Perhaps the antibiotics were kicking in. Would DI James charge the Gibsons with owning a dangerous dog? Was he checking the electric toothbrushes? And I needed to see Phil Cannon again.

Hey, slow down . . . I told myself. You are ill. Enjoy this rare moment of being cosseted.

The door opened and the nurse came in with a tray. She smiled cheerfully. 'How are you feeling, Miss Lacey?'

I pretended to have just woken up, did a yawn and stretch. 'Lovely sleep,' I said.

'You sound better. Here's some tea and I've brought scones and jam. You may not have had any lunch.'

'No lunch. No breakfast either.' I managed to sit up and she helped me, plumping pillows. No one had ever plumped pillows for me before. I could get used to this treatment.

'The doctor will be along to see you soon,' she said. 'I'll bring you some fresh water. You need to drink a lot.'

She poured out the tea. The cup and saucer were rose patterned. She added milk from a small jug. It was so civilized. I nearly swooned with enjoyment. Is this what marrying Jack would mean? Milk in a jug? But I doubted it. Jack was one of the roughest characters in Latching. He might drive a big flashy car but I bet he poured milk straight from the bottle.

She left me to snack on scones and tea. I was ravenous and the light-headed feeling had gone. My mind felt normal and in thinking mode. This was a good time to re-think my cases.

1. Following Brian Frazer was over. Invoice on hold. Who electrocuted this poor man/Shirley Bassey clone was not my business. Yet I felt I ought to know. No one could stop me digging deeper.

2. Phil Cannon had to get a move on with a DNA test. Nesta had hinted that she and Dwain's father were still an item, but I'd never seen him visiting their home, coming and going as if he lived there.

3. Lydia Fontane's trail was ancient dry. Although I felt immensely sorry for her, what could I do? Her two sons were murdered ten years ago and the police had closed the case. Or had they? DI James might still be working on it. He would not tell me.

He'd never tell me anything. He had left home without taking any possessions, had to start from scratch. He had encased his feelings in cement. Something much worse must have happened.

The bedroom was en suite so there was no excuse for wandering along the corridor, seeking a bathroom. I could pretend to be looking for a book. We blue-stockinged academics, never happy without the written word.

I did a little light-headed walking along the corridor, noting that Gill Frazer's room was two doors down. Did she still eat in her room or was she promoted to the dining room? They had built a glass conservatory on to the back of the house and I could see it was furnished with small tables and each was laid for a meal.

On hearing footsteps I scuttled back to my room and flung myself into bed. Only just in time. They were coming into my room.

'Here's Dr Marshall,' said the nurse.

'I've seen you before,' I said.

It was the same young doctor from the hospital, the one who had so swiftly signed me out. He was moonlighting. Two jobs, one in the private sector and one in the NHS.

'Ah, yes, maybe,' he said.

'Perhaps I'm mistaken,' I fluttered feverishly, a little confusion does no harm.

'And how are you feeling, Miss Lacey,' he said, looking at my chart. Then he took my pulse, felt my forehead, sat down and looked at me. 'You're looking a lot better.'

How did he know if he had not seen me before? No problem, doc. I went along with the charade.

'I'm still feeling hot,' I said. 'And this is hot.' I touched the dressing.

'Ah, yes,' he repeated. 'Too soon yet for a complete recovery. I think another twenty-four hours should see a big improvement. Just rest and drink plenty.'

'I will,' I said. 'Could you send up some wine? Red, Chilean or Australian Shiraz. You could phone Miguel's Mexican. They do an excellent Chilean.'

He laughed. The nurse laughed. Red wine in a nursing home. 'We'll see what we can do,' he said on his way out.

Another twenty-four hours and a big bill for Jack. No way, I was out of here tomorrow morning, straight after breakfast. This was more than five-star treatment. It was twenty-five star, shut your eyes when you pay the bill treatment.

Things quietened down in the nursing home after the doctor's round. I could feel the settling. Some people slept early after supper in their rooms. Supper came to me on a tray with pretty china. Salmon quiche and a green salad. Sliced banana and yogurt. A cup of Horlicks. But it was way too early for me.

About nine o'clock, I started to creep around. Gill Frazer was not in her room. It felt strange to be standing there in her empty bedroom. Her personality was not there either. She was passing through in some different state, in or out of her mind.

Then I saw the photos by her bedside. I went over and looked at them. Two photos, but in one frame, were of three children. Three? Then it dawned on me who they were. The oldest boy was Max, her own son, who was at present on walkabout somewhere in Latching. The other two were very small boys.

Of course I knew. They were Lydia Fontane's two sons. The sons that they said she had murdered. Gill Frazer had their photos beside her bed.

The door opened. Gill came in, wrapped in her camel dressing gown, her hair awry. She did not seem surprised.

'What are you doing here?' she said.

'I'm looking at your photographs,' I said. 'These are Mrs Fontane's two sons, aren't they?'

'Yes,' she said.

'You were charged with killing them.'

'I didn't kill them,' said Gill. She went over to the flask and poured herself a glass of iced water.

'Why are their photos beside your bed?'

She looked at me, kind of astonished. 'Because I knew them,' she said. 'Leave me alone. It's none of your business. Get out, please. You're not allowed in here. I'll ring for the nurse if you don't go.'

Seventeen

I could get nothing more out of Gill Frazer. She went into a clam-like state. Shutters came down over her eyes like the prize-winning arc bridge over the Tyne. It was difficult to understand but then she was disturbed and ill.

'So who did kill them?' I asked.

'I don't know what you are talking about,' she said. She suddenly becoming intent in wiping thick night cream over her face.

'The two boys. Lydia Fontane's children. Don't you remember? You were their nanny and they were suffocated. You were asleep in the house at the time.'

'I don't remember anything about it,' she said. 'Would you mind leaving? I should like to go to bed. I'm very tired.'

'Of course. I'm sorry to have kept you up. Sleep well, Mrs Frazer, with your dreams . . . or are they nightmares?'

She shot me a look that was pure sanity itself. In a flash I knew that she knew what she was doing. This current disability was another facade. There was nothing wrong with her.

I meandered back to my room, via an empty TV room, finished up what was left of my salad supper and pondered on the Fontane case. Gill Frazer was not that ill. It was first-class acting on her part. I wondered how long she could keep up the role. She was some actress. She even knew her words.

A nurse came in with my antibiotic. I'd not seen her before. All their staff seemed to be part-time. She was new, dewy-eyed, fresh-faced and straight from a decent night's sleep.

'Hello, Miss Lacey,' she said brightly.

'Hi, there.' I was feeling with it, streetwise, fever receding. The nasty dog wound was starting to heal even though my legs were aching. Bonzo's germs could not withstand modern medication.

'Please take your antibiotic.'

'Of course.'

I took the pill with some water, settled into bed, pulled up the duvet. There was not much else I remembered. It was as if I cut all ties to the world. A sort of instant letting go.

I was not aware of when DI James came into my room. He was sitting by my beside when I surfaced from a washed web of mixed-up clogging dreams. I tried to hang on to them but they went, fragmented and elusive. It was so strange, finding him there. He was dark and concerned, yet the lines on his face were not of my making. Something else had etched a new concern.

And the room looked strange, different somehow. There were blinds at the windows instead of curtains. I could swear there had been summery flowered curtains before, blowing in the summer breeze from an open window. I tried to absorb the sense of the room but it escaped me.

'I was wondering when you were going to wake up,' he said. 'Jordan, Jordan, wake up. Come on, girl.'

I tried to put words into my mouth but they would not form. My tongue was swollen and coated. Puzzlement came into my eyes. I could not speak properly. A sudden panic swept through my body as though I could not feel anything. I could be sweating but I was not really sure. It was a different bed, narrower. Where was I? What had happened?

James was holding my hand and slapping the back of it, quite smartly. I could hear the slap. 'Don't go away again, Jordan. Hey, hey, Jordan, wake up. Stay with me. Hold on.'

There was an urgency in his voice. That much got through to me. But the rest was frightening. I tried to curl my fingers round his but they would not respond. My hand was in his and I could do nothing more about it. I could not seem to move anything with ease. I tried my hands, my feet. It was terrifying. At least I was breathing but for how much longer? There was nothing wrong with my mind. The thoughts were razor sharp.

I was on a saline drip again. That much I could see clearly.

'Listen to me, Jordan. Can you hear me? Can you nod? No, not into nodding. Now, don't worry, don't panic. Jordan, can you blink? That's it, girl. Blink at me. Lots of blinks. Terrific with blinking.'

I could blink. I was blinking like mad. It seemed to be the only thing I could do. And cry. Tears were filling my eyes and one trickled down my cheek. James leaned forward and wiped it away.

'Don't cry, Jordan. We'll get you better. You are back in Latching hospital. I brought you back here last night. Did they give you any medication at the nursing home? Blink once for yes, twice for no.'

I blinked once. The nurse had given me an antibiotic. But I could not tell him that. What was the matter with me? Last night? My eyes pleaded with James for some sort of explanation.

'Was it a pill?'

Blink.

'How many pills?'

How many? I couldn't remember. Did the doctor give me one when he came to see me? How could I signal: I don't know. I blinked once, paused and then blinked again.

'Maybe two . . . is that what you are saying, Jordan?'

Blink.

'You've been given some kind of drug or poison, Jordan. We are not sure what it is yet but the results of the blood test will be back soon. Then we'll know.'

Drug? What kind of drug? A street drug? Ecstasy? Could

I have died? Was Jack involved in this? No, no way, Jack would never harm me. If he was involved then he had been duped into it. I knew Jack was innocent.

'I want to find out who moved you from the hospital to the nursing home. Did you know the person?'

Blink.

'A man?'

Blink. I sensed James settling back with resignation. This was going to be a slow business. A dark stubble was already growing. He was patting my hand casually now. The slapping had stopped.

'How am I going to scale down your male checklist to one name, Jordan? Impossible. You probably have a dozen boyfriends that I know nothing about. I don't know where to start. There must be a short cut. I can hardly go through the Latching phone directory.'

I tried to help him but I did not know how. I started to blink rapidly, hoping to get my meaning over to James.

'Right, I think I've got it, Jordan. You are going to blink the alphabet, yes?'

Blink. Thank goodness he understood.

'OK, take it slowly. It's a long time since I was at school.'

I blinked ten times. I could still count.

'J.'

Blink.

'A.'

Three blinks.

'C. JAC. Is it Jack? Is he called Jack?'

Blink.

'Well done, Jordan. You're a star. Jack, whoever he is, moved you to the nursing home. Am I right? And is this Jack a boyfriend?'

Was he a boyfriend? I didn't know what to call him. Jack thought he was, hoped he was, but he wasn't. I shook my head.

175

I was sure I did it, a sort of off-balance sideways movement. Had James seen me? Yes, he had and his response was
electrifying.

James leaped up and grabbed me. 'You shook your head!
She's moving. Jordan's moving. Hold on, I've got to go and
get the doctor. Keep moving, baby.'

He was out of the door. Now I realized I was in a private
side room at Latching hospital. It was all a mystery to me
how I got there but I was moving my head. It was sheer
pleasure. We take everything for granted and now I knew
how precious something as simple as movement can be. I
prayed that it was all coming back to me. I wanted to walk
the pier, walk the beach, feel the wind and the rain, get back
to being a human being.

I lay in the hospital bed, reliving the utter terror of the last
hour. And James had been there, holding my hand, something
to remember but I was not sure if it was the kind of embrace
I'd want to remember. I did not like being left alone in the
room. I was scared and tried to call out.

'James,' I murmured. There was some foreign voice
coming from deep down inside of me. My vocal chords
were returning but reluctantly.

The fear in me was more than I had ever known in a
physical situation. This was me, in a bed, with little control
over my body, except the tiniest movement of my head. I
could not wash my face, brush my hair, clean my teeth. I
was inside a white shell. Trapped.

James came back with a doctor, another doctor. Not the
young one who had let me leave Latching hospital, only
to turn up later at the nursing home. The moonlighting
doctor, augmenting his NHS salaries. What was his name?
Dr Marshall.

'This is good news,' said the doctor, taking my pulse,
turning up my eyelids. He was a heavyweight type of doctor,
buttons straining on his jacket. 'The sight seems good. Can
you see me, Miss Lacey? Can you nod?'

I nodded, quite definitely a nod.

'Good job we pumped her straightaway. There's no anti-dote except immediate pumping.'

James could see the panic return to my face. He smiled reassuringly, ocean eyes bright with encouragement. 'You're going to be all right, Jordan. This is Dr Sprightman. He's been taking care of you since you were brought back. Thank goodness you did not know you were having your stomach pumped. Not a very nice experience but it has saved your life. It got rid of the poison.'

I was tired of blinking. The concentration was beyond me. 'Poison . . . ?' I managed to whisper.

'Hemlock, we think. Conium is the other name, a very poisonous chemical. The stuff grows wild. It can be used to make a salad. It even looks like salad. The leaves resemble parsley. Did you have anything like that to eat?'

I nodded. The delicious supper, which I had finished up to the last shred. I should have left the parsley.

'You had a salad in the nursing home? Was it brought to you by a nurse? OK, we'll make some enquiries. Don't worry, Jordan. You are going to be all right now.'

James got up to go. This was a man going back to work. James was going to leave me. It was unbelievable. He couldn't go. I would not let him.

'Why . . . ?' I croaked.

'Why? We are not really sure. You obviously know too much about something, but what sort of something we don't know. There's a police officer outside the door of your room now, so don't worry. No one can come in here and whisk you off again.'

'I'll leave you to rest,' said Dr Sprightman. 'There's a bell on the end of this cable. Can you press the buzzer? Excellent. Don't worry, the feeling is starting to coming back.'

There was no light in the room now, only some slants of late sun penetrating the blind. I did not want the harshness of electric light. My eyes ached. I did not want James to go but he was preparing to leave. With my one-word vocabulary, how could I make him stay a little longer?

'James . . .' The name made him stay for a few moments. It was sheer willpower. He sat down by my side and smiled. He smiled so rarely. His eyes glinted like sapphires, not coldly but with a new warmth. I wanted to say more.

'Thank . . .' I began.

'I know,' he grinned. 'Thank you, Detective Inspector James. You are wonderful. You are Superman himself. I shall make gallons of home-made soup for you, get out my best soup bowls and old-fashioned soup spoons and we shall sit together on the floor and have second helpings.'

He had remembered that time, last year. He had remembered my big white, gold-edged soup bowls and the antique silver soup spoons. They were all that were left from some magnificent dinner service from a big Edwardian house. And I tried a smile back. My mouth was moving again.

'Soup,' I said, nodding.

'It's a date,' he said.

Shopping list: mushrooms, celery, swede, parsnips, lentils, garlic, herbs, crusty bread, Stilton, French butter.

'And Jack? Is he a boyfriend?' The man was curious.

'Arcade,' I said, shaking my head again.

'Of course, I remember. The amusement arcade on the pier? You threw yourself on to a robber in the arcade and made the headlines. Overnight heroine. That was the Jack, the owner, who moved you from the hospital? I suppose he thought you deserved more comfortable surroundings. That makes sense. He's a very generous man. He gives a lot of money to charities, including the police benevolent fund. Nice guy.'

Nice guy. Yes, Jack was a straight A guy. 'How . . . you?' I began.

He was on to my thought wave immediately. 'How did I find out you had been moved from here? It wasn't me. It was DS Evans. He came to visit you and went ballistic when he found you had gone. We found the doctor who had discharged you, then we tracked you to The Laurels Nursing Home, stormed in and found you in a coma. Hemlock causes paralysis of the muscles. You had to have your stomach pumped out immediately, sorry. They had to get rid of the poison. You'll be all right now. But don't go anywhere for a while and be careful what you eat.'

A nurse bustled in and I recognized her from one of my previous fleeting visits. 'Would you like a cup of tea?' she asked. 'You must feel horrid after that wash-out. I'll also bring you a mouth rinse.'

'Could I . . .' I began.

'I know, weak with honey. That's the way you like it.'

James had told her. I knew instinctively. I made to thank him again but he had gone. I suppose he had better things to do than sit with a woman who couldn't tell parsley from hemlock.

But DS Evans had rearranged his shifts so that he could visit. He pulled up a chair, leaned over and kissed my cheek. It was the most I could expect after a stomach pump, hemlock and mad dog fever. It would be a wonder if anyone ever kissed me again.

'How are you, darling?' he said, looking at me fondly.

'Getting better,' I croaked. 'Thank you for setting off the red alert.'

'I thought you had been kidnapped by the Gibsons.'

'Just as well you found me or I would have been a goner.'

'But you are not and that's what's important. You are going to be fine. Back to your old self in no time. You'll need a nice long holiday after all this, somewhere sunny. Fancy coming on holiday with me?'

'Heavens,' I sidetracked. 'I don't remember when I last had a holiday. It was years ago.'

'Then all the more reason to take one now. Where do

you fancy? Barbados? Bermuda? Bahamas? You can choose. Somewhere hot and interesting, eh?'

'It's hot enough here. We're having a lovely summer now. A late start but it's improved. They say the high temperatures might go on into the autumn.' Speaking was suddenly normal.

'Don't start talking like a weather forecaster. I've just asked you to come on holiday with me. You don't need to pack much. Just a bikini and a nightie.'

'I haven't got a bikini.'

'All the better. Just pack your nightie.'

'Don't rush me,' I panicked in seconds. 'Let me think about it.'

'Take all the time in the world. But make the answer yes, Jordan. We could have a great time together.' His eyes behind his glasses were sparkling with enthusiasm.

I nodded. This was fast tiring me out. All this emotion and decisions to be made. I did not want to have to decide about anything.

'Tell me about the Gibsons,' I said. 'Have you been round to their house?'

'Sure. Bonzo is now wearing a very attractive leather face mask. Should keep him out of trouble. Nearly took a bite out of the leg of my WPC. Mrs Gibson had hysterics and started throwing things at me. We found a few interesting items which we took away, but the rest was junk.'

'What did you find?'

'Hey, Miss Lacey, you know I can't tell you.'

'I told you about the box of brand new electric toothbrushes in the bathroom.'

'OK, toothbrushes, hairdryers, food mixers. We believe they are a couple of fences, handling stolen goods.'

I enjoyed Ben's company. He was so easy to get along with and there was no tension, at least not on my part. A holiday would be nice but I could not afford it and I was not into sharing some two-bedded identikit room with basic shower. Not yet.

'Darling, I think you should try and get some sleep,' Ben said. 'You've been through an awful time. Rest all you can.'

Two darlings in one visit. This was heady stuff.

'If you say so,' I murmured.

He kissed me again, vaguely, somewhere on the cheek. We might have been married for years. Marriage. I'd never thought of marriage with anyone, not even with my DI James. I doubted if Ben Evans had such thoughts. People didn't marry much these days.

I was too afraid to sleep in case something else happened to me. Yet I could see the figure of a police officer sitting outside my door. Who could I trust? Had the young doctor been involved or the young dewy-eyed nurse? I did not know who I could trust now. I was sure I could trust Jack, yet he had some dodgy friends.

My feeling was coming back. My legs and arms belonged to me once more. I wanted to try them out, walking, but it was scary. I moved my legs cautiously to the side of the bed and rolled them over. My feet felt the coldness of the floor. That was reassuring. It was an effort but I pulled myself up into a sitting position and eased into being upright.

I was standing. But not for long. The effort was too much and I fell back awkwardly, sweating profusely. But I'd done it! And so I could do it again. It was a question of getting stronger. And I knew I could handle my recovery.

I had little idea if it was day or night or what was the time. My body clock was not working. It needed winding up. Now that my brain was starting to function, there were two more things I wanted to ask James. Who and why? Who had decorated my salad with hemlock? And why did they want to get rid of me?

Eighteen

The hospital eventually let me go home. They did a series of tests, confirming that my system was clear of the poison and that I was out of danger.

They lent me some casual clothes to go home in. I did not dare to think where the skirt and shirt had come from. At least they were clean. They had been through the hospital's laundry thrashing machines, boiled to extinction. My own clothes were at The Laurels Nursing Home. I did not fancy making a call to pick them up. I could bump into the wrong person. They might try the poisoned dart routine next time.

The taxi dropped me outside my shop. I had been forty days in the desert. It was important to check my answerphone and mail. Hopefully a client might have paid. A cheque would be nice. My bank manager would be pleased.

There were two cheques. Phil Cannon had sent me a postdated cheque; Gill Frazer had sent a cheque for fifty pounds on account. A note said she had not received an invoice but thought she must owe me something. It seemed an odd thing to do. Perhaps she thought I would never get round to cashing the cheque.

Someone had fed me hemlock. Gill had been under the same roof. Who else knew I was there? Young doctor, young nurse, Jack, the Gibsons? Maybe they had tracked me down.

Doris put her head round the door. She had brought a bag of apples, a carton of soya milk and a bar of chocolate. 'Been in the wars again, have you? What was it this time?'

'Hemlock.'

'Yeah, yeah. Pass me the belladonna.'

'No, I'm serious. Someone tried to poison me.'

'Killing you off type poison . . . ?' Doris looked dubious. She did not know if I was kidding her. 'Jordan, have an apple. It's not poisoned. I'm your friend and you're no Snow White.'

'I don't know who my friends are any more.' I sounded scared. And I was. I was out in the big world, on my own. No burly Sussex policeman on guard outside my door, no Jack to rescue me, no DI James, no DS Evans to hold my hand. No, it was James who had held my hand. I was still confused.

I thanked Doris, went back into the shop and locked the door. This was no way to carry on. I had got to sew myself back together. I threw off the hospital clothes, stuffed them into a bag, put on my own jeans and a red T-shirt, trainers. The ladybird was parked in the back yard. I got in and drove her to Findon, parked on the ridge road, then climbed the steeply stepped path to the top of Cissbury Ring.

The verdant view of the Downs and the distant sea sparkling with summer sun was amazing. The fields were ripening with acres of corn and rape seed and wheat. The colours rolled from dew pond to hedge, from barn to cottage, from clump of trees to chalky path. A light breeze rustled through the crops and my nose was filled with their essence. The windswept trees and overgrown bracken on Cissbury Ring moved in the breeze, resident ghosts from the Iron Age peered through the branches. Rabbits darted back into their burrows, whiskers twitching, tails bobbing.

The Iron Age fort was steeply double-ditched for massive, unscaleable protection. I walked along the top ridge letting the clean air blow away my fears, taking care I did not fall down one of the Neolithic flint mineshafts. No way was I going to hide away, wrapped in cotton wool. Fear was suffocating. I had my job and I had to get down to doing it.

Shopping list: courage. Where could I buy it?

I'd find it from somewhere. This episode was not going to dominate my life. I'd been in scrapes before but no one had actually tried to kill me. Locking me in a hermit's cell had not been in quite the same category.

It took a while to walk the mile round the highest ridge of the sixty-acre site of Cissbury Ring. The formidable timber of the original fortifications had long been laid to waste but the hill-top site was still impressive. People had lived there in compounds, been born, bred children and died, living short, harsh lives in a tribal group.

I hoped I might find a bit of pottery, a bent coin or link of broken jewellery, some sort of Iron Age goodwill token, but no such luck. Walking downhill is always more difficult. Slipping and sliding on the dry grass, I slithered back towards the car park, life and work.

One cheque was banked and my balance rose. I brought my notes up to date and restarted my card system. I wrote everything down on separate cards, put them on the floor and moved them around into different configurations. Sometimes it worked or sent my brain off into a direction that had not occurred to me before.

I made a sandwich of Leicester cheese, spring onions and mayonnaise. I'd gone right off salads.

It was time to have another chat with Phil Cannon. I called him on his mobile and made an appointment for that evening. We were going to meet at a pub that I had never been in before called The Fox in Hand. It was a few miles inland from Latching and away from my normal patch.

It was a pub with a legend. Seventeenth-century history decreed that during a hunt, a panting fox had taken shelter in the pub and its life had been saved. I'd heard a similar legend from Lincolnshire, when a hunted fox, fur bedraggled, had leapt into a farmhouse oven, only emerging when he had dried out.

It was an old L-shaped pub with worn red bricks and creeper, low ceilings and beams, tables outside in a flower-filled garden. It was relaxing. Phil was already sitting at a table. He had a half of beer in front of him and he'd bought me an orange juice.

'Oh, is that for me?' I said, sitting down. Such generosity. How could I ever thank him?

'I knew you'd be driving.'

'Right. Thank you.'

'I've done what you said. Got the DNA, like you told me. And I've got the results.'

'That's good and you've got the results already? That's quick work. But I'm very glad that you've had it done. What's the result or can't you tell me?' He did not look upset so it must have been the result he expected and wanted.

'Like I told you, I ain't the father. Look, I've got the results here from the laboratories. Paid the bloody cost and all, I did,' he said. He looked more upset about having to pay up.

'It was the only way,' I said, sipping the juice. 'I'm really pleased. OK, so you've had to pay for the tests, but look how much money you are going to save now. You won't have to pay a penny more to Nesta.'

'That's true,' he said smugly. 'She won't get another penny out of me. She can go to hell. Dwain ain't mine. She can look after the brat herself. Not me.'

'Well, that settles it, doesn't it? It's what you wanted so you must be happy,' I went on, grinding the organ.

'Course I'm happy. Won't have to pay you any more either. That'll be even nicer.'

What a charmer. My favourite kind of client. He could have been a dab more pleasant. He had got what he wanted, after following my advice. If he had had the test done earlier, he would not have received further bills from me. There was no way I was going to give him back the money. I had earned it. And he'd sent me a postdated cheque – tricky. Sometimes these had a funny way of being cancelled.

'Perhaps I should have a copy of the results from the laboratory,' I said. 'It would be safer to keep them on file, in case Nesta makes a fuss at some future date.'

'As long as I don't have to pay storage.' He did not look completely convinced. 'You mean, photocopies?'

'That's right. They cost ten pence a copy at the library. Better safe than sorry. You might lose them. They could get mislaid or, worse still, stolen.'

'Wotcha mean? Nesta might steal them?'

This had obviously not occurred to him. He digested the outlay at the library and decided ten pence might be worth it.

I got up. As far as I was concerned, the case was closed and I was not sorry. Phil Cannon was a difficult client. It would be a pleasure to put his file at the back of my filing cabinet and mark it 'CLOSED'.

'Goodbye, Mr Cannon,' I said. 'Just drop the photocopy in at my office any time. No need to make a special journey.'

He seemed surprised that I did not want to linger in his company. I bet if I had offered him a drink he would have ordered a straight malt whiskey and a double.

'OK. Right. I'll do that.' He finished off his half pint. No offer of another drink. No thank you. He swivelled off the seat and made track for the bar. He was obviously celebrating. He was going to be pounds in pocket now that the payments could stop.

I drove carefully on my orange juice. There might have been a double vodka concealed in it. A sudden moment of generosity by client in celebratory mood.

I would have to go back to The Laurels Nursing Home. They could hardly feed me hemlock a second time. It took half an hour to drive back to Latching, my mind pondering imponderables. It was luminously light, that still magic of a summer's evening with a sky like a Turner watercolour.

I parked outside the nursing home. The front entrance looked like open jaws. Think Cissbury Ring and courage.

The receptionist nurse was surprised to see me. She was

willing to talk. Yes, they had been quite upset when I was taken ill. Yes, Dr Marshall worked for them in a private capacity as well as at Latching hospital. The young nurse? Oh, yes, that was the new Mrs Marshall, sweet young thing.

'And Mrs Frazer . . . is she all right?'

'She went home today. Checked herself out.'

'I expect the cost was a drain on her resources,' I said. 'I know nursing homes have to charge a lot. It's the heavy upkeep.'

'We have such a high standard,' she agreed.

'Gill Frazer was lucky that she had private health insurance. Do you know which scheme she was in?'

The nurse shook her head briskly.

'Ah, that's classified,' she trilled to cover her anxiety. 'We never disclose private arrangements.'

'Of course not. Quite right too. But I knew anyway.'

'I'll get your things,' she volunteered. She came back with a neatly folded pile of clothes. They do everything with style when you are paying several hundred pounds a week. She was also carrying a huge bunch of red roses. There was no card.

'These came for you,' she said.

'Heavens,' I said, drifting into the heady perfume of the velvety roses. A list went through my head. James, Ben, Miguel, my trumpeter . . . 'I can't think who could have sent them.'

'He was driving a flashy blue car. No, no, he came earlier, sorry. Not with the roses.'

Jack brought me roses? Not quite his style. 'Ah, so not my benefactor.'

I started to leave. 'By the way, who would have prepared my supper the other night?'

'The cook, Mrs Niki Shiko. Did you want to speak to her? I should think she has gone home by now. She's on shift work.'

'Yes, I would like to have a word. Perhaps I could have her address or a phone number.'

'I'll get you her phone number.' She turned her back on me and keyed up some information on the screen.

I sensed I was outstaying my welcome. She wanted to get rid of me before I asked any more awkward questions. I pocketed the post-it note with the number, thanked her again, and left. She was busy on the phone the moment I went out.

I was tired by now. Having a tube put down your throat ruins the appetite. A little chicken soup might be appropriate. Maeve's Cafe was closed. I drove along the coast road. The tide was out and the sea a distant line. Sea Lane Cafe was closed. Had a war been declared in my absence?

I found a late night supermarket still open at the back of town. Four tins of branded chicken soup were expensive. So was everything else. I could not afford to shop there often. But I did treat myself to a chocolate marshmallow. It looked decadent even with a barcode.

The light was beginning to fade as I drove home, chicken soup on the passenger seat, roses on the floor of the car. The sky was glowing with rays from the setting sun, a glorious peach sundae of ice-cream clouds and golden juice.

He was waiting on the pavement outside my bedsits, leaning against the new parking meter. As always, he was wearing black. Black trousers, black silk polo neck, dark jacket slung over his arm. His trumpet case stood at his feet.

'Hello, sweetheart,' he said softly, folding me into his arms. 'Did you like the roses? Why were you in a nursing home? Had you got hurt?'

He always arrived without any warning. It was something I accepted with the sweetness of seeing him again. The BB band had been on a world tour. He'd landed at Gatwick and taken the train down to Latching for the pleasure of seeing me and blowing a few notes at the Bear and Bait.

'But I'm jet-lagged, Jordan. It was a long flight. I may fall asleep.' He brushed his floppy hair from his eyes.

'You can sleep here. I have room for you.'

'I may take you up on that offer. Let's blow a bar or two and then break away. I haven't played for you for a long time.'

'A hundred years,' I said wonderingly.

'Is it as long as that? Well, that's how time flies. You look as if you need a drink. What's been happening? I had a devil of a job finding you. Policemen all over the place.'

'A bull mastiff bit me and then someone gave me hemlock in a salad,' I said, cutting a long story short.

'This Latching place seems too dangerous for an innocent young woman like you,' he said, tucking my arm through his, swinging his case in his other hand. We walked to the Bear and Bait, catching up, talking twenty to the dozen like the long-time friends that we were. My energy surged back. I was his number one UK fan. He was still happily married and apparently his wife had gone with him to the States.

'Where is she now?' I asked, expecting some glamorously svelte creature to emerge from the shadows, all New York glitz.

'She's gone straight home. Got to water the plants or something.'

The Bear and Bait was capacity full. Their usual jazz quartet greeted my trumpeter with the good-humoured banter of jazz musicians. The crowd round the bar parted to allow him to order. They wanted to hear him play.

'The best red for the lady,' I heard him say. 'Chilean. Open a new bottle if you have to. And a bitter shandy for me. Draught. Nothing out of a can.'

I found a corner seat, tucked away behind some massive rugby players. Their shoulders would block my view. I'd forgotten all about chicken soup and being hungry. But he hadn't. He came back with a big glass of ruby wine and a plate of sizzling potato skins and a sour cream dip.

'I guessed you hadn't eaten.' He winked wickedly. 'I always know everything about you.'

I hadn't eaten and I hadn't seen him for months, nor heard

his magical trumpet. I knew my priorities. I was swimming in happiness and nothing else mattered.

When he began to play, tentatively at first, following the sound of the other players, the chattering died away. Only a fool would talk through this class of jazz. He eased in with their melody, always the polite visiting guest, waiting till an opening came for his sheer genius to burst into improvisation.

He moved seamlessly from the haunting 'Samantha' to the peerless 'Harry James' Carnival', rocking to 'Shiny Stockings', then slowing into 'I Only Have Eyes For You'. I had slipped down on to the floor due to massive rugby shoulders in front of me. It was necessary to watch this man's face and his fingers as he poured his soul into the drifting tones he was feeling for, see the golden glint on his brass. The wine and the potato skins came with me. They were delicious too.

Time vanished into matter. He wiped the mouthpiece and began another piece, the clear high sounds making my spine tingle. Cadences found notes I did not know existed. The name of this piece of music eluded me but it was sheer joy and sweetness and somehow captured the murmur of the sea.

When the last notes died away, everyone started clapping. He cupped the microphone but he was looking at me.

'That last number was new. I wrote it for a dear friend. I call it 'Lacey'. Now, folks, if you don't mind, I need to put my head down fast. Time lag is catching up with me.'

'Lacey'.

He could hardly keep his eyes open as he cleaned and carefully packed away his precious trumpet. There was nothing I could do to help. I stood around.

'Are you sure you've got room for me?' he wheezed. His breath had gone. Blown away. He would not make old bones. This gutted me.

'Plenty of room,' I said, like I had a mansion.

We walked back to my place, my hand in his. He was fighting sleep and we did not talk. I took the roses from the car and unlocked the front door. I guided him upstairs, step at a time. His feet were leaden.

'I'll put some clean sheets on the bed,' I said, propelling him towards my bedroom. 'The bathroom is over there.'

'Don't bother, sweetheart,' he said. 'It's too hot, too damned hot for sheets. I'll just roll on top of the bed. I'll be out . . . like a light.'

And he was. He flaked out on top of the duvet, his breathing falling into sleep pattern instantly. I took his shoes off, unfastened a belt clip, smoothed his floppy hair out of his eyes, put his glasses safely beside the bed, and switched off the light. I would never have dared touch him in daylight nor dare I curl up beside him now. I watched him sleeping. It was hard to leave him. But I had to. He was not mine.

I tiptoed out clutching my clock and an extra pillow. I would sleep on the floor of my sitting room. There were plenty of cushions. My alarm was set for six a.m. so I could get up and move my car. I did not want a parking ticket.

Nineteen

B reakfast was two black coffees. It was strange having him wandering around my place, using my bathroom, looking through my tapes. I had Jazz FM playing on the radio. He listened for a while.

'They play the same old stuff,' he exploded. 'Why don't they move on? That's wallpaper jazz.'

'It's smooth jazz,' I said, defending my favourite radio station.

I'd never seen him in the morning, pacing about. My bedsits were too small for him. He was an evening man, dusk and night time. He only came alive in the evening. I drove him to the station. My car amused him but he had to go home, he explained. Commitments.

'Sorry, sweetheart,' he said, leaning across and kissing my cheek. 'Don't leave it so long next time.'

Me leave it so long! When I never knew where he was in the world. Still, that was the star mentality.

'Take care,' I said, moved because he had written a piece of music for me. A tune called 'Lacey'. Pretty cool. An underwater stillness froze my heart. I might never see the man again. He could die. Jet-setters die from DVT.

'No more hemlock salads, baby,' he smiled, touching my face. 'Promise?'

'Promise.'

Then he was gone, swallowed into the forlorn station, its bleakness like chloroform, back to London, to wife, back to celebrity concerts, Bond film tracks, Hollywood razzmatazz, a man with a magic trumpet. I would press one of the roses between the leaves of a book of poems. Someone might find the dry petals in years to come and wonder who loved who. I drove back to the shop and parked the ladybird in the backyard.

I slid into a void.

First Class Junk had a good morning. I sold a blue Delft china jug, a WWII gas mask, and a pile of old sheet music. The woman was ecstatic.

'I used to sing all these songs when I was young,' she said, almost breaking into a song and dance routine in the shop. 'But I've forgotten the words. Now I'll be able to learn them all over again. It's wonderful. Thank you so much.'

She handed over six pounds without a second thought. The power of music.

I got out my portable typewriter and fed in a sheet of paper. This was crunch time, unzip brain. I typed:

```
FRAZER - FONTANE
1.Frazer was Fontane's nanny.
2.Frazer was in house when Fontane's sons
were murdered.
3.Fontane has been paying Frazer £250 a
month ever since.
4.Frazers buy garden plot next to Fontane.
5.Frazer's husband is murdered.
6.Frazer is unhinged by death.
7.Someone feeds me hemlock in nursing
home.
8.What does this mean?
```

I sat back, the fog clearing. Gill Frazer had obviously been blackmailing Lydia Fontane for years, hence the standing order. Blackmailing her about what? What did Gill know? Maybe they did not even buy the garden plot. Was it another sweetener from Lydia when she realized she could not increase the payments?

They did not like the new house much. Gill had never turned it into a home. It was if they were passing tenants.

Then I understood. Gill wanted the big house. She was waiting to move into Lydia's lovely home. And the face at the window. I knew who that was now. That was Max, Gill's son. He had already moved in. It was time to pay another visit to Lydia Fontane.

The door to the shop opened and a customer came in. I took the paper out of the machine and put it in a drawer.

DI James was peering at the collection of old WWI medal ribbons. They sold well to collectors.

'Hi,' he said, coolly. 'Had many of your friends sleep over lately?'

It was like a blow in the solar plexus. He was wearing his cold face. Eyes masked. The inquisition had arrived.

'I beg your pardon?'

'Your overnight guest.'

'That was my musician friend,' I said. 'The trumpeter. He was jet-lagged and he flaked out.'

'On your bed, no doubt.'

'Yes, so he did, fully clothed. But I slept on the floor in the other room. Anything else you want to know? Does he snore? I've no idea. I only know he arrived late from the States and played at the Bear and Bait, then almost passed out with tiredness. Did you expect me to leave him to sleep on the pavement? I suppose you would have found him a cell.'

'There are plenty of hotels in Latching.'

'He was beyond checking in at a hotel.'

'Naturally. No need with a besotted fan at his beck and call.'

'Not at all,' I smarted from the insult. 'He's a friend. I'd do it for any of my friends. Even you.'

He ignored the comment. 'You should be more careful who you have sleeping at your place. It isn't safe and you could get a bad name.'

'My name is no business of yours,' I said, starting to move

things around in the shop. My hands needed something to do or they might do the unforgettable and throttle the man. 'In fact, none of this is any business of yours.'

'I'm glad it isn't. Your life is chaotic and a minefield. I have enough trouble at the station.' He took out his notebook. 'I just want to check a few things.'

'Is this a social call, official visit or have you come to buy something?' I snapped.

'I'll buy something if that'll make you happy,' he said, looking round the shop with complete disinterest. 'What have you got that is clean, authentic and unique? I guess it would be pretty rare in this shop.'

He was being stroppy and I was fast losing my temper. It was unforgivable. OK, he was stressed as usual, tired, traumatised by some kind of deep secret from the past, a nasty divorce, etc. But that did not excuse him for his behaviour this morning. He'd arrived in a filthy mood and it was getting worse.

'I think you had better go,' I said, taking a deep breath and counting to seven. There wasn't time for ten. 'I may do something I would regret, like slapping your face or tipping my expensive coffee over your head.'

'Typical juvenile behaviour,' he said.

'Would you take yourself and your despicable manners out of my shop? I don't know, nor do I care, whose bed you got out of this morning but it was obviously on the wrong side.'

'Still making cheap jibes,' he said, slapping the notebook shut and thrusting it into his pocket. 'Call me when you've grown up.'

'I'd rather call Saddam Hussein,' I shouted at his departing back.

I stood knee-deep in the wreckage of my life. Static crackled through my head; shards of his words cut my breath. I needed a couple of puffs of Ventolin but the inhaler was back at my bedsits. Somehow I made my legs move and I bent over a chair to ease the breathing. It was an automatic reaction. My brain was not working. It had gone into a negative station. It was not responding.

My hand shook as I poured out some strong black coffee. It was too hot and burnt my mouth but I hardly felt the pain. I did not care anyway. I was beyond feeling any physical pain. Everything else hurt too much.

We had quarrelled. James. My precious James. He would never speak to me again. It was over. Finished. Life had moved on. I did not know how I would manage without him.

Someone came into the shop and bought something. I don't know what it was, automatically wrapped item in tissue paper. And I gave them too much change.

My typed list of that morning made no sense. The words were almost a foreign language. I blinked rapidly, making myself focus before going out. The sun was scorching hot, light dancing off glass, but I had to put on a sweater.

I almost forgot to lock the shop and put up a sign. I put up CLOSED FOR DECORATION. It was as if I had closed down. People in the street pushed past me, heedless. The invisible woman.

Footsteps hurried after me on the pavement, like ghosts. They barely registered. I'd forgotten my sunglasses and the sun blinded me.

'Jordan. Hey, Jordan, what's the hurry? Slow down.'

DS Ben Evans caught me up, his face beaming. He looked nice and normal. His clothes were normal, a lightweight suit, white shirt, loosened blue tie.

'Sorry.'

'Are you all right? You look a bit pale.'

'I'm all right.' My mouth formed the words somehow. It felt all stiff and unnatural. The top lip would not move.

'To be expected,' he said, falling into stride beside me. 'You've been through a lot.'

'I have, haven't I?'

'Has the guv been giving you a rough time? He looked like thunder when I passed him.'

'A minor explosion of some sort occurred,' I said, trying to instil some lightness into my voice but it didn't work.

'Don't take it to heart. Some of the big guns from London have come down and taken over the dead fisherman case. It's tied into something bigger.'

'Drug running?'

'Don't ask. And don't let's talk work. It's too hot. Let's talk holidays.'

'Forced, shared, solitary, disaster or idyllic?'

'Idyllic shared,' said Ben, taking my hand. His skin was warm but not sweaty. 'I've been cruising the Internet. There's a bargain 10-day holiday in Cyprus on offer, quite reasonable as it's a late bargain. Four-star hotel, right on the beach. Do you fancy it, Jordan?'

'OK,' I said recklessly.

'Hey, that's wonderful,' he said, hardly believing what he had heard. He spun me round on the pavement, unable to contain his enthusiasm. No one got knocked over. 'I didn't really think you'd come with me. We'll have a great time. Swim, sunbathe, dance, walk. Lots of places to visit. I promise you, sweetheart, you'll come back a new woman.'

'I want to be a new woman,' I agreed.

'It'll be fun.'

'What sort of sharing is shared?' I asked, some sense returning.

'A twin-bedded room, en suite, of course. Saves on the single supplement charge. Do you mind? I won't peek. You can have all the privacy you want.'

Twin beds. I could move some piece of furniture and put it between the beds. Like the wardrobe.

'Have you got a passport? Is it up to date?'

Here was my chance to lie my way out of the situation. No passport, out of date, mislaid, confiscated by the police, eaten by the dog. Except I don't have a dog. Could I blame it on the bull mastiff?

'Yes, I have a valid passport.' I'd had to get a passport in a hurry when my parents were killed in France. The Passport Office had pulled out all the stops and issued one in hours. It was one of the many kind things people did for me then. I had not used it since.

'Shall I book the Cyprus holiday when I get back to the station?'

I remembered James' face that morning and the stark disapproval on it. But I could not understand why. I had done nothing wrong.

'Why not? Go ahead, Ben. Book it.'

'Wonderful, Jordan.' He was beaming, ear to ear. How could I hurt this nice, trusting man? It was only for ten days. I'd survive.

A tall, gangling youth opened the door of Lydia Fontane's house. He had a round, amiable face and pale gingerish hair gelled into spikes. He was wearing the uniform of youth – baggy trousers and even baggier sloganed T-shirt. It was a rock band shirt.

'Hi,' he said.

'Hello. Is Mrs Fontane at home?'

'Nope. She's gone out.'

'Do you know when she'll be back?'

'Nope. Do you want to come in and wait?' He smiled at me and I smiled back. 'I'm Max.'

This was a young, trusting ten-year-old living inside a twenty-one-year-old body. Nothing visible, just the feeling of innocence and unworldliness. He shuffled backwards, his trousers in folds over his unlaced trainers.

'Come in. You can wait in the kitchen. Would you like some tea? I can make tea.'

He seemed eager to show off his skill. He was already filling the kettle.

'That would be nice,' I said, sitting on a chrome high stool at a formica counter. It was an Ideal Home kitchen; everything carefully planned and coordinated. A dream in cream and ceramics.

Max got out two mugs and a tin of biscuits.

'I'm going to have a biscuit. I'm allowed to,' he said. 'Do you want one?'

'Lovely, thank you.' I took a ginger crunch and I don't like ginger biscuits. Perhaps he would not mind if I dunked.

'This is my favourite,' said Max, taking a chocolate finger and sucking the chocolate off. 'You can have one if you like.'

'This is fine,' I said, nibbling.

He made the tea competently although it was too strong for my liking. I added some extra milk.

'Are you at college or working?' I asked.

'I go to a special crafts college,' he said happily. 'Because I'm a bit slow at learning. The teachers are nice.'

It was easy to get Max talking about his college. It was nearby and he could walk there. He prattled on about what he was learning. He had been making clown faces to go on T-shirts. He liked doing that and the teacher gave him a highly commended mark.

'That's very good,' I said.

'Do you want to see one?' he asked eagerly.

'Yes, please.'

Max rushed out of the kitchen, almost tripping over his laces. I took the opportunity of a quick survey of the kitchen, looking at the engagements calender hanging on the wall, looking in the letters rack, opening a few drawers and rifling through the contents. The perfect guest.

A clutch of unpaid bills were in my hand when Max returned but he did not seem to notice. He was wearing his clown T-shirt. The clown was bold and brassy with a big red nose and arched eyebrows. It could sell well in souvenir shops. Perhaps he had a career ahead of him as a designer.

'That's wonderful,' I said, meaning it.

'Would you like one? I can print them off at school.'

'No, really. But thank you, Max. That's a kind thought but perhaps I'm too old to wear a clown T-shirt.'

He stared at me and then grinned, twisting the hem. 'You're not too old at all. You're just the right age. I'll print one for you.'

This child-boy did not know what he had said or what it did to me. I could have kissed him except that I did not want to kiss a boy. There were lots of other people, mostly men, I would rather have kissed. But he had stirred something frail inside of me that had been badly hurt. Of course I was just the right age. I was the right age for anything. There were years ahead of me and I was going to use every one of them.

'Max, thank you,' I said. 'I've had a lovely time talking to you. Thank you for the tea and biscuit. But I must go now. I've got lots to do.'

'I've got lots to do, too. I do lots of things for Mrs Fontane. You will come again, won't you?'

'Yes, I'll come again.'

'It's been nice having someone to talk to. I like you.'

'I'll see you soon.'

He was pushing up his sleeves, intending to wash up the mugs. His upper arms were covered in cuts, half healed, but some of them were still raw and weeping. They were self-inflicted. Max was a boy who mutilated himself. That bloodied shirt in the bin had belonged to him.

I walked down the leafy driveway, out on to the street, quickening my step, deeply distressed by what I had discovered about Max. Nor did I want to be caught near the house. The bills were still clutched in my hand. I hoped they would bear fruit. Pineapple or melon. It was immaterial.

The son, Max, was a revelation. His parents had not been able to cope with him, I suppose. Brian had gone off into some feminine dreamland. Gill had denied everything. Only Mrs Fontane had seemed to be able to accept him for the child that he was. And she had given him a home.

The air hung like a viperous cloud. It was difficult to breath. Something was going wrong with the climate in West Sussex. But no one had any idea or even noticed. The beach was crowded with people, sunbathing, picnicking, paddling, building sandcastles, fishing, canoeing, surfing and windsurfing. A normal summer's day at Latching when the tide is out.

I took off my trainers, tied the laces together and began to walk along the beach, far out towards the shallows. The water was cool and refreshing to my feet. The stones had to be avoided. The small, sharp ones could be painful. Some patches needed careful negotiation. Little wavelets are so pretty and gentle. They wash around your feet in baby ripples, kissing your toes, stroking your ankles. It's easy to get carried away.

Something made me look up. A sudden absence of birds. The seagulls are usually everywhere, squabbling on the sand over the dead fish heads. But not now. There was not a bird to be seen. They had vanished.

Far out to sea, on the horizon, was a thin dark line. It seemed to be moving, coming towards Latching. I watched it for some moments. It was definitely moving nearer. Odd.

The weather was changing. The sky had gone a peculiar pewter colour and it was starting to rain. I did not know what was coming or what to do. But some primeval sense told me to get away as fast as I could.

So I ran across the sand towards the shore, but not nearly fast enough.

As I ran, the sharp stones cutting my feet, I suddenly knew why James had been in such a bad mood this morning. He had been jealous. My James had been stricken by the green-eyed monster called Jealousy.

But even this knowledge was washed to the corners of my mind. Something ominous was happening. Out at sea. And I did not like it.

Twenty

The tidal wave hit Latching at 2.31 p.m. in the afternoon. A gale of wind whipped up sand and paper. People ran screaming from the beach. Swimmers tried to get out of the sea but were engulfed by the huge wave that towered over the sloping shingle.

The sky had gone a peculiar dark colour and it began to rain, droplets as big as coins fell from the clouds. The sunbathers were running in all directions, leaving their clothes and possessions on the beach. The wall of water was rushing past the high tide mark and surging across the promenade and on to the road.

'It's a freak,' I gasped, stopping at the top to stare.

Tidal waves don't happen in Latching. But this was happening. And I was going to be submerged if I didn't run too.

The force of the wave had swept swimmers out to sea, overturning canoes and windsurfers. Some were floundering, helplessly. Others, the experienced surfers, were clinging to their boards waiting for the atrocious weather to subside.

It surged over everything in its path: deckchairs, bikes, pushchairs, litter bins, even threatening the palm trees that the council had newly planted along the front. It spread down roads, going inland, flooding shops and offices.

I was knee-deep in water, flung against a wall, holding on to a railing so that I would not fall over. It was too much like the watermill for comfort. I could hear crashing glass as the wave hit the windows of shops and cars. A car slewed across the road, narrowly missing people who were running. Other cars had stopped, their engines flooded, passengers staring in fright out of the windows.

Then I saw the canoe. It was upturned and someone was clinging to the hull. It was being washed out to sea in the deep trough behind the wave. I heard a faint cry for help, hardly audible in the noise of the wave smashing into the town.

I waded through the water and was soon out of my depth. I struck out towards the canoe. There was no way I could let the man drown in front of me. I'd been swimming before I could walk, an inherited trait. The trick was not to get tired and not to swallow water. A steady crawl took me near the canoe, but already I could feel a downwards sucking pressure from the wave's energy.

Now I could see why the man was in trouble. He had a gash on his head which was bleeding profusely. He was too weak to either right the canoe or climb in. His limpet hold on the hull was a mechanical reflex.

And, dammit, in spite of the bloodied hair and face screwed up in pain, I knew the man.

A plank of tarred wood floated past. A fisherman's runner. I grabbed it and steered it towards the canoeist.

'Grab this,' I yelled. 'Hold on.'

He was conscious enough to understand and took hold of the other end unsteadily. In that second I leaned over the canoe, pulling on the far edge so that it righted in the sea. Water cascaded out nearly drowning the canoeist again. He had the sense to grasp on to the near side but was unable to heave himself into the canoe.

I swam round to the other side so his weight would steady the canoe as I climbed in. I practically fell into the vessel. It had a lot of water in the bottom and would sink with my weight if I didn't bail and fast. But what with?

My trainers. Useful again. I remembered when I had burned a pair in the cinema to attract attention. I go through trainers and mobiles so fast I ought to get a discount.

203

Two-handed, or was it two-footed, bailing got rid of a lot of the water. But I could see the man would soon be slipping away from sheer exhaustion. I had to haul him into the canoe. I chose a moment when a following ridge of water lifted him high enough.

The canoe shook with the impact and threatened to capsize again but I managed to steady it with frantic side to side weight replacement.

We were quite far from the shore. No one would see one small canoe in the rainy mist. It was still chucking it down but beginning to ease off. The tidal wave had disappeared inland, causing thousands of pounds worth of damage to the town.

Then the rain stopped, just as suddenly, and the sun came out. It was as if nothing had happened. The sky was a pale washed-out blue, exhausted by its own turbulence. Sparkles danced on the water, hopping about like mischievous water elves.

The man stirred in the light.

'What the hell was that?' he groaned.

'A tidal wave,' I said. 'A freak wave. I read somewhere that they are caused by one wave sucking in energy from its neighbours and mutating into a monstrous rogue wave.'

'Ouch, some mutation . . . My head hurts.'

'You got hit by something. It's bleeding.'

I took off my T-shirt and ripped off a wide bit of hem. It made a reasonable length of bandage and I practised my first-aid skills on his head, the blonde hair sticky with blood. Then I put what was left of the T-shirt back on. I could hardly paddle back to shore in just a size 34B bra.

Paddle. It would have to be my trainers again. But his were bigger. I took his size tens off the unprotesting man and started to polish up my paddling technique. I was pretty rusty. We were making no headway at all. The pier looked even further away. Had we somehow entered a parallel universe?

'Do you feel strong enough to help me with the paddling?' I asked hopefully. 'We've got to get you to the shore.'

'I'll try,' he said, struggling to sit up. We took one side each and tried to get some coordination going. Even injured, he was stronger than I was. But we were still being washed further and further out to sea. It was frightening.

'Do I know you?' he said.

'I don't know,' I said. 'But I certainly know you. You're Roy Dinglewell and you are supposed to be dead.'

He managed a smile. 'Yes, I'm Roy Dinglewell.'

'There were a lot out to get that boy, mark my words.' Mavis had said when the diver's body had been found. But here he was now, bloodied but alive, looking better by the minute despite the circumstances.

His hair had been roughly bleached and he'd grown a wispy moustache and beard. Otherwise he was the same strapping Roy Dinglewell I had glimpsed on the beach, hauling in his fishing boat, *Bluebell*.

'So I'm not dead,' he said. 'Is that a problem?'

'People have been grieving.'

'Who?'

'Mavis, for one.'

'Mavis who?'

I left that one to simmer. 'Your family for instance.'

'They knew. It's no secret from them. I suppose I owe you some sort of explanation since you've saved my life.' He stopped and looked at the stretch of sea between us and the shore. He both wanted to talk about it and not talk about it. 'You are saving my life, aren't you?'

'Keep paddling,' I said. 'There's been a freak tidal wave. I know no more than that. The sea has got to settle down soon. Latching is not an unnatural phenomenon zone.'

'But can I trust you?'

'You've no option, Roy. Now tell me why there's a diver in the morgue wearing a toe tag that says Roy Dinglewell.'

It was easy to feel sorry for him. He wanted a drink desperately. I wanted a drink. No water bottles floated by.

Roy cleared his throat, searching for saliva. 'You know

I fish. You know I dive. Diving in wrecks is my hobby.'

'Keep paddling.'

'I was wreck diving. There are so many wrecks in the English channel, it's like a car dump under all that water. I got suspicious about what was going on. It wasn't natural what I saw. Then it dawned on me that some foreign lot were smuggling drugs into the country, using the wrecks as a halfway point. They were leaving bags of the stuff tied to wrecks, to be picked up later, by another lot, when it was quiet and clear.'

'Then they found out that you had found out?' I was streets ahead of him.

'Yeah. I got threats. Lots of threats, nasty ones from this drugs ring. Like being carved up if I interfered. No one threatens a Dinglewell.'

The sea was misty now, a haze on the horizon. There was no sign of any other vessel. Everything had disappeared. No colour in the sky, only this washed-out blue, drained of all energy. I wondered if this was actually me, in a canoe, paddling with a trainer. I could have missed myself on the way.

'So what happened?'

'I was out diving and I found this poor chap who'd been caught in some dredging machinery. It might have been an accident or something more sinister. I don't know. I saw a chance to disappear, for a while, anyways. I ripped the name tag off his wetsuit and exchanged neck tag chains. He's wearing mine now. I threw his in a bin. It was some foreign name.'

'He'd been in the water a while?'

'Not that long but I know what water does to a face, bloats it out, doesn't it?. In twenty-four hours he would be unrecognizable. What do they call it?'

'Adipocere. It's because the body reacts with the water, developing a waxy substance. The fatty tissues of the body

206

become a sort of soap. Do you mind if we don't talk about it? I am still getting over an enforced stay in hospital.'

'So they fished the body out. My name tag on a chain round his neck. Same height, weight, similar age group. They thought it was me. My family identified the body as me. They shut their eyes and said yes, sir, that's poor Roy, though I'd managed to get word to them first. So everyone got happy. I was happy because I was not dead. My family were happy because I was not dead. The druggy lot were happy because they thought I was dead.'

'And what next?'

'I'm gonna lie low for a while, keep out of sight. Then when everyone has forgotten all about it, I'll resurface, say it was all a mistake, my DNA clone. Been loafing around the good life in South America or somewhere. By that time, the drug ring may have got caught by Interpol or whoever and I'll be safe.'

I did not tell him what DI James had hinted about a cross-Channel drugs connection. It was not much anyway. But it seemed that West Sussex were not stupid and knew what was going on and were on their track.

Roy suddenly looked straight at me, despite all the blood over his face and the sodden bandage. 'You won't say anything, will you?'

'Cross my heart. I'm more concerned about getting back to shore. Your private life is your private life. I have already forgotten what you told me. Never heard a word. The waves are far too noisy.'

'There's a strong south-pulling current,' he said, seawise.

'What are we going to do? I don't feel in the mood for tax-free shopping in a French supermarket. We need help.'

I was sitting on something hard. It stuck into my bottom. It was Jack's mobile. The one he had thrust on me in case of an emergency. But water cascaded out of it.

'Mine is in the locker,' said Roy. 'It's in a waterproof Aquapac.'

I dialled zero, zero, one, zero, hoping it would work. I got a recorded message. 'Jack? It's Jordan. I'm in the middle of the Channel in a canoe, trying to paddle with a trainer. Can you get some help? My French is pretty hazy.'

'Don't worry, Roy,' I said, clicking off. 'Jack is reliable. He'll hire a helicopter or the *QE II*.'

It was not exactly the *QE II*, slightly smaller in size, no cabaret or guest lecturer. But we were just as pleased to see the Shoreham lifeboat zooming towards us, the sturdy bow cutting through a swathe of spray. The loudhailer boomed, 'Hello, there? Jordan Lacey? We're coming alongside. Get ready to board.'

Strong arms hauled us aboard and secured the canoe to the deck.

It was cocoa and buttered current buns all round, being wrapped in blankets. Lots of weather-beaten men in yellow oilskins doing their job. The radio crackled into life and there were reports of a yacht in trouble. Two yachtsmen were picked up from a capsized dinghy. It was more cocoa and buns. Quite a party.

I identified myself for their log but said that the canoeist had lost his memory, due to the bang on his head. It seemed to be accepted. They let me curl up on a bunk, deep down in the lifeboat and I fell asleep instantly, worn out by everything. I didn't care where they took me. Timbuktu would do.

An ambulance took all four of us to Shoreham hospital. It made a change. Latching hospital could not cope with the sudden number of injuries. But there was nothing wrong with me and they let me go quite soon. I did not see Roy Dinglewell leave A & E for an x-ray upstairs. Some charity fund gave me enough money for my train fare to Latching.

'I'll pay you back,' I said. 'I'll send it by post.'

'That's fine,' said the woman at the desk. 'When you've got time. I hope you get home safely.'

'Thank you,' I said.

She saw I was shivering in my half a damp T-shirt and came after me with a cardigan. 'Borrow this,' she said. 'I always keep a spare one in the office.'

It was shapeless, handknitted, in some vague mouse colour but just then it could have been a priceless garment designed by Versace. It was as warm as the woman's good nature.

'Thank you,' I said again.

The trains were still running but not at their scheduled times. Many tracks of line were flooded and a sort of shuttle service between Brighton and Littlehampton was in operation.

'Half the roads are closed,' said the sales clerk. 'Better to wait for a train. You'd never get a taxi.'

'Thank you,' I said. Apparently I only knew two words now. My vocabulary had shrunk. The train, when it arrived, was a snorting two-carriage dragon but I was glad to see it. Field upon field was flooded. Seagulls were swimming inland, looking bewildered. Lots of gardens were water-logged. I suddenly remembered my shop and my stock. And I was not insured. No one insures junk.

First Class Junk was not under water. The two steps up to the front door had saved it from liquid penetration.

'Excuse me but do you sell umbrellas?'

It was a customer, putting a distressed head round the door. The freak weather in Latching had obviously unnerved her.

'Sorry, I don't sell them,' I said. 'But I can lend you an umbrella. You can return it any time.'

She came in gingerly as if she expected the Mafia to strike. 'I'm only here for a week, on holiday,' she said. 'I'll bring it back on my last day.'

'Sure.' I went out the back to look through my collection of unwanted umbrellas. I picked out a blue one with daisies. She looked like a daisy person.

The woman was peering at some elderly glassware. 'I like this old scent bottle,' she said. 'I collect them, you know. Scent bottles. It's certainly not a Lalique or Roger et Gallet but it's very pretty. Ahmn, you can still smell the perfume. Amazing how it lingers. How much is it?'

I wouldn't know a Lalique if it was waved under my nose.

'Six pounds.'

'I'll take it. A nice addition to my collection.'

For no reason at all, while I was wrapping the bottle, a small cracked green bottle with a stopper, I decided I should take another look at The Limes.

As the streets were still in the throes of receding flood, I walked. It was quite a way but the exercise was good for me. I had not walked for ages. It was time I had a good tramp over the Sussex Downs, beheld a few views.

Phil Cannon was on the other side of the road, strolling with his hands in his pockets. His moon face looked cheerful. It was a surprising sight.

'Hi there,' I said.

He did a double take as if he had forgotten me already. Put me on the back of a sell-by shelf. I was the disposable PI.

'Er . . . hi there,' he said.

I crossed over. He looked too cheerful. It was not natural.

'Everything all right?' I asked brightly.

'Sure. Hunky-dory.'

'That's good.'

I hung about. He was not telling me everything. His face had shrouded over. Decidedly suspicious.

'You're looking very pleased with yourself,' I said, coming straight to the point.

'Oh? Do I?' There was an inward battle going on. He was undecided whether to tell me or not but the sheer glory of it all got the better of him.

'I've been on to the social services people,' he said casually. 'About the DNA. And they said I'm entitled to a refund or something. Like, it being proved now and being legal. So, it can't be bad, eh?'

'Great,' I said. 'I'm very pleased for you. So it was worth coming to me after all, wasn't it?'

'Why? It wasn't you who did the test, was it?'

It was medal time for not clouting the man. But I restrained. So Phil Cannon was going to get a refund. It would be quite substantial. Fair enough, I supposed, but he could have been more grateful.

I stood outside The Limes, wondering whether to knock on the door or use the key taken from under the birdbath.

Mrs Fontane came to the door. 'I've been wondering when you would come to see me,' she said.

Twenty-One

It might be intuition or some sea fairy tapping in my head. Lydia Fontane could have gone to the jazz concert in Falmer Gardens.

'Thank you,' I said. 'Yes, I'd like to ask you a few more questions, to confirm some points. It won't take long. There's one or two things I'm not quite sure about.'

'Ah.'

'I was wondering if you can tell me if you were anywhere near Falmer Gardens the day that Brian Frazer died so tragically? Did you see anything unusual? Anything that seemed strange or anyone acting oddly?'

'Heavens no, I wouldn't have gone within a mile of Falmer Gardens that afternoon. All that discordant rubbish. Not my style at all. I prefer classical music.'

'We all have different tastes,' I said, quite calmly for an ardent jazz fan.

'Of course, but you don't have to inflict it on other people.'

'But if you weren't there, it wasn't being inflicted on you.' I was quick.

She moved very slightly, stroking down a fold of her summery dress. It was a totally unnecessary movement. She was wondering if she had said something which could be picked up on.

'Quite true. Is that all you came to ask me? I am very busy.'

'Not exactly. I was in the office of the *Sussex Record* the other day, looking up old cuttings. Fascinating.'

'Totally biased reporting. She should have hung for it.'

'I didn't say I was looking at the trial cuttings,' I said.

'But you were, weren't you?'

This was one tricky lady and I was not sure why. She was hedging in a refined sort of way. Her eyes were not meeting mine. Her gaze was firmly elsewhere. Any minute now she would say she had to go to a committee meeting.

'Do you think we could talk about this some other day? I have a meeting of Age Concern to go to. I'm on the committee and I really don't have time for this.'

'You asked me to investigate the deaths of your two small sons ten years ago and that is what I am doing,' I said, wondering if Max was upstairs. 'I have to find out as much as I can. If someone else is also interested in the case, then that could be suspicious.'

'If you say so. But the murderer is obvious. I just want it proved.'

'Is Max around?' I asked casually.

She stopped in her tracks. She turned very slowly, her face pale, an eyelid twitching. 'Max?'

'Yes, Max. Gill's son. I saw him here the other day. A very nice young man.' I put a slight emphasis on the word 'young'.

'I don't know . . . he may have come by for a drink or something. Now, where did I put my driving glasses?' She opened and shut a drawer.

'He seemed very much at home for someone who was just coming by for a drink.'

She was gathering up things at speed. Handbag, gloves, her glasses, keys, slim black document case. Gloves for a committee meeting? It was an impressive display of efficiency. She was some committee member.

'I really must go.' She was hustling me out now. She filled a tumbler with sparkling Highland water from a bottle in the refrigerator, drank it, and put the glass down.

'One last question,' I insisted. I don't know why I said it.

A remembered newspaper photograph flashed into my head without any warning, the way thoughts do. 'Do you possess a pink cocktail dress, made of silk and chiffon, very classy, with roses on the bodice?'

But she was ready for me this time. 'Do you really expect me to remember every dress I have ever worn? Good heavens, I've probably had a dozen pink dresses.'

'This one had deep pink roses sewn across the front.' I waved vaguely over the top of my chest. I tried to look as if it did not matter what the answer was, that it was immaterial.

'Very glamorous. And what do you do with your dresses when you've grown tired of them? Do you pass them on perhaps . . . to friends or hard-up relatives?'

She was opening the front door for me, rigid as steel. 'I'm sorry, Miss Lacey, *tempus fugit*, as they say.'

'Not for Brian Frazer, it doesn't,' I said. 'Time has stopped for him.'

I was breathing hard. Everything had gone pie-eyed. I had gone to see Lydia Fontane, meaning to ask her certain questions and ended up asking completely different ones. But it had not been wasted time. The fog was beginning to clear. As the song goes, I was beginning to see the light.

I went straight to Latching police station, marched up to the desk and asked to see DI James. Outside the sun was shining fit to burst into flame like a golden omen. Latching's council gardeners were busy tending the municipal flowerbeds. They were a riot of organized colour and design.

'He's busy, miss.'

'Tell him it's Jordan Lacey and I've solved the Brian Frazer murder,' I said, very sure of myself.

'Please take a seat.'

I calmed down as I sat waiting, longing for a drink of water, reading all the new notices. Perhaps I had not solved the murder but I had a damned good theory. And it was one the clever DI James, the man who ignored me, would not have thought of in a thousand years.

'Jordan . . .' He came impatiently into the corridor, his feet like lead. He ran a hand through his short hair. 'You want to see me? Make it brief. I'm up to my eyebrows.'

'I think I know who murdered Brian Frazer,' I said.

'Can you prove it?' He was not impressed.

'No.'

'Then don't bother me. I've enough crackpots coming into the station.'

He turned away so that I only got sight of the back of his head. Even the way he was holding his neck showed it ached, like it might splinter at any moment. There was no possibility of me stroking his neck to ease away the stiffness. The man had distanced himself from me.

'I'm not a crackpot,' I said firmly. 'Don't class me with the station groupies, James. I can't prove it but I can produce a lot of evidence. You could at least listen to me. What have you got to go on?' This was pure guesswork. 'Nothing! Absolutely nothing. Go on, admit it. You are up the creek with this case. Right?'

He came back to me, glaring. 'If this is a wind-up, Jordan, I will throttle you. I do not have time for this.'

'I demand the courtesy of an interview room and a cup of your disgusting cheap tea,' I said, making myself every inch of five foot eight, even in trainers.

'Make her some tea,' James groaned to the desk sergeant, leading the way.

We went into an interview room, the usual dreary, colourless square-footage of space. Two plastic chairs. A table. A window. The same ancient, well-thumbed *Hello* magazines on a shelf. I would donate them some *Country Life*.

'OK, Sherlock Holmes. Tell me,' he said.

His eyes were always the quicksilver ocean blue that fascinated me, but they were guarded now. What had happened to our almost friendship? Then I knew. Somehow a rumour had spread about a certain holiday to Cyprus. I couldn't remember what I had agreed. It was beyond recall.

'Brian Frazer was murdered, not because of his singing, but because he looked like his wife, Gill Frazer.'

'Clear as mud.'

'Someone who has to wear quite strong spectacles for driving can't focus long distance properly,' I said. 'So people, back view especially, can be mistaken, especially in pink silk.'

'If you say so.'

'And that's what he'd got on. Brian was wearing one of his wife's dresses.'

'Jordan, are you still on medication?' James was not joking.

'The pink dress is one which Lydia Fontane had passed on to Gill Frazer at some time but Brian Frazer was wearing it. He often borrowed his wife's clothes. Mrs Fontane thought Brian was Gill and so she fixed an electric shock. Maybe it was just to give Gill a fright. She was never sure who had killed her children, but Gill was always the prime suspect. I don't know how she knew what she was doing with the transformer, but she's an intelligent lady and Brian would have trusted her if she had approached him on the stage.'

'How do you know it was Mrs Fontane's dress?'

'I saw a photo of her in the *Sussex Record*, taken years ago, wearing the same dress. It was in the newspaper. The Mayor's Ball. Unmistakable. This was her dress and at some time she'd passed it on to Gill. So she thought Brian was Gill. I think I even heard her voice in the crowd, that unmistakable classy tone.'

'This is only heresay. I need proof.'

'It's your case. I don't have to prove anything.'

James was showing a degree of interest, a slight flicker. 'You're saying that Mrs Fontane murdered Brian Frazer in a moment of mistaken identity? But why would she want to murder Mrs Frazer?'

'Gill Frazer had been blackmailing her for ten years and

216

she was almost milked dry. The only asset Mrs Fontane had
left was her house and she wasn't giving that to the nanny
who may have suffocated her two sons. She was avenging
her children's deaths at last. She thought it was justice in a
twisted way.'

'Blackmailing her? Are you sure?'

'I've proof of it,' I said triumphantly. I could not conceal
the wicked glint in my eyes. A moment of triumph. 'Bank
statements galore. Two hundred and fifty pounds standing
order every month for ten years, regular as clockwork. Three
thousand pounds a year, thirty thousand pounds so far. Work
that one out, buster. Quite a hefty sum. Where's that tea?'

'It's coming.'

As we talked and I drank tea, we pondered the blackmail.
Why was Gill blackmailing Mrs Fontane if Gill had suffocated the two children? It did not make sense. No, the
blackmail was because of something else. She had some
kind of hold over Lydia.

'Gill is blackmailing Mrs Fontane because of something
only she knows about.'

'And how are you going to find out?'

'Me?'

'Anything to do with the two boys is your case, isn't
it?' James relaxed for the first time. He was passing the
buck. A glimmer of a smile cracked the ocean frostiness.
For a moment the old James was there. It was heartening.
I remembered the odd moments, only moments and not long
ago, when he had shown me some affection . . . a touch, a
joke, saving me from something.

'Mrs Fontane has hired me to do something I can't do,' I
confessed. 'She wants me to prove that Gill suffocated her
two boys. It's impossible. A hopeless task. There's nothing
tangible to go on.'

He nodded. 'Try to reconstruct exactly what happened
that night, minute by minute. Find flaws, inconsistencies,
contradictions. Talk to everyone who was around then.'

'That's asking a lot. It was a long time ago. Mrs Fontane is tight-lipped. Gill Frazer is twice as tight. And Mr Fontane is dead. Who else was there?'

'Max, the son?'

'But he was only eleven years old. Hardly a reliable witness and probably fast asleep at the time.'

'Mr Fontane died leaving a lot of financial problems. He and his partner had borrowed heavily to build a multi-screen cinema and it all fell through. That's another route to take.'

'I'll try,' I said. 'Thanks. I'll see what I can do. But I don't hold out much hope.'

'Thanks for the pink dress lead. There's a lot of prints on the transformer. We'll isolate them all. We only need to find one of hers, to put her there at the scene.'

'Mrs Fontane wears gloves,' I said.

'You really believe she did it, don't you?'

'She's got a motive. A strong motive. Even if she killed the wrong person.' I suddenly made up my mind. 'I can get you a set of her prints if you really want them. Do you?'

'Not breaking and entering, surely, Jordan?' He was mocking me. 'I shall have to caution you about your devious ways.'

'Not breaking and entering.' I didn't add that I had a key.

I checked whether her BMW had returned to the garage at The Limes. The garage was empty. In a moment I had let myself in. It was still there, the tumbler on the kitchen table. She had not had time to wash it up before rushing off to her committee meeting.

I put it carefully into a plastic bag, sealed the top and let myself out. It would have been useful to have a good look round the house but this was not the time. I did not want to be caught.

On second thoughts I dashed back into the house, raced through to the kitchen and took the bottle of Highland water carefully out of the refrigerator, holding it by the neck. Lydia Fontane was going to be really puzzled. Bottles of water don't walk by themselves.

'The things I do for him,' I said, talking to myself as I hurried away from the scene of the crime. 'DI James, you definitely owe me one.'

Twenty-Two

It was all going to depend on matching arches, loops and whirls. I delivered the items to Latching police station clearly addressed to DI James, both labelled and dated, packed in a box marked 'FRAGILE'.

And if that wasn't cooperation, then I didn't know the meaning of the word.

It was back to the drawing board with the Fontane case, that is the mass of newspaper cuttings. I laid them out on the floor of my office, corners weighted down with pebbles stolen from the beach and unpacked my brain. I had missed something and it might be staring at me.

Lydia Fontane and her husband had certainly led a very active social life. Most of their photographs were shots taken at various prestige events in West Sussex. Edgar Fontane had been a man of some standing in the county and although several years older than Lydia, they looked a happy couple.

I took my magnifying glass and began an inch by inch search of the photographs. It was a playback from my training days when we had to identify sets of fingerprints. Not that I was looking for fingerprints on newspaper cuttings. But I was looking for something identical.

The background detail was fascinating but before I got too engrossed in memorabilia, a slightly blurred face appeared in the crowd several times. I started to scribble:

a. Know this face. From past. Whose past?

b. Face always looking towards Mrs Fontane.

c. Significant other?

The third note wrote itself. My hand was guided. Joke . . . there is nothing spiritual about detective work. It is slog, followed by slog, often boring and mainly unrewarding.

I'd seen that man's face somewhere before. Tall, grey-haired, distinguished, upright bearing. I began category thinking, that is, all the places and groups beginning with an A first . . . art gallery, Americans, local associations, antique shops, Admiralty. Then B . . . beach, barbecues, banks, birthday parties, burials, bachelors, businesses and so on.

Time was consumed by this lengthy process. I made coffee when I got to C. Visited Doris for soya milk when I got to D. Kicked myself awake when I got to K. By the time I got to P for pier, I was nearly comatose with boredom. Jack was hardly tall, distinguished with an upright bearing. He was the total opposite. I could remember none of his clients, not even the shady ones at the barn boot.

Police station. The answer hit me with a small electrical shock. There was a framed photograph upstairs on the wall near DI James' desk. The same distinguished face and bearing, in uniform. He was part of the West Sussex police organization. I could not recall his rank. But some time ago, this man may have been in charge of the area.

Naturally he would have been invited to all these official functions but why was he looking at Mrs Fontane? Why does a man look at a woman? Once, twice perhaps. But every time? I counted the shots in which he was somewhere in the background. There were eleven. A bit over the top for normal interest. Or was he on surveillance? Was he guarding her?

That was a creepy thought. But a high official would not take on such a duty. It would have been dished out to some lower rank.

There was only two people I could ask. Mrs Fontane herself or Gill Frazer. I decided on reverse alphabetical order. It seemed sensible in the circumstances.

I walked to St Michael's Road, stiff after sitting on the floor for so long. As I went to the front door, a curtain twitched. She was in, even if in hiding. I set the chimes going and I was not going to go until I saw her.

Eventually Gill Frazer opened the door. She looked dishevelled. Her cardigan was on inside out. For some reason this reminded me to do some shopping for my holiday.

'Yes?'

'May I speak to you for a moment?'

'I suppose so.'

She was packing. The hall was stacked with half-open boxes. The rooms were in a shambles. Not that there was much to pack but she was making a right mess of the job. Things all over the floor. No organization or method.

'Are you moving?'

'Yes, I can't stand this place a moment longer. That woman was round this morning, ranting on about me telling the police about some dress she gave me. Oh, it was ages ago. I never wore it. What would I do with a dress like that?'

'I know that you didn't tell the police,' I said. 'It was me. I told them. I spotted Mrs Fontane wearing the dress in an old newspaper photograph and recognized that it was the pink dress that your husband was wearing when he was killed. I thought the police might be interested in this very small item of information and passed it on.'

'It was you? Then, do you think they may know who killed Brian?' Gill looked relieved and a couple of degrees of face frost thawed.

'It might help with their enquiries,' I said, using the well-worn spokesperson phrase. 'May I come in? I have a few private things to ask you. And you don't want Mrs Fontane to see me on your doorstep, do you?'

'Come in, then. But I am busy.'

'So I can see.'

There was nowhere to sit down. All the chairs were piled with items brought from upstairs, linen and towels and loo rolls. So I stood.

'I want to ask you in more detail about the night that the two boys were suffocated,' I began.

'I've told you all this before,' she blustered.

'But you didn't tell me about when Mrs Fontane came back to the house and let herself in,' I said. 'You didn't mention that, did you? There was no sign of a break-in so the person who came back had to have a key. It was Mrs Fontane, wasn't it?'

Lucky guess. I could have suggested Edgar Fontane. But I went for the lady first.

Gill's face went pale, then blank. 'I never said so.'

'But she did, didn't she?'

'Yes, she came back. It was quite late. I'd already gone to bed. Then I heard something and thought perhaps it was the wind rattling one of the window ventilators. They are old-fashioned and can make a noise. But it wasn't the wind.'

'It was Mrs Fontane. She had left the mayoral party?'

'Yes.'

'And . . . ?'

Gill was having quite an internal tussle. I could see she wanted to tell me and yet she did not want to tell me. Her face was twitching and her hands plucking at the mud-coloured skirt. She had changed since she first came into the shop. Gone to pieces. No longer completely in control. I felt sorry for her.

'So Mrs Fontane had left the mayoral charity event on some excuse and had come home.'

'She said she had a headache.'

'So she took an aspirin and went to bed?'

'No.'

'What did she do?'

'I-I don't know. I didn't see.' But she had seen. Gill was now quite agitated and it was pretty alarming. I didn't want her to start screaming again and the neighbours to call an ambulance. We'd all had enough of that. She sat down on a pile of blankets that threatened to topple her on to the floor.

I cleared a chair at speed. 'Sit here, Gill. That doesn't look safe.'

'Thank you,' she murmured, hanging on to the arm of the chair. I went through to the kitchen. More chaos. There was no method in her packing. Half the cupboard doors were open and their contents stacked on the floor. I filled a glass with water and took it through to her.

'Drink some water,' I said. 'I won't ask you anything more if it's going to distress you. I'll just make sure you are all right and then I'll leave you to your packing.'

She nodded, taking sips of water. Her mouth was not quite in control and dribbles ran down her chin.

'Where are you going to move to?'

She shook her head. 'I don't know.'

'I should stay here for a while, till things settle down. It won't be so bad,' I said hopefully. 'You can't move if you don't know where you're going.' I am not one of life's natural counsellors. It was the best I could do.

'I don't know what to do . . .'

'Then it's easier to have a good night's sleep and think about the future again in the morning or next week. There's no hurry and it's such lovely weather. You should be out on the front, walking the beach and enjoying the sea. It's quite calm now.'

'That would be nice,' she agreed vaguely.

'Promise me that you will have a nice, relaxed day tomorrow. No more packing for the moment. Have a cup of coffee at the pier cafe. Go and see Maggie at the theatre. She'd be pleased to see you. You might think again about doing some voluntary work at the theatre. They always need people.'

'I suppose I could. Brian would be around there, in a funny way.'

Gill was calming down. Her hands were steadying. It was time for me to go. At least I had confirmed that Lydia Fontane was the person who had returned to The Limes late that night. But it didn't solve the murder of the two small boys. That was still a mystery.

I went to let myself out of the door. Gill was taking off her cardigan and folding it neatly. She was beginning to look more her usual self. Any minute now she would fix her hair.

'Take care, Gill. Look after yourself. You don't have to tell me anything more. I've worked it out. Lydia Fontane was not alone, was she? She had brought a man friend back to the house with her and you saw them together. And he was pretty high up in the West Sussex police force, wasn't he?'

Gill said nothing. She was intent on folding a pair of plain white pillowcases.

'And that's why she's been paying you £250 every month ever since, isn't it? To keep your mouth shut. She did not want this man's career destroyed. She must love him quite a lot.'

She shot me a look of pure malice. 'She doesn't know the meaning of the word,' she snarled.

Twenty-Three

I asked Dr Sprightman to check out the sprig of parsley that I had picked from Gill Frazer's garden. The tests came back that it was the hemlock plant.

'It grows wild all over Europe and North America,' he said. 'You had a very lucky escape.'

Mrs Niki Shiko, the Asian cook, was genuinely upset that I had been taken ill. She had made my supper that night and delivered it to my room, she told me. She could not remember if the salad had parsley on it.

'I was short of parsley that day,' she said. 'But Mrs Fontane said she'd bring some from her garden. She'd been visiting Mrs Frazer. She's such a nice lady.'

I'd been talking to Gill at supper time, before my short visit to the TV room. Long enough for a quick addition to my supper plate. Had Mrs Fontane meant the hemlock for me or for Gill? Maybe she got the room numbers mixed. Easy enough to do in the stress of murdering. One first floor room looked very much like another.

'Mrs Fontane has gone away,' said Max, opening the door. He grinned. He obviously remembered me. 'I'm looking after the house. I do lots of things for Mrs Fontane. Do you want to come in?'

'Thank you,' I said, following him into the kitchen. 'But will they let you stay on in the house on your own?'

'Who do you mean? I don't see why not. It's my home. Mrs Fontane looks after me.'

'Don't you live with your mother in the house next door?'

'My mum doesn't like me much, so I live here. She keeps getting ill. Mrs Fontane likes me. That's why I do things for her.'

Max was happily scratching the wounds on his arms. It did not seem to worry him that his arms were a weeping battlefield. I wondered if he cut his legs as well.

Max was making two lemonade drinks. He added ice and a slice of lemon. I hoped he wasn't using the same knife.

'Here you are,' he said cheerfully, popping in coloured straws. 'A Max lemonade special.'

'Thank you, Max. Well done. This is lovely for a hot day. Tell me some of the things you do to help Mrs Fontane.'

Max began reciting a long list, from finding her glasses to saving the crossword in the paper, making tea, watering house plants. It was a catalogue of small tasks that he could cope with.

'And I grant her wishes,' he went on, stirring his lemonade with the straw. 'Once Ben and Izzy were crying late at night, after some party, and Mrs Fontane was upset and saying she wished they would stop crying so I made them stop. I went into their bedroom and made them stop. It was very late and very dark. Of course, she didn't know it was me. I never told her. You won't tell her, will you?'

I looked at the boy with his young, innocent face but I was unable to smile. 'No, I won't tell her.'

I decided to do nothing. Mrs Fontane was already being questioned about Brian Frazer's death. Max could not stay on in the empty house on his own now. Soon the welfare machine would gather him in and harvest another lost soul.

A card arrived, covered in old-fashioned blown garden roses and bold gold writing. He'd remembered my birthday but not the right date. My birthday was late next week. Still it was near enough not to matter. And inside the card was a ticket to the Watermill Jazz Club at Dorking. My trumpeter was guest playing with the Don Weller Big Band.

It was a long time since I had heard him play in a big band although he toured the world with the famous BB Band. And so many other great players were to play that night as well as the legendary sax player, Don Weller. He of the bushy beard and immovable black beret. It was unmissable.

I looked at the date. It was the day I was flying out to Cyprus on this holiday with Ben. The holiday that I was not sure when I had agreed to. The flight was scheduled for 22.30 from Gatwick airport. We would arrive at some unearthly time in the early hours of the morning but this was the price for a cheap flight. But in Cyprus the night would still be warm and balmy.

Dorking was not far from Gatwick. I could make it. I'd go to the jazz, already packed, and leave in time to drive over to Gatwick. Meet hunky Ben at the check-in desk and fly off to paradise beach hotel.

It looked good on paper but the reality scared me witless. Shopping list: new T-shirt, new bikini (modest), new pants, new jeans, new mascara, SF30 tan protection, book.

Book? I'd got a shop swamped with books. Help yourself, Jordan.

It was while I was in Marks & Spencer, dithering over plain cotton, high-cut pants in white, fuschia or cornflower blue, that I noticed a couple round the corner buying undies like they were going out of fashion. The woman was taking hanger after hanger of brief lacy pants off the rails with matching wired bras and camisoles. Her arms were piled with every colour in stock, black, blue, lilac, buttermilk, white, pearl grey.

Then she moved on to the nightwear section and was becoming ecstatic about satin nighties, long and short, with matching wraps. This was serious honeymoon shopping.

''Ere, Phil, what about these crazy striped satin nightshirts?

Do you think they're sexy? They've got Foxy Lady embroidered on the pocket, smashing.'

I knew that voice. I ducked down behind some matronly flower-sprigged creations, keeping out of sight, fascinated with ghastly growing curiosity.

'And you're one foxy lady,' said another voice I recognized. 'Get two, babe. The black and the red. I'll buy you anything. You deserve it.'

'I'm having a really smashing time,' said Nesta, tripping to the counter with her arms full of goodies. 'I usually buy my undies down the market.'

'Nothing's too good for you now, dollybird baby,' said Phil Cannon, getting out his wallet and following her.

Dollybird baby. I'd read that phrase before on a scrap of paper that I'd thrown away in a rash moment. In my bin bag raiding days.

I watched as Phil paid cash for this loot. And loot it was. It was his use of the word *now* that made the connection. This was a very clever scam and I'd aided and abetted in the scheme. I did not know where to look as the truth sank in.

Phil Cannon had come to First Class Investigations with his honest face, asking for help in proving that he was not the father of Dwain. He had had a nagging doubt for years, he'd said. He'd hinted at a new girlfriend.

I knew who she was . . . Nesta Simons and not so new. The two of them had thought up a very neat swindle. Phil Cannon was the father of Dwain and had been dutifully paying for the child's upkeep. Till he got fed up with paying. He'd got me to investigate the paternity, supply written reports while he had, in a very gentlemanly manner, delayed having a DNA.

My detailed reports had proved to some degree that his doubts were genuine. He had probably sent copies of them, and my invoices, to the CSA.

The eventual DNA test had proved he was not the father. I'm not sure how they'd fixed that one because the DNA factor has to be supplied with a witness present. OK, so

Dwain's had been a legitimate sample taken in the presence of a doctor. Somehow, Phil had fixed his. Sleight of hand. Dodgy witness. Samples switched. I couldn't prove it but I was sure that's what he'd done.

But however he'd managed it, the result was what they wanted. He was not the natural father and the order was overturned. Child Support Agency kindly refunds him all the maintenance he has paid in the past, out of taxpayers' money.

The CSA officials would not ask Nesta to return the payments. She named him the father of Dwain in good faith, she would say.

Hence the celebratory shopping spree. Phil was due a hefty five figure refund. Dwain was twelve years old. Phil had been paying for twelve years, that's over 600 weeks. My maths could not cope with the final sum.

I took my multicolour packet of pants to a different counter. I felt chastened and sick. I did not like being set up and taken for a fool even if I was one. Then I remembered the cigarette end which I had saved in a specimen bag. It was in my filing cabinet, labelled Phil Cannon. Someone at the CSA might be interested. Some official.

My packing took all of ten minutes. I put my plants in the bath with three inches of water, locked up my bedsits, locked up my shop and said goodbye to Doris.

'Cheer up, Jordan,' she said. 'It's only a holiday, not till death do us part. Go and enjoy yourself. Have fun while you're young.'

'Yes, Doris,' I said dutifully. 'I've got a good book.' I tapped Tolstoy's *War and Peace* on the cover. 'It's about time I read it.'

'You won't have time to read,' she warned cheerfully.

'Be back next week,' I said. 'Bye.'

'Got your burn lotion?'

I nodded. 'Got my burn lotion.'

I drove the ladybird towards Gatwick on the A24; circled the long-stay car park to find out what I had to do that night in the semi-dark. I hoped she wouldn't mind being left with all those strange cars. At least the airport had an international flavour and there were dense trees on the fringe. Not too alarming.

The Watermill Jazz Club was held in a local social club. Upholstered armchairs were set out in rows. Very civilized. I usually sat on the floor or on stairs. The band were setting up their equipment, the sound man busy with mikes and amplification. Three rows of seats and stands were placed for the musicians. It was going to be a big band. A tremor of excitement hit me for the first time that evening.

Don Weller was wandering about in a pink shirt, checking everything, his black beret firmly on his head. Did he ever take it off?

Four trumpets, five saxes, four trombones, piano, double bass, drums and Don Weller himself. My trumpeter was standing in the back row. He spotted me, sitting in a comfortable chair, nursing an orange juice. There was the merest wink. Perhaps he liked my baker's boy cap and off-the-shoulder cotton peasant blouse. Weird with jeans but it worked on some fashion level. No one else would have seen the wink. But he knew I was there and that was enough. The hall began to fill up.

It was a hot evening and all the windows were open. The music would pulverize the air for miles. They began to play and the sudden surge of sound was electrifying. I almost shot out of my seat. My spine shivered in expectation.

This was improvised jazz of the highest quality. The soloists were seamless and impassioned. My trumpeter was producing a cacophony of sounds that I had never heard before, spurred on by the brilliance of the other musicians. Alan Barnes was superb.

A pale-faced woman was standing near the back. She looked fragile but obviously loved modern jazz so much, she was prepared to stand for the whole show. During the clapping, I beckoned her over and gave her my seat. She shot me a smile of pure gratitude.

I went and stood at the side of the hall, my bottom hitched up on the windowsill, keeping the brass row at the back in view. I didn't have a seat now but at least I had shelf space for my glass. That I kept slipping off the sill was a minor disadvantage.

But the titles of the pieces were new to me. 'Fruit'? 'Bongate Song'? 'Bearded Gravy'? 'It'? Yes, it was a title. I didn't know these numbers. 'High Force' was named after a waterfall in Cumbria; the sound was almost out of control, going faster than the beat. It was great and powerful.

Because the music was hard to follow, I had to concentrate. It was not like the standards and classics in which it is easy to get floated away. The kind of music that he always played at the Bear and Bait. Then the trumpeter began to play 'The Man with The Horn', and I melted with pleasure. My mind went off into the land of cerebral processing where the magical sounds of that piece were retrieved from my memory and I relived the first time I had ever heard him play.

The Bear and Bait.

Latching!

Ben . . . DS Ben Evans.

I came down to earth with a dynamic shock and the shock wasn't the music. I was supposed to be at Gatwick airport. Now. The clock on the wall behind me was very bad news. It was 9.25. I had about an hour in which to drive to Gatwick, park in the long stay, bus in, find Ben, check in and board the plane to Cyprus. They would be boarding soon. I'd never make it in an hour without breaking my neck in several places.

I did not want to break my neck.

I slipped out of the hall and stood in the grounds to think calmly. It was still light and the sky was a glorious colour but I had no time to admire it. There was a phone number on the ticket for enquiries. I keyed in the number. I was praying for a serious flight delay. But the flight was on time, the operator told me, and would be boarding in about 30 minutes.

I was in bad trouble. I'd left it far too late.

Ben would be at Gatwick, waiting, searching the crowds for my face. I cringed at the awful hurt he would feel when I did not turn up. He would think that I had ditched him, cottoned out at the last moment. He'd never believe that I had simply forgotten the time, listening to jazz.

My feet took me slowly back into the hall. The music could not cheer me but it numbed the pain while I thought of what I would have to do. As soon as I got my head together I would phone Ben. I'd have to tell him the truth.

But the truth was, I was relieved. And I couldn't tell him that.

Music stole the minutes, confirming my cowardly delaying tactics. I had almost forgotten the trumpeter, blowing his heart out. If he looked my way, then I wasn't looking at him and that would be a new experience for him.

The band were taking a break, the sweat pouring off them. They needed a beer or whatever. I fled outside. This was the moment. I switched on my mobile and it immediately began ringing.

'Jordan, Jordan, I've been trying and trying to get hold of you.' It was Ben. His voice sounded taut and urgent. 'Your phone's been off. Then it was engaged. What's been going on?'

'Sorry . . .' I began.

'Listen, Jordan. I really hate this. I know you must have been wondering where on earth I'd got to. There was nothing I could do about it. I just hoped you hadn't already boarded the plane, though I couldn't blame you if you had.'

'Got on the plane?' I repeated. This was one crazy conversation.

'I can't make it, sweetheart. All leave has been cancelled.

Some terrorist alert in London. Cyprus is off. But you go ahead if you want to. Have a good time.'

'I wouldn't dream of going without you,' I said faintly.

'It's orders. All leave is cancelled.'

'I understand,' said the brave little woman, sinking back on her heels.

'You're wonderful,' said Ben.

'I know I am,' I said, thanking the guardian angel of reluctant holidaymakers. Later on, the music sounded so cool. I stayed for the whole programme, talked some jazz with the band, then drove back to Latching through the countryside in the dark, my heart singing, thinking of a certain Detective Inspector who might, might possibly, be glad to see me.

At least for one lucid moment.